Allison & Busby Limited
11 Wardour Mews
London W1F 8AN
allisonandbusby.com

First published in Great Britain by Allison & Busby in 2019.
This paperback edition published by Allison & Busby in 20...

Copyright © 2019 by Sarah Hawkswood

Hostage to Fortune

A Bradecote
and Catchpoll Mystery

SARAH HAWKSWOOD

First
This publication

.
0.

The moral right of the author is hereby asserted in accordance with
the Copyright, Designs and Patents Act 1988.

A CIP catalogue record for this book is available from
the British Library.

First Edition

ISBN 978-0-7490-2478-9

Typeset in 11/16 pt Adobe Garamond Pro by
Allison & Busby Ltd.

The paper used for this Allison & Busby publication
has been produced from trees that have been legally sourced
from well-managed and credibly certified forests.

Printed and bound by
CPI Group (UK) Ltd, Croydon, CR0 4YY

Hostage to Fortune

By Sarah Hawkswood

Servant of Death
Ordeal by Fire
Marked to Die
Hostage to Fortune
Vale of Tears
Faithful unto Death

For H. J. B.

Chapter One

Christmastide 1143

The Severn was running high, for there had been heavy rain in the preceding week, and there seemed little chance of the man, whose head was being held under water, being found. The current ought to take him swiftly southward to where none would recognise him, and none would mourn him as more than a soul lost to the river's power. The flailing, which had been uncoordinated, ceased, and his assailant, breathing just a little heavily, let him go and turned away into the darkness. Thus the man did not see that the body merely floated to catch between two skiffs that strained against their moorings, to be discovered with daylight.

William de Beauchamp, lord Sheriff of Worcestershire, was not known as a generous man, nor one particularly concerned at the happiness of his vassals. He had, however, been considerate, and not made his undersheriff wait over long for a decision upon his request to wed the lady Christina FitzPayne, widow of Corbin FitzPayne of Cookhill. This had been less to do with any wish to earn Hugh Bradecote's thanks and devotion than a desire not to have an undersheriff whose thoughts would be inclined to wander, and whose resentment would rise if his ladylove was kept tantalisingly out of reach. A pragmatist, not a romantic, de Beauchamp worked upon the principle that once the woman was his, Bradecote would settle back into normality and not be found gazing at nothing, and with that untypical vacant smile upon his face. He had given his approval at the end of Bradecote's feudal service early in Advent, and had declared that they could be wed come Candlemas, but it was several weeks into December before the undersheriff was able to meet with his betrothed, and give her the good news in person.

Hugh Bradecote had returned to celebrate the Feast of the Nativity in his manor, showing his accustomed charity to the poorest of his peasants and arranging for a hog to be roasted come Twelfth Night. Undeterred by a cold easterly wind, and flurries of snow, he collected Christina from Cookhill on the feast of St Stephen, and took her to his manor at Bradecote, there to view what would become her new home, to be seen by all and sundry, and to be introduced to his son, now a lusty infant of nearly five months. He had been concerned that she might find it a melancholy thing to hold a babe in her arms, having lost the child she was carrying when her husband had been killed. He need not have worried. She took to Gilbert from the moment that he held out his pudgy baby hands to tug at her coif and blew bubbles at her, and she was reluctant to give him up to the wet nurse. The natural demands of an infant to be cuddled found a maternal response in her that was heightened by seeing his father in him. Bradecote, who saw no resemblance at all, truth be told, relaxed.

'I see that I have already been supplanted in your affections by a younger suitor.' He shook his head in mock complaint, and she laughed. 'They say a woman's heart is fickle, but so soon?'

She drew close, with Gilbert pulling at her earlobe, and smiled up at him, which made his heart beat the faster.

'You are the only man for whom my heart has ever stirred. This little mite, oh yes, draws mother love, but mother love is not what I feel for you.'

She laid her free hand on his chest, and her eyes were full of promise.

'I do not value power or possessions, but I hold you above everything, above any duty or loyalty. You two are the focus of my life now.' His voice was low, and he took her hand and kissed the fingers, one by one. She gripped his hand, and there was a tremor in her own voice as she spoke.

'I had never thought to mean so much to anyone, my lord.'

'Well, you do to me.'

There was a tension, a frisson. There were those who considered that the binding of betrothal gave a man full rights, and at that moment Hugh Bradecote was very aware of the desire to take whatever she was happy to give.

Gilbert, perhaps sensing that he had been forgotten, gave

a bubbly gurgle that broke the spell. They laughed, just a little self-consciously.

It was the only difficulty between them. Bradecote was determined that she should not feel pressured or forced in any way, and for her part she feared that offering herself to him might seem to indicate that, as a woman twice widowed, she did not value either her body or the deed. In a way that was true, for bitter ill use had inculcated the former, and the absence of love, and indeed positive loathing of her first husband, had debased the second. She wanted this union to be special, and the anticipation was acute. It promised so much, and she was caught between wanting to wait and a very physical need.

After a couple of days it was verging on the unbearable, and the summons from the lord Sheriff was almost a relief. A man-at-arms arrived on the last day of the month, calling Hugh Bradecote to Worcester.

'De Beauchamp is at the castle, and thankfully the castellan is away, which lightens the atmosphere.' Bradecote smiled at her. 'The sheriff is never in a good mood when living cheek by jowl with Simon Furnaux, and I am not sure that I blame him. Will you come with me?'

'Is that a request or a polite command, my lord?' She smiled back.

'A request, of course. The lord Sheriff has said that, investigations notwithstanding, there will be a good night's feasting, come Twelfth Night, and if I am to miss it here . . . Oh, let us be honest, I just want to see you, be with you when I am able. It is an odd sort of wooing, my love, but there it is.'

* * *

10

Parting from Gilbert cost Christina a pang she had not anticipated after only a few days, but her spirits were lifted by the presence of Hugh, riding so close that their knees touched as the horses walked side by side. They arrived with the sun casting its lacklustre rays from three fingers above the horizon. The fur-lined hood of Christina's cloak framed a face pale and pinched with cold, and Bradecote was glad to see her bestowed in a chamber with a brazier already giving a steady heat. He himself went straight thereafter to the sheriff.

'Good to see you here, Bradecote. Enjoying your betrothal?'

Bradecote coloured, which made de Beauchamp laugh.

'Looking forward to Candlemas, my lord,' Bradecote mumbled.

De Beauchamp raised an eyebrow, but said nothing, and continued smoothly to the matter in hand.

'I called you in because we have trouble brewing, and if we do not bring the culprit in soon, we may have problems with the burgesses. If they cannot trust the coinage it disrupts trade, and since it bears the King's head, it casts doubts upon his power also.'

'I am sorry, my lord,' Bradecote tried to make sense of de Beauchamp's rather cryptic utterance, 'what exactly has been happening?'

De Beauchamp drew a hand across weary eyes.

'Far too much, and none of it good. There's silver coin in Worcester that might as well be lead with a silver coat, and the merchants and artisans are all in a fuss, like chickens with a fox among 'em. Heaven knows the coinage is not as good as it was under the old king, for he made sure there was more silver in it, but this is not just a little light, it is not fit to call coin of the realm.'

'But surely we just arrest the moneyer whose die marks the false coin?'

'Now why did I not think of that?' The sheriff's voice dripped irony. 'Of course that was what we did. But Master Osbern is no forger. He has been a moneyer here, oh, must be a good two dozen years. I would say longer but that he still has both hands, and a daughter of twenty, so he cannot have been in the trade when King Henry took his justice upon the moneyers.'

Back in 1124 there had been an issue of silver pennies. There had been many complaints at its poor quality, and King Henry, determined to assert his authority, had called in all the English moneyers and the majority had lost their right hand and chance of fatherhood. It was a salutary lesson, and one that was not forgotten the best part of a generation later.

'There is no doubt?'

'None. Catchpoll has never had a sniff of anything corrupt about the man in all his years, and when he brought him in, he was patently as mystified as frightened. You can smell guilt.'

Privately, Bradecote wondered whether William de Beauchamp could really tell the difference between guilt and fear, but nodded anyway.

'We checked the die. The forged coin was not as sharp, not quite, according to Catchpoll, who has the eyes of my best hawk. He thinks a copy was taken, which would be simple enough in wax, and passed to the forger. And then, to cap it all, Osbern's journeyman was found floating in the Severn. Now, he might have been drunk, but it all tallies rather too well. It seems it was probably a killing, but I doubt it was by his master.'

'There cannot be many moneyers in Worcester, my lord, if it was another.'

'Five. We have spoken to all, and none seemed more than horrified at the forging. We have no proof to link them, and obtaining a confession would be . . . difficult.'

'When was the journeyman found?'

'This morning, just after sunrise. We have one innocent man, and four seemingly so, and need an end to this.'

'Could not a man who has been a journeyman to a moneyer elsewhere, and knows the craft, have come to Worcester, then befriended our drowned journeyman and . . .'

'Just happens to have secret access to a supply of lead and silver and a hidden furnace and . . . Must I continue?' The lord Sheriff sneered, and Bradecote looked embarrassed. 'You set that hound after a scent that leads nowhere. Speak to Catchpoll, and let us make an end to this before the good burgesses send too great a complaint.'

Serjeant Catchpoll greeted his superior with a nod that was half obeisance and half greeting.

'I thought as the lord Sheriff would be sending for you to join the pack. If nothing else, it looks good to the moaning merchants.'

'Such confidence.' The undersheriff smiled wryly. 'Am I meant to be rendered speechless with joy?'

'No, my lord. It was the lord Sheriff's thinking I was voicing. My thought is, the more, the merrier. My bones are too creaky to enjoy chasing around Worcester in the sleet, with men-at-arms whose brains froze long before their feet, and just Walkelin with any sense. Another pair of legs with a brain attached is mighty useful.' Catchpoll grinned. 'And you've got mighty long legs, my lord, if I speak truth.'

Bradecote smiled back, but then grew serious.

'So we have forged silver pennies that are more dross than silver, an innocent moneyer in the mire, and a drowned journeyman. You don't think the last might have been an accident?'

'Accident?' Catchpoll made a derisive sound.

'The lord Sheriff said it was always possible he was drunk and fell in.'

'Well, he might have been drunk, for a drunken man is easier to get to the water and push, but if so, he wasn't so drunk he didn't struggle at the last. I reckon as his head was held under and when they was sure he was dead, they pushed the body right in. There is a bruise on the inside of one arm, not a place that gets bruises in day-to-day living, but might if someone was holding you down with the other pushing your face in the water. I am sure, but the lord Sheriff is trying to be not quite convinced.'

'The coincidence of the death seems too much. I am with you.' Bradecote paused. 'Who have we spoken to since?'

Serjeant Catchpoll noted the 'we', and resisted the urge to smile.

'The journeyman lived in Osbern's house. He had an aunt

in one of the streets off the Foregate, but all she does is wring her hands and say as he was a good lad. Osbern is a widower, and his daughter keeps house for him. According to him, the two did not speak much except over meals, and he had no complaints about his journeyman, other than he thought he had itchy feet to move on at the end of his indentures.' Catchpoll turned, aware that someone had come in quietly. It was the lady FitzPayne. He made her an obeisance a little self-consciously.

'Forgive me, I . . .' She coloured. Whatever she had intended to say was set aside, and instead she took a breath and looked directly at Serjeant Catchpoll. 'I could not but hear what you just said. Was the journeyman ill-favoured, or of disagreeable temperament?'

'Didn't look too pretty after a night in the river, my lady, but he'd have been comely enough breathing, and well, we haven't asked if people liked him particularly, more if any really had reason to hate his guts. Why do you ask?'

'Because if there was a young man in the house and he was comely and agreeable, it sounds very odd to me that he and the daughter did not at the least flirt a little. That the father thinks they barely spoke looks like a pretence to lull him. Perhaps the girl did not think he would favour a match with the journeyman? If it had got that far.'

'You think the father found out and killed him?' Bradecote enquired, frowning, but she pursed her lips and shook her head, as if despairing of male intelligence.

'No, my lord. But I think if someone was to ask the girl about the journeyman, away from her father's presence, you might find out far more than you would expect.' Her voice softened. 'Lovers tell secrets as well as keep them.'

Catchpoll gazed at the floor, face working as he considered the matter. Hugh Bradecote kept his eyes on hers.

'And . . .' she looked down, avoiding Hugh Bradecote's gaze and said, hesitantly, 'she would tell another woman, before she showed her broken heart to a man.'

Catchpoll was quick enough to grasp her meaning.

'You're not a sheriff's ma—officer, my lady.'

'No, Serjeant Catchpoll, but I am soon to be a sheriff's officer's lady, and the quicker this is solved, the more time for' – she paused, and her eyes betrayed a twinkle – 'discussing the future.' Bradecote actually blushed. 'Put me in the way of the maid and see what happens. If I fail, you have lost nothing, and if I succeed in finding out anything you may take it further. It is not hazardous. Please?'

Serjeant looked to the undersheriff, who rubbed his hand over his lightly stubbled jaw, and then nodded.

'We can do that easy enough, my lady. And grateful we'll be if anything comes of it, for sure.'

They arranged to visit Osbern the Moneyer in the morning, for the short, winter day was drawing to a close, with sullen grey clouds hanging heavy over Worcester, and the wise shaking their heads and presaging snow. Hugh Bradecote was torn between pride in his betrothed's intelligence, and a strong dislike at her involvement in any shape or form with his work for the shrieval authority. That the last time had brought her to a dagger's point still brought a shudder when he contemplated it. He voiced his disquiet when they were alone.

'This is not your concern, my sweet, though it was clever of you to think of—'

'It is your concern, my lord, and I would have you free to think of me.'

She dimpled playfully, and teased him with a cheek close enough to kiss, but he was not so easily distracted, and took her by her arms, firmly but gently, and held her from him. She pouted, and he frowned.

'I would not see you set at risk, you know that.'

'What risk is there in talking to a girl about a secret swain?' She sniffed disdainfully. 'Women do such things every day.'

'Not when the "swain" has just met a violent death. I am serious.'

Her face lost the smile.

'So am I, my lord. I want to be part of your life. This is one aspect of that life. Oh, I know that usually I will be of no use to you, but here I can be so, and at no real risk, you must admit.'

He drew her close then, cheek to cheek.

'You are not just a "part", you are far more, and you will always be of use to me, because thinking of you will make me content when the world is otherwise grim.'

'Merely content, Hugh?'

His kiss answered her.

Osbern the Moneyer had a neat burgage plot in Gloveres Strete. Christina could tell, just by peeping into the open workshop, as she 'happened' to pass by, that though the owner might have no wife, he had a woman who kept it clean and orderly. She wondered if he would have been happy to give his daughter up to any man, not just his journeyman.

Catchpoll introduced his superior to an obviously worried man, who still feared that the law might arraign him for murder if not the equally capital crime of forging. He gave his full attention to the questions that the undersheriff posed, even if he had answered them all before. His fear meant that he did not wonder why the lord Undersheriff was accompanied by a lady. The whereabouts of his daughter were discovered with a casual question, which elicited the information that she was laying out washing at the drying ground to the rear and would not disturb them. Christina FitzPayne excused herself from 'men's talk', and had a momentary concern about how she would explain what she, an unfamiliar face, and clearly not one used to menial tasks, was doing among washing, but was spared any complicated lie by the girl herself. She was as neat as the house she kept, but her cheeks were marred by a smudge where she had wiped a grimed hand across tears, and her eyes were red. An expression of sisterly sympathy had Christina sat with an arm about the girl's shoulder and hearing the outpouring of her misery in moments. The tears alone told much. Hawise could not grieve in her father's presence, but her heart and hopes, she cried, lay in pieces. It took little or no coaxing on Christina's part to find out that she and Edmund, her father's journeyman, had planned to wed, but that there had been harsh words in recent weeks between master and man, and Edmund had taken them badly and had turned his thoughts to leaving as soon as his indentures expired at Lady Day, and taking her with him. He had even made provision should he not find employment in his trade in

Hereford or Gloucester, he had said. Much more was made of how wonderful he had been and how cruel fate was to take her chance of happiness from her. Christina, with a genuine wish to give comfort, listened at length and said, though it might comfort her little now, that she herself had met with sorrow, but had found happiness later.

'It can seem so black, the future, but do not think it will turn out to be so. Quite unexpectedly, all can change.'

Christina thought of how true that was, how her own life had altered so very swiftly, and for a few moments she forgot Hawise, forgot her mission. Only three months past she had been the peacefully contented wife of a man who inspired respect but no passion, but had been glorying in a new chance to be a mother, and with the hope of a child she could love and, at last, see flourish. Husband and hope had been swept away in one blow, as sharp as any axe, casting her back into the abyss in which she had once before languished, and yet, in that despair and misery, Hugh Bradecote had appeared, and taken her life and expectations into the light. She loved, and was loved; she would have a child to care for, even if it was not of her own womb, and—It struck her, the revelation, and she gasped as if winded. The thought in her head was as clear as a command at her shoulder, and if she did not obey it, she knew her dearest hope would crumble to dust. Her lord, as he would so soon be, would not like it, but there was no avoiding what must be done. She blinked and stiffened, and the girl felt her do so, and looked at her, dragged from her grief by curiosity.

'Who are you?'

'I,' Christina smiled, and her voice did not sound her own in her ears, 'I am just a pilgrim.'

Christina's information to Catchpoll and Hugh Bradecote stopped short of revealing this intention, but was otherwise a true account.

'She did not say that she knew what it was that her lover intended to do to make provision for their departure. She might not know, of course.'

Catchpoll tugged at his ear, and pulled a face.

'It would depend greatly upon how he thought she would react to his stealing from her father, though if the dies were simply copied, he might have persuaded her there was no theft, just a crafty borrowing. He need not have told her the end result of that "borrowing".'

'How foolish would she have to be not to . . .' Bradecote shook his head, but paused at the look on Christina's face, and his voice petered out.

'A woman in love is blind to many things, my lord, and may choose to be blind to more.'

There was an edge to her voice, defensive as she was for her sex. She did not want him to think women weak-minded, as all men thought them weak of body. Catchpoll coughed, uncomfortable at the thought of some lordly lovers' spat. It drew Bradecote's attention back to the matter in hand, and he was grateful to avoid what he too feared might be a feminine huff, which he could neither combat nor comprehend.

'Many's the time I've come across the family of criminals who cannot see how their son or husband, aye, or daughter even, could be guilty of as much as a minor misdemeanour. They close their eyes to what they would see as obvious in others. So what the lady says may well be true. If he did not tell, well, she would not ask.' Catchpoll sighed. 'Pity, if that is the case, since if he told her everything, we could have our forger under lock and key before the Matins bell tomorrow.'

Chapter Two

The serjeant's gloomy prediction proved remarkably accurate. When the sheriff's men spoke to her the next morning, Hawise was initially afraid and then affronted at their suggestion that Edmund had been engaged in a serious crime.

'It is a wicked thing for you to cast blame on a man when he cannot defend himself. He was a good man, my Edmund, I'd swear an oath on it.'

Bradecote tried to smooth her ruffled feathers, suggesting that perhaps he had been deceived by another, a person who had then killed him to prevent him revealing all when he found out the truth. This settled far better with the distressed damsel.

'Did he have to have dealings with other of the moneyers in Worcester, or their indentured men?' Catchpoll tried to sound casually interested. 'As part of the trade?'

'Well,' Hawise creased her delicately arched brows in concentration, 'I suppose he must have had some with all of them at one time or another.'

'What about recently, Hawise?' Bradecote did not want to frighten the girl, and spoke gently. 'Do you recall him going out on your father's business, or indeed upon his own, when work was finished?'

'We met when we could,' she murmured, 'when Father was out. Edmund did not go off to the alehouse, if that is what you mean. He stayed here, except of course when he went to visit his aunt. He was a good nephew, and she has been ailing of late.'

Catchpoll glanced at his superior. When he had seen her, the dame had looked in robust health.

'So he was good to his kin. Tell me,' Catchpoll sounded nonchalant, 'if he had gone to an alehouse, which one do you think he would have gone to?'

'Not where Father sups, for sure,' she sighed. 'The sign of The Moon down by the quays, I suppose, which he knew from youth, as his father used it. But, as I said, he did not go drinking. He was a good man.'

'A good man who was almost certainly putting his master's neck in a noose by stealing his dies to make forged pennies,' muttered Catchpoll, as they left, collecting Walkelin, who had been detailed off to keep Osbern engaged in conversation, 'and her father must have the eyesight of a mole not to notice those red-rimmed eyes of hers.'

'Perhaps she claims it is the peeling of onions,' suggested Walkelin, with a grin, which was met with a quelling glance from his serjeant.

'So,' Bradecote was determined to sound positive, and ignored Walkelin's jest, 'we are off to the Foregate to see the aunt and visit a nearby alehouse, just in case.'

'We are, my lord. The aunt looked a sturdy, fit woman to me. I would guess the "visits" were not to her, but we had best check, before wasting our time in alehouses.'

'I did not think to hear you say time in an alehouse could be wasted time.' Bradecote grinned.

'Now there, my lord, you are wrong. I happen to think a lot of time is wasted in such places, idling, and "home brewed, home drunk" is better.' Catchpoll made a fair assumption of righteous innocence.

The aunt was indeed far from enfeebled, and declared, with some pride, that she had not been laid sick in her bed for a single day in the last five years. Their next stopping point was thus the alehouse, where the host was cagey. He had come within Catchpoll's orbit sporadically over the years, and was not keen to be helpful. However, the lordly undersheriff was not the sort of personage who entered his premises, and Bradecote played off his rank shamelessly, standing tall and looking both arrogant and powerful.

'I take it you will not waste my time with lies.' He conveyed a sneering boredom that the man had never before encountered. 'Had you seen Edmund, the journeyman of Osbern the Moneyer, with anyone in particular these last weeks?'

'Edmund . . .' The man spoke the name as if he had never heard it before, looked at the wall, and then the floor, glancing only briefly at the undersheriff, but jumped as Bradecote brought his hand down with a sharp crash upon the table. The tankards set upon it rattled as if nervous.

'Don't . . . keep . . . me . . . waiting.' The words held menace, and the alehouse keeper trembled.

'My lord, I . . . he . . . Well, there were one or two fellows he spoke with more than others. I did not recognise the first. He was a stranger in the parish, though he turned up on four or five occasions. The other was one of his own craft.'

'I want the name. The moneyers of Worcester are known to all who trade.'

'My lord, it was Geoffrey, the son of Herluin, him as works in Meal Cheaping.'

The undersheriff, noted Catchpoll approvingly, did not express his gratitude for this information, but rather 'suggested' that the alehouse keeper keep his memory sharp for the next time he should be visited by the law, and stalked out. Catchpoll almost rubbed his hands in glee.

'Now, that, my lord, was very well done. Just the right degree of power, threat and downright malice. Did me good to see it. You mark that, young Walkelin.'

'Before you praise me so much my head swells, Catchpoll, I want Walkelin to the Bridge Gate, and you stay here to watch the Foregate. I am heading back to the castle and will set men on the other gates and reliefs to you both. We meet in Meal Cheaping, as soon as we can, but not directly in view of our suspect. Whereabouts is the man's workshop? '

Catchpoll gave him directions and he set off, his stride long and purposeful, but not running, lest it draw remark that might yet set the quarry to flight. The thought that the moneyer would have been wise to flee Worcester as soon as

25

he had disposed of Edmund was supplanted by that which said the lord Sheriff had not begun a murder hunt upon the discovery of the sodden corpse. It had been treated as accidental drowning, and so keeping calm was the best course. Wavering between hope and anticipation of failure, Hugh Bradecote entered the castle and immediately set about ordering men who were native to Worcester off to the gates, with instructions to question those leaving and to watch for Geoffrey, son of Herluin. His was a well enough known name and face to be noticed. He then returned through the bustling streets to Meal Cheaping to await Catchpoll and Walkelin. He would have been disappointed, had he known, that a lad had been sent from the rear of the alehouse under the sign of The Moon as soon as he and Catchpoll were out of sight, with instructions to inform Geoffrey the net was closing about him, to remind him that he had most certainly not passed poor coin into circulation through the alehouse, and to receive a generous reward for the information.

It was not long before Walkelin arrived, and thereafter Catchpoll, who looked a little breathless.

'Let's hope our man is still within. Walkelin, go round the back and make sure there is no escape route that way. Count to thirty as you go, as will we, and then go in fast. Off you go. One, two, three . . .'

When they entered the premises there was no sign of Geoffrey. Walkelin suggested hopefully that he might have simply gone out to purchase food, but Catchpoll shook his head, gloomily.

'Look about you, lad. What do you see?'

'Well, normal things, Serjeant. There's a loaf and a beaker and the furnace is ali—Oh!'

'Yes, the furnace is aglow, but there are no signs of tools, and why leave it fired up if he was planning to be out in the streets this morning? Especially unattended.'

'Should he not have a man working under him?' queried Bradecote, frowning.

'He did, my lord, but he died just before the end of Advent, and no doubt it was natural. He slipped on ice and broke his thigh. There's a few that live after that, but most do not. I knew of it, but he was not pushed, and it was no business for the lord Sheriff. I doubt Geoffrey would have replaced him yet.' Catchpoll's eyes narrowed. 'If he has gone to ground today, I would swear an oath it was these last minutes, which means he was warned. I'll have that conniving slug from the sign of The Moon by his—'

'By nothing until we have conducted a search of Worcester, Catchpoll.'

'Search Worcester, my lord? All of it? We could be chasing the bastard in circles for days. There are not enough men in the castle to go through every house, outhouse and stable, and not let him slip past and turn up behind them.'

Bradecote muttered imprecations under his breath. What Catchpoll said was true.

'It is possible he got out through the gates we had not covered straightaway, but if we ask at them, we ought to be able to find out if he was seen at one. Otherwise he is still in Worcester. If we cannot flush him out with numbers, well, he cannot make his escape either, and if we put out patrols in force, he must turn up somewhere over the next few days. We go to any known kin, or friends, and check them thoroughly. If he is hiding, as opposed to being hidden, he must emerge at some point for food, if nothing else. We patrol day and night, and he has to fall into our hands eventually.'

Catchpoll detected the note in Bradecote's voice, the one that was trying to persuade himself this would work. He sighed.

'I suppose even if we do not have him yet, he cannot put out any more false coin, so that will limit the damage with the burgesses, at the least. But the lord Sheriff will not be best pleased. And I will have the alehouse keeper in my charge at the castle, because if he warned him, my lord, then he knows far more than he told, and playing coy with the law is what I won't have.'

'Fair enough, Catchpoll. Do you want to drag him in yourself, or get Walkelin to do it?'

'Do it myself, from choice, my lord. And if the good citizens of Worcester see me kicking him all the way, well it does no harm to remind 'em that I am still . . . er' – Catchpoll's thin lips spread in an unpleasant grin – 'alive and kicking.'

Whilst the sheriff's men had been checking who was leaving Worcester and Serjeant Catchpoll was making life most unpleasant for the alehouse keeper, a party entered, making its way towards the Cathedral Priory, where, having been greeted with suitable deference and respect, and having had private conversation with Prior David, its leader went to pay a call upon William de Beauchamp.

28

Samson of Bec held no abbacy, but he was influential, being a friend of the Archbishop of Canterbury from his days in Normandy, and was employed as his envoy trying to mediate with Bernard, the Bishop of St David's, with whom Archbishop Theobald was engaged in a long dispute. He therefore travelled with the entourage befitting an important churchman. De Beauchamp had little interest in the religious world, but Theobald had power and influence and was now aligned in the Empress's camp. It would be a foolish man who did not extend his envoy less than every courtesy. Nonetheless, it was the sort of superficial meeting that left William de Beauchamp grinding his teeth in frustration at such time-wasting. Father Samson was not one to be rushed, and though not personally vain, was very full of the importance of his mission and of his superior. His voice was low, and he spoke slowly, in the sing-song manner of one who had spent a lifetime reciting the Offices in church, and, in the ears of de Beauchamp, he sounded patronising. The lord Sheriff did not appreciate being treated like a child, by anyone. He was thus in a far from pleasant humour when Bradecote and Catchpoll returned. Expecting the worst, Catchpoll sent Walkelin off to the kitchens to scout out some bread and cheese, thus keeping him from hearing his seniors given a rare trimming.

Father Samson was still expatiating upon the intricacies of his mission when they were ushered into the chamber. For a moment, William de Beauchamp's face registered relief, and he held up a hand to stem the cleric's flow. Father Samson was caught mid-sentence and registered his displeasure with a frown. The lord Sheriff's apology fooled nobody, but he did invite the archbishop's envoy to return to bless and partake of a fine dinner. Father Samson could do nothing but thank his host and withdraw with a good grace. De Beauchamp's brief expression of pleasure was quickly followed by a scowl, as his undersheriff and serjeant revealed that they had probably worked out who had killed Edmund and copied Osbern the Moneyer's dies, but that the suspect had slipped through their fingers. He made growling noises like a mastiff with toothache, as Catchpoll described it later to his friend Drogo, the castle cook.

'And I will say this for our undersheriff: he does not shrink from getting an earache off the lord Sheriff as his predecessor did. My lord de Crespignac was not as bold in the face of the de Beauchamp ire.' Catchpoll grinned, accepted the proffered beaker of beer, and took a good swig, wiping the back of his hand across his mouth. 'And,' he added for good measure, 'he can curse in the English something beautiful. Your average lord, well he can make himself understood and can master a few choice comments, but it trips off my lord Bradecote's lips like he took it as mother's milk. No trace of Foreign in his speech, and no need to explain slow, what someone says.'

'Want to adopt him, do you?' Drogo chuckled, and ducked as the empty beaker was lobbed at his head.

Christina FitzPayne had kept her own counsel since the previous day's interview with Hawise. She needed time to try and work out how her aim could be achieved, and spent the morning coming upon dead ends. In each case she knew that she would face Hugh Bradecote's prohibition, and prohibition that was well founded and sensible, as she had the honesty to admit to herself. Defy him she might, but not foolishly. She had not initially paid much attention to William de Beauchamp's visitor, until she heard a lay brother talking to a man-at-arms in the inner bailey. She approached, and both men acknowledged her presence with a respectful nod.

'Forgive me, Brother, but did I hear you are travelling to Lincoln?'

'Indeed, my lady. Father Samson is on his way to discuss his mission with the lord Bishop of Lincoln, who is currently within his see.'

'And when is it that you depart, brother?'

'On the morrow, my lady.'

'And do you take the route that meets the Fosse Way?'

'I have not been told so, my lady, but I would judge it likely. If the weather is like to get worse, Father Samson will want to use the best roads and reach Lincoln betimes.'

'Thank you, Brother.'

Thus it was that Father Samson was waylaid upon his departure from the shrieval presence. If at first he frowned and shook his head, it was clear that he was persuaded to change his opinion. All Christina need do now was inform her betrothed, and she pulled a face at the thought.

Bradecote was contemplating how to create the impression that the patrols and searches were not just a random and desperate effort to find their culprit, when Christina found him. He smiled, but it was perfunctory, and then 'confessed' the morning's failure.

'But is the lord Sheriff not pleased that you know which moneyer is responsible?'

She sounded perplexed, and he pulled a wry face.

'He does not see things in your charitable light.' He sighed. 'Until this matter is settled, I cannot escort you back to Cookhill, my lady. I am sorry for the delay.'

'I was not intending to return there straightaway. I . . .' Her voice became uncertain, for she did not relish the reaction she knew her words would elicit from this man, this man whom she loved. 'I am going on pilgrimage.'

'You are what?' His voice was raised in surprise and disapproval, all thought of Geoffrey the fugitive cast aside.

'I want to go to the shrine of St Eadgyth at Polesworth, before we wed, my lord. I need to, don't you see? No child of my body has lived to full age, and I am afraid.' She came very close, looking up at him, her eyes pleading, taking his hand and placing it below the girdle at her waist. 'Holding Gilbert, seeing you in him, I want your child, our child, and I want it to live. If I go on pilgrimage, the blessed saint may intercede for me. My grandmother ended her days there, and prayed to the blessed Eadgyth for my mother to have a son after she had produced but four daughters. My brother was the result. This is important to me. Can you not understand?'

'And cannot you see that I am marrying you because you are you, not to bear me sons?' He stroked her cheek. He saw the worry gnawing within her, but he had worry of his own. 'Wait until I can accompany you. You know I will be free as soon as we have the forger. It is midwinter, Christina, the roads

32

are treacherous, even without the risk from outlaws and lordless men in these times.'

'My dear lord, I would not wish you to accompany me. No, do not look like that. If you were with me, what hardship would there be, however harsh the weather?' She smiled tremulously. 'It would be a pleasure to me. And if there is no hardship, or risk, how have I proved myself worthy of the saint's blessing?'

Her eyes pleaded, but he saw only the hazards.

'You do not comprehend the risks, and would put yourself in harm's way for a whim,' he said softly, though she took his tenderness as patronising, and then he made an even greater blunder. 'It is not as though the case were desperate. I have an heir. I love you. I really do not care—'

'You do not care for me to carry your child? Is it because I carried Arnulf de Malfleur's? There, I said his name.'

She was losing her temper. She stiffened, and her eyes glittered.

'Don't be foolish.' He scowled. 'That chapter of your life is closed to you, and as if it had never been to me. Those things were not of your choosing and I do not – could not – think you "sullied" by them. Of course I want children with you. I keep telling you that I love you, don't I? But I love you so much I do not want to lose you, and needlessly.'

'I have to go, Hugh.'

He shook his head, and spoke with finality.

'It is simply too far and too dangerous. I forbid it.'

The stiffness became rigidity, and her pretty mouth set in an uncompromising line.

'You forbid? Well, since I am not yet your possession, you cannot forbid, my lord Bradecote. Father Samson's party departs in the morning, bound for Lincoln, and I have already obtained his permission to travel with them. You see, I am not foolish.' She tossed her head. 'I have thought this through and I shall be perfectly safe. Who would threaten men of God?'

She pulled away from him and stormed from the room. He swore beneath his breath at the mule-headedness of women, and sighed heavily. He considered going to the churchman and asking him to refuse Christina's request, but deep down knew that if he did, a black chasm would always thereafter exist between him and the woman he loved, and he wanted nothing between them at all. To keep her close, he had to let her go, however much it fretted him.

Chapter Three

Hugh Bradecote did not spend a good night. Christina had been in a brittle mood at dinner, showing herself the demure and pious widow before the churchman, but casting him defiant, and almost petulant, glances. She had excused herself early from the meal, upon the perfectly reasonable premise that she should get a good night's rest before the commencement of her arduous journey. There had been no opportunity for him to catch her alone, to make his case with soft words and apologies, though he had rehearsed them well enough beforehand. Then, to cap it all, de Beauchamp had decided that a full search of Worcester would take place on the morrow, overriding his instructions to Catchpoll. He had therefore tossed and turned, frustration, anxiety and anger jostling in his mind for pre-eminence. When he awoke with the dawn, he was heavy-eyed. He went to her chamber, but was greeted with the news that she had already left it to break her fast in the hall, and he found her there, simply garbed and coifed. Unadorned, she still had a beauty that took his breath away, and that very beauty made him fear the more for her, travelling without guard, in the company of men whose only defence was their calling. His disquiet made him frown.

'You have not changed your mind, then? Have not seen reason?' His disapproval remained.

It was an unfortunate choice of words, and the smile in her eyes faded.

'I am unreasonable?' There was an edge to her voice, though she did not raise it. 'Because I want to do this or because I do not submit to your command?'

'It is not a matter of submission. Sweet Jesu, Christina, I am thinking of you, of your safety and well-being. I do not say you must not go, but not go now. I will send for my own men-at-arms, as soon as it looks less likely that the weather will be foul, and if you will not have me at your side, then you shall the security of men I trust to protect you. All I see is a mad determination to prove your independence by taking unnecessary risk. Do you doubt my judgement?'

She made no reply. His fingers gripped the edge of the trestle table so that the knuckles showed white. He had meant to cajole and he had fallen into the trap of sounding self-important. He looked down at his hands and shook his head.

'I cannot stop you, not without putting between us a wound that would fester. Why do you have to make this so hard for me?'

She reached out a pale hand and touched his larger one, tentatively.

'I am sorry, my lord. Truly I am. But this . . . This has to be. I did not plan it so. The idea came as a revelation, a compulsion that I dare not disobey, even if it costs me your displeasure. I will be an obedient wife, I swear it. I want us to be happy, to be blessed. All will go well, you will see, and afterwards you will laugh at your concern.' Her voice had softened, and unconsciously he laid his other hand over hers. 'I must go, Hugh. I was to meet Father Samson's party at the Sutheburi Gate just after the bell for Prime.'

'I will escort you that far at least. You will not deny me that?'

'No, my lord.' She shook her head. 'In my heart, I would deny you nothing.' She moved her hand from his hold and went to collect the few things she was taking upon her pilgrimage. He was concerned that she gave her fur-lined cloak and hood into his keeping, and took a simple woollen one.

'Need you risk the cold so?'

'I am a pilgrim, my lord. The trappings of wealth, the comforts of privilege, have no place upon such a journey.'

'But must you be a pilgrim who catches her death of cold? There is snow in the clouds. They are heavy with it.'

'I have a second cloak. I may place it over the first at need. Two thin layers will do well.'

They descended to the bailey. The bell of the Cathedral Priory rang for Prime. Little as he relished it, she must go. He assisted her into the saddle, helped her arrange her skirts decorously, surreptitiously kissing her hand. Then he walked at her side as she left the castle and clip-clopped to the Sutheburi Gate. As they drew up, the dark-clad Benedictines were approaching from the priory, most of them mounted on mules.

They reminded Bradecote of crows, and he was filled with an inexplicable foreboding. He looked up at Christina.

'I will not be easy until your return. Come to Bradecote, not on to here. Christina, my heart . . .'

'You have kept the hour well, my lady.' Father Samson hailed them and nodded at the undersheriff. 'I admit to some surprise.'

There was no time for more private words. Bradecote gave her a speaking look.

'I will pray for your safe return.'

It sounded so trite, so formal, and yet was so heartfelt. She smiled back at him, though her lip trembled, and she nodded, wheeling her horse to take station in the middle of the party.

Bradecote watched the group long after it had gone through the gate and was making its way up the hill on the road towards Stratford, and it was a grim-faced, tight-lipped undersheriff who strode back into the castle yard a few minutes later, and snapped at the men-at-arms guarding the gate.

Serjeant Catchpoll had enjoyed removing the keeper of the tavern with the sign of the moon from his business in full view of his customers, and then making much of exhibiting him through the streets to the castle. His initial interview with the man, whose name was Roger, was of limited use in the hunt for the evasive Geoffrey. Roger was weighing the misery of interviews with the serjeant against the misery of being hanged if he confessed to knowingly passing false coin. Trying to steer between the two evils was not easy, being helpful without revealing that he had any involvement with the man other than as a customer, and his replies were muddled and even contradictory. Catchpoll spent a very frustrating couple of hours and then reported back to de Beauchamp, who was anticipating how best to both placate the burgesses and yet still sound perfectly in control, more as something to while away the time than achieve anything useful.

'Trouble is, my lord, the snivelling nithing is confusing himself now. I don't say as how he should go without punishment if he is guilty of a crime, but . . .'

'The alehouse keeper?'

'Aye, my lord. If these coins have got into Worcester, well it cannot be through the usual exchange of new for old. It would be too obvious. I reckon as Geoffrey would want to try out how easy it was to filter them into circulation. The amount that has turned up is significant enough in number of pennies to have caused the burgesses to panic, but not so much if you add it together in worth. If he and Roger are on such good terms that Roger warns him of our interest, I would not be surprised if it was through the alehouse that the coin was passed. He only had to pay for any tuns not of his own brewing with the odd forged coin among the good. What doesn't sit well with me, is that the coin that has turned up would pass a first glance but is not that good. Geoffrey has always minted perfect coin, certainly good enough never to call down complaints from the King's Exchequer. These are just plain poor standard.'

Bradecote, who had walked in as Catchpoll finished, was frowning. Serjeant Catchpoll was not sure whether this was from general ill humour, or concentration upon his pronouncement.

'What advantage could there be from producing forged pennies so easy to spot? Once the authorities are alerted it could only be a matter of time before the net closes around the forger, and that would limit how much he could make. Sounds too risky an enterprise by half, unless . . .' Hugh Bradecote paused, thinking through the logic of what had occurred to him. 'If you do not wish to make a profit from the coins, there must be another motive.'

'What other motive could there be?' William de Beauchamp snorted, but Catchpoll's eyes narrowed.

'What is it you're thinking, my lord?'

'Well, to whose advantage is it if there is a loss of faith in the coinage?'

'Not the moneyers, nor the burgesses either.' The lord Sheriff shook his head. 'Nobody profits by it.'

'But whoever the moneyer might be, one thing is on all the pennies, and that is the King's head. Devalue the coin, you devalue the kingship. There are coins in the Empress's image aplenty in Gloucestershire. Would it not aid her to have all the western shires prefer her head upon their coinage?'

'I pray you are wrong,' William de Beauchamp groaned.

It put him in a difficult position if true. He had supported the Empress Maud these two years past, but still held the shrievality in the King's name, clinging on by a mixture of the claim that it was inherited through his grandfather Urse d'Abitot, and because he did nothing in his sheriff's role to give King Stephen cause to hunt for a replacement. De Beauchamp was no fool, and the shrievality was profitable. He collected the King's taxes, from which he was entitled to a percentage, and it gave him power in the shire that he would not wish to lose. If pressed, he argued that the 'King's Peace' was to be upheld whoever the king, or there would be mayhem. He was quite straightforward about it, and the thought of undermining a king by creating distrust of the coinage was underhand and ignoble. If true, however, it would put him in a position where both Stephen and Maud would expect his support.

Bradecote grimaced, but Catchpoll was clearly thinking. His face worked, the muscles twisting the features.

'It might be so, my lords, it can't be denied. Yet it is not the only answer. Look at it this way. Geoffrey puts out coin in another moneyer's name, poor coin that attracts attention. Folk will look to a man they can trust if they bring hacksilver to exchange for pennies, enabling him to produce even more forgeries of a better finish.'

'Seems a bit complicated,' mumbled de Beauchamp, scratching his chin, 'but I would prefer it as an option. Have another go at the alehouse keeper.'

'Well, whatever the answers he may give, we are more likely to get to the bottom of it once we have Geoffrey in our charge, so we sweep the streets for any report or sign of him.' Bradecote sounded morose. 'Catchpoll, as far as I am concerned, it is information on Geoffrey's likely hiding places I want most. Have you set the men-at-arms into parties and given them areas to search?'

'No, my lord, seeing as I was with Roger of the Moon, but I did tell Walkelin to do so, upon your authority, him being no higher than them and like to receive short shrift from many of his fellows. He will be awaiting your final commands by now,

I should imagine. He's Worcester born and bred, and should have a nose for rat holes. I will join you if I get anything of use from the prisoner, my lord.' Catchpoll pulled a wry face. 'And though it goes against the grain, my lord Sheriff, can I offer to look the other way over the passing of any false coin he was dealing?'

'By rights he should lose a hand at the least, if charged,' de Beauchamp growled.

'Aye, and the fear of that keeps his mouth either shut or gabbling like one moon mad, which is almost funny, with the name of his alehouse. We need the answers he may have in his cringing skull, sooner rather than later. I could get them the hard way, but it might be slow.'

'Fair enough, though you can tell him from me, if he ever so much as waters his ale and comes to my attention, I'll have the contents of his codd for earrings for my lady.'

Bradecote, turning to leave, bit his lip. How the sheriff's wife might react to being given a man's testicles as jewellery was hard to imagine. Somehow, he did not think she would be delighted.

Walkelin was flustered. As Catchpoll had surmised, he had received a considerable amount of ribald response from the men-at-arms, who knew he was essentially still one of their number, and lacked any official seniority. 'Apprentice in Serjeanting' gave neither an increase in pay nor power. He was in the uncomfortable position of having to use his superior's rank to get order out of the chaos, and by the time Bradecote arrived on the scene, Walkelin was flushed of cheek and looking harassed. Complaining to the undersheriff, however, would smack of running to Mother with tales, so he kept his own counsel.

The men-at-arms themselves had stiffened into more alert and bellicose poses at Bradecote's arrival. The whisper had already run round the garrison that the undersheriff, who was known as a reasonable individual, was like a man with the toothache this morning, and had best not be crossed.

Bradecote assessed the situation in a glance. He would not make Walkelin's position worse. He therefore spoke to him in the same tone he would have used to Catchpoll, and let Walkelin show that he had used his initiative.

'Are the men aware of what we need to do?'

'Yes, my lord. I have divided them into groups of five men, so that, as they go through an alley, one man stays in the street while a pair searches the building either side. If we keep a steady pace, then if our quarry makes a bolt from the rear of any building he will bump into the next search team to the side.'

'Very good, Walkelin.' He spoke clearly so that all could hear his approbation. It certainly sounded as if it would work, though the reality would be far more muddied, and opportunities for Geoffrey, son of Herluin, to evade capture would present themselves. 'We commence before the castle itself. Oh, and if he does run for it, try and ensure he does not claim sanctuary in any of the churches. We need this man in our custody, and able to answer questions, so do not worry about causing him injury, as long as it is not life-threatening or prevents speech.'

Bradecote gave a twisted smile, which impressed the men-at-arms with his toughness, but which was in fact his recognition that he had sounded as much a hardened and cynical bastard as Serjeant Catchpoll. Being the sheriff's officer was eroding his morality. Six months ago he would not have suggested being rough with a man not yet found guilty of a crime.

He roused himself, aware of the eyes upon him once more, and, with a jerk of the head towards the castle gate, led the search party out into the town. They ignored the priory, though Bradecote had already spoken to the sub-prior and requested that a search be made of the claustral buildings, in case their suspect had taken shelter without wishing to claim the entitlement of sanctuary. The sub-prior had assented willingly, for using the enclave as a place to evade the law, not claiming sanctuary, defiled the sanctity of the House.

The men-at-arms fanned out into their allotted positions. The real problem lay in that there would not be enough of them to guarantee the ends of the line covering the full width between the river and the gated wall. Bradecote wished there had been enough to form a second line, just in case, but he had all the men that were available. He looked along the line, and gave the nod to start. The squads took the northward streets and the back alleys behind the burgage plots, with the instruction to halt at the first cross street, and work along that before advancing north again.

It was a process that took time, and was not greeted with universal approbation. Barely had they begun when an old woman beat a man-at-arms over the head with her broom, haranguing him for creeping into her home, and accusing him of having designs upon her bony person. The man looked more shocked by this than the beating. It caused brief hilarity among his fellows, until Bradecote, stalking between the patrolling men-at-arms, quelled them with sharp words and a hard stare. He was in no mood for jocularity. The men exchanged looks.

In the castle, Catchpoll was finding Roger difficult to persuade. The man was so terrified that the serjeant could smell the rank fear on him, and was repeating for the third time that if he had 'mistakenly' been persuaded to pass forged pennies in his dealings, this would be overlooked if he gave information on the whereabouts of Geoffrey, son of Herluin. The staring eyes gazed at Catchpoll like a fieldmouse mesmerised by a snake.

In desperation, Catchpoll shook the man.

'Sweet Jesu, are you taking in one word of what I say?'

Roger blinked.

'Say something, addlebrain.'

The man did not speak but nodded, repeatedly.

'Then tell me where we find Geoffrey.'

The alehouse keeper licked dry lips and whispered, so softly Catchpoll could not catch the words.

'No. Tell . . . me. I don't want to guess.'

'He has a woman, a woman he uses, off the yard by William Potter's place, in Gloveres Strete. If he has hidden himself, it is where I would think he would go, though I do not know. 'Tis but my guess.'

Catchpoll sighed in relief.

'Your guess had better be good, my friend. For if it is, you leave here a free man. However . . .'

The sheriff's serjeant then went on to pass on his superior's warning, so graphically that Roger felt physically sick, and unconsciously clasped his hands protectively before his manhood. Catchpoll left him, secure in the knowledge that even if Roger did leave the castle a free man, everyone he met would realise you did not want to be brought within its walls for questioning.

He headed, as fast as his dignity would permit, into the busy streets of Worcester, catching up with the men-at-arms as they reached Cokenstrete, and was pointed in the direction of the undersheriff.

'Any luck with the keeper of the Moon tavern?'

'Aye, my lord, at the last. He says that Geoffrey has a woman off the yard by William Potter's place in Gloveres Strete.'

'That is near the eastern wall, yes?'

'Yes, my lord, and north of here. With luck, news of the hunt has not reached the woman's ears yet, but we would be best to make haste.'

Bradecote raised an arm and beckoned those men he could see, Walkelin among them. He sent a man to warn those guarding the nearest gate, and then the whole party set off at the lope to the yard by William the Potter's premises, dividing so that the back as well as front were covered. A lank-haired brunette was seated in the doorway of an unobtrusive house in one corner. She was apparently engrossed in rubbing hard skin from one heel, shamelessly revealing one leg to the knee. Catchpoll wondered what Geoffrey saw in the wench. Perhaps she was just cheap, and him unwilling to pay more.

Some sixth sense clearly alerted her as Catchpoll and Bradecote approached. She got up slowly, smoothing her skirts down, and gazed at them warily, with alert eyes under drooping lids. Bradecote had no time for preamble.

46

'We are here for Geoffrey, son of Herluin, to take in upon the charge of minting false coin.'

She looked at him, assessed her chances of lying successfully, shrugged, and stepped aside. Bradecote let Catchpoll take two men within. There was the sound of a scuffle, and shortly after the trio emerged with Geoffrey firmly held between them. One man-at-arms looked as if he had a black eye in the offing. Bradecote stared coldly at the prisoner.

'Hard to find, aren't you, my friend? Now, we are taking you into custody upon the charge of minting false coin, and falsifying the mark of another moneyer.'

Bradecote was not sure the second was actually a crime, but it sounded serious, and reasonable. The man had stolen another's good name, which was a valuable thing, especially to a man making money.

'The woman, my lord?'

Catchpoll indicated the slovenly brunette. Bradecote stared at her for a moment, sniffed, and shook his head.

'As you wish, my lord.'

Serjeant Catchpoll got far closer to her than Bradecote would have wished, but then, he had seen such, and worse, often enough.

'We've been looking for this man, and all Worcester knows it. You knew, and I know you knew, so best you pick your men more careful in the future, and don't you come within my suspicioning for as much as stealing a feather from a cock's tail.'

The woman gave back stare for stare, but then dropped her gaze and nodded.

'Good,' Catchpoll smiled, which made one of the men-at-arms whisper to his fellow that he almost felt sorry for the wench.

Nobody took any notice of a pedlar, a cloaked and hooded figure crouched in the far corner of the yard, attempting to sell kindling; nobody saw that although his clothes were ragged, his boots were remarkably good.

Chapter Four

William de Beauchamp greeted their success with barely more pleasure than if they had returned empty-handed, in Bradecote's view. He nodded when told of the capture, but said only that it made up for their previous failure. Catchpoll was not surprised. Years of working with, and for, the lord Sheriff of Worcestershire had taught him that de Beauchamp was a man who thought praise was better spent on a hound, since it gave men an overinflated idea of their worth and prowess. The glance he gave the undersheriff gathered that Bradecote had expected more. There was a crease between his brows as they went to interrogate the forger.

'You didn't expect the lord Sheriff to clap his hands and jump for joy, I hope, my lord.'

The sombre look on the undersheriff's face was replaced by a wry smile.

'Not exactly, Catchpoll. Hardly his style, I think.'

'Well, he ain't one to whom praise comes easy. Giving a tongue lashing, now that's a different matter. It has always been his way, as long as I have known him. We might raise a "well done" if we gets a nice healthy confession from our man, though.'

Geoffrey, son of Herluin, despite being in the castle cells, was strangely calm, which both Bradecote and Catchpoll found oddly disconcerting. As Catchpoll admitted, putting one's head in a noose, if he was lucky, and facing a hard death if he was not, would hold a man back from offering a confession at the outset, but Geoffrey had what could almost be described as an arrogance about him, a confidence that his situation should not have given him. He had the odd bruise consequent to resisting arrest, but was otherwise almost cheerful. The answers he gave them were evasive, and he denied any knowledge of forged coin, suggested Roger the alehouse keeper had been imbibing too much of his own ale, and claimed Osbern's journeyman had poured out his troubles to him because his maid was playing hard to get, no more.

Despite a natural urge to ram Geoffrey's grinning teeth down his lying throat, Catchpoll suggested that a night of contemplation in the far from salubrious castle cells might loosen his tongue adequately, and that they resume their 'cosy chat' next day.

Father Samson was not lingering on his journey to Lincoln, taking it in easy stages. He regarded the discomfort of a long day in the saddle as good for the soul, if not the body, and took a certain pride in his aches and pains, though he was guaranteed a decent bed at every religious house at which they halted for the night. The words, 'envoy of Archbishop Theobald' had worked wonders right across South Wales and into the English shires. They spent the first night after leaving Worcester at the Benedictine abbey of Alcester, which was only eighteen miles distant, but the short winter day and frozen ground meant that they could not guarantee reaching the Austin canons at Kenilworth. That was intended to be their stop for the second night.

The road from Worcester towards Stratford was, of course, well known to Christina, and the brothers were not only quiet in obedience to the Rule, avoiding chatter, but clearly discomfited by a female presence. She therefore had the oddest sensation of riding alone, whilst being among a group of men. It gave her time to contemplate matters. Part of her thought she owed it to her pilgrim status to think pious and religious thoughts, but that proved impossible, since Hugh Bradecote loomed large in her head as well as her heart. That he had been concerned for her welfare above all, she knew well enough. It had rankled, the manner of his expressing it, but she forgave him so very readily. Her sin, she thought sadly, was having such a temper. She prayed, most devoutly, that she would be given the strength to quell it when married. Hugh Bradecote admired her spirit, that was clear, but what lord would want a wife who ripped up at him, or rebelled against his wishes? She smiled to herself, and hoped the brothers did not see into her mind. The art of being a good wife was to persuade the husband to one's way of thinking before ever a command was issued, and she thought the task of persuading her new lord would be both exciting, and frequently successful. That thought led naturally to the reason for her journey. If the blessed saint would but smile upon her devotions, she could give Hugh what she longed for, and what he must, as a man, also desire. Marriage was for the bringing forth of children, though for the first time in her life, Christina had realised that the very act of conception need not be a trial, an unpleasant foretaste of the trial that ended in birth. It had always been so for her, and yet now her blood seemed to run the hotter at the mere thought. She reddened. She wanted to feel his child, their child, quicken within her, to see his face when she presented him with another son, to watch the child grow and flourish; she also relished the thought of the pleasures that must precede these things. Such thoughts were truly unsuitable for one upon pilgrimage, and she resolved to wear only the one cloak next day in penance.

They set off after Prime the following day, with the abbot's benediction carried after them upon the chill wind, which made Christina shiver, and half regret her previous day's resolution. The second cloak, however, remained rolled behind her saddle. They were only perhaps a mile or two beyond Stratford itself when they heard the sound of hooves at speed behind them, and drew to the wooded side of the trackway to let pass whoever was in such haste. It sounded as if it must be some body of soldiers, for there were certainly many horses. The idea that there was any risk would have been discounted, for they were humble men of God, without wealth worth the stealing, and protected by their calling. The horsemen were alongside them before any realised they had drawn swords, and were not going to overtake them. The vanguard swung round, blocking any advance, and the undergrowth was too tangled a mass of briars to allow any escape into the trees. A hand was thrust out to grab Father Samson's bridle. He remonstrated, but was met with a callous laugh, and was struck. Even as he rocked in the saddle, a younger monk tried to manoeuvre his own mount between his superior and the assailant, and so far forgot his calling as to flail a fist at the attacker. The man laughed, avoided the blow, and brought his sword crashing into the side of the Benedictine's head. It was as much a battering from the crosspiece as a slash from the upper part of the blade, and if it did not kill, then it rendered him unconscious as it struck. The brother toppled from his mule into the undergrowth with a lifeless thud. Father Samson's eyes bulged in horror at this violence, but even as words rose to his lips, fear froze them in his mouth. As a man of God, he was prepared, far more than most, to meet his Maker, but had a very human inclination to delay that encounter as long as possible. The swordsman smiled, which was not in any way encouraging.

Christina, confused as much as shocked by what was going on, was not foolish enough to risk injury when her own reins were grabbed, but flashed the rough-looking man whose grimed hand grabbed them from her a look of haughty anger, which he seemed to find amusing. He grinned, baring gapped and discoloured teeth.

It all seemed to happen so fast that they were being led back and then taking a narrow pathway through the coppicing before they could contemplate fully that they had been abducted.

There were perhaps a dozen kidnappers, scarcely many more, but well-armed and easily able to control the seven unarmed Benedictines and the lone woman. Christina knew it was fruitless trying to work out their direction, threading their way as they were through the trees to skirt Stratford, and common sense screamed at her that this was folly, for the only things of value the group possessed were their mounts. She wondered, with concern, if the quality of her own horse might mark her out. Her garb might be that of any reasonably fortuned dame, a merchant's wife or widow, perhaps, not clearly a lady. Her horse was a tidy beast, and few of the mercantile class would possess such an animal.

Thinking as calmly as she could, Christina tried to weigh the situation, and decide how best to both preserve her safety, and give her the greatest chance of being freed. Robbery was not the motive, that was obvious. The likeliest alternative was that whoever had taken them had followed the group for some time and knew the importance of Father Samson. There was a chance they also knew her identity, but it was the merest chance. Should she reveal who she was, and hope that fear of bringing the wrath and power of the shrievality down upon them at a personal level would make them let her go? She looked surreptitiously at the man who seemed to be the leader, and decided against it. Better to remain a nobody and hope that she would merely be numbered among the Benedictine brothers, held so as not to reveal the who and why.

The man she studied had hard eyes, so pale a grey that the black pupils took on a sharp malevolence that made her shudder within. She knew such a face of old: Arnulf de Malfleur, her first husband, had been as cold of visage, and a man in whom kindness was entirely absent, and evil as natural as breathing. Christina FitzPayne had truly thought all the horror of the past could be buried, but her head told her that she must face it again until such time as Hugh found her. He would find her; she no more doubted it than that the sun would rise above the horizon in the morning. How he would do so, she did not know. She did not know where they were, whether they would be held in some hideaway, or moved day by day. At least that way there might be an opportunity to leave some sign to aid pursuers. She prayed, silently but fervently, aware that at this moment only her prayers, and those of the Benedictine brothers, stood between them and an abyss.

They crossed the salt road along which the clerical party had come to Stratford, and a glimpse of the sun just beginning its descent made Christina think at least one prayer was answered, for heading westward meant being closer to Worcester and Hugh. As the afternoon progressed, she also knew they were still north of the Avon. As the shadows lengthened into eventide, a man was sent ahead to scout out any shelter. He returned with news of a grange, scarcely half a mile ahead. Reynald de Roules lifted a hand, and the men behind him halted. Beckoning his lieutenant to his side, the pair of them reconnoitred the grange. It looked as if it was poorly tended, and they wondered, briefly, if it might even be uninhabited. There was a single mule in the stable, however, and, upon closer inspection, a thread of light from within behind the heavy wooden shutters at the window of the dwelling. In the near darkness, de Roules grinned at his companion. This would be easy. He nodded, and the other man drew the hood of his cloak over his head, bent to look cold and weary, and knocked upon the door. A wary voice questioned who might be there, and he replied in a tremulous voice at odds with his healthy frame.

'I beg refuge, Brother, on a cold night, for I am lost and assuredly will perish if you do not show me charity.'

There was the scraping sound from the lifting of a wooden bar, and the door opened a few inches. A lay brother peered out, at a disadvantage looking from comparative light into the gloom.

'Of God's grace, Brother?' The voice pleaded.

The door opened another foot. No more was needed. The hooded figure straightened and stepped forward smartly, the steel of his knife catching the light, but without him doing anything more, de Roules pushed past, sword drawn. He did not so much thrust as slide the blade into the unsuspecting brother so that he died with no more than a widening of the eyes and a hiss. Even as the man crumpled, de Roules pushed past, dragging back the blood-wet sword, and faced the second occupant, who grabbed a staff and brandished it half-heartedly. Reynald de Roules smiled broadly.

The waiting horsemen heard nothing until called forward, and urged their mounts into the clearing before the ramshackle grange. Their hostages were dragged from their animals, some stumbling where the cold had numbed their feet, and pushed unceremoniously into what was barely more than a cottage. They blinked first in the light, and then with undisguised horror at the cowled forms in the corner like a heap of rags. The wide-eyed stare of the first brother showed from the dead face, and de Roules was wiping his blade on the skirt of the other brother's habit. The Benedictines crossed themselves.

'How could you . . . ?' Father Samson mastered his voice.

'Very easily, and if you don't want to find out how, you'll shut up.' Reynald de Roules looked at the religious with near loathing. 'I cannot abide sanctimonious fools who haven't the courage to take life and shake it. It is all threats with you, threats and empty promises, disguising your own guilt.'

The look of horror on Father Samson's face was replaced by blank incomprehension. He could not conceive why this man should spout such venom. Seeing it, de Roules scowled and clamped his lips into a thin line, as if regretting giving so much insight into his thoughts. There was an almost nervous silence from both captors and captives alike. A monk sank to his knees, taking refuge in prayer even if it angered the dangerous individual who held them, and one by one the others followed suit. De Roules turned away, his lip curling, but said nothing more. It gave a chance for the tension to ease.

Christina was somehow divorced from the scene, half forgotten in the background. There was no possibility of escape, for she knew she could not slip away entirely unnoticed and she had no idea where she was, but she tried to make sense of what she was watching. She had certainly been correct in her first assumptions about the leader of the gang, whom a man had addressed as 'my lord'. He was no common criminal; perhaps he had committed some crime and been declared outlaw in the past. He was cold enough, but not totally cold. His words to Father Samson had been bitter, and from deep within. She wondered if they had been targeted specifically because they were a group of religious. Her first thought had been that they had been taken for ransom, but if this man hated so much, it might as easily be to satisfy his bloodlust, and where did that leave her? There was a cold, sick feeling in the pit of her stomach. When he had finished with the Benedictines, he would not be letting her go free.

De Roules was speaking quietly to his right-hand man, the one he called Guy. There were practicalities like food and water to be considered. There was a well to the rear of the building and one of the men was sent to draw enough to boil for a pottage. One man unpacked a sack, and then muttered and spoke to Guy, who stroked his close-cropped beard, smiled and nodded. The man grinned and brought the bag of barley, onions and dried herbs to Christina.

'Here. A woman is good for two things. Since we ain't being allowed the one, you can give us the other. Cook the dinner.'

Christina did not demur. Nor did she reveal that her experience of actually cooking a meal was almost non-existent. She had overseen feasts and the daily provision of meals in a manor, but not stood over cooking pots. Well, if she hoped to maintain the deception of her being but a merchant's widow, she would have to show at least some nearer experience and ability. She said a silent prayer and hoped that a simple pottage could not go wrong. Had it not been so serious, it would have been almost funny that her future might depend upon her cooking skills.

The fire was fed, the iron cooking pot hung over it and Christina FitzPayne, twice the widow of landed lords and the betrothed of the lord Undersheriff of Worcester, sliced onions that brought tears to her eyes. The smell, at least, was promising. She even heard a stomach rumbling. Her addition of herbs was probably the most decisive element, when she might turn a reasonable effort into something that would either draw praise or be spat into the embers.

She was only able to relax when the pottage was ladled into bowls and a murmur of approval ran among the kidnappers, and even the brethren. It also meant, however, that Christina was appointed cook for the party. She hoped they would not expect variety.

The normality of eating seemed to calm nerves. The threatening atmosphere lessened, though de Roules would not have the corpses moved. He thought it amusing, watching the Benedictines, who were divided between those who averted their eyes and studiously avoided facing the corner, and those for whom the sight had a mesmeric fascination. Christina assumed that, after the meal, the details of a night watch would be made, and then everyone would settle to rest as best they could. It was most unexpected when the leader got up and addressed them.

'You may be wondering why I have gathered you here . . .' He paused for effect, and Christina wondered whether he meant 'gathered' as a man gathered witless sheep, 'because I promise you, I do not hunt your sort for pleasure; poor sport it would be. However, you are of use to me; at least he is.'

De Roules pointed at Father Samson, who tried to outstare him, and failed. The lupine smile returned to the thin lips. A couple of the brothers shifted uncomfortably, for there was malice in the expression.

'William de Beauchamp, Sheriff of Worcestershire, holds something I want, so I need to get him to hand it over. I know him of old, and so taking just anyone is no use. I have to hold someone he dare not shrug and let me kill, rather than give in. Fortunately for me, here is the Archbishop of Canterbury's envoy passing through, and de Beauchamp dare not be seen to throw him to the wolves.' He laughed, and gave a wolf howl, eyes sparkling.

Father Samson looked at him with the growing realisation that there was a dangerous madness to the man.

'Who are you, my son?'

'I am Reynald de Roules, and no son of your getting.' The reply was spat. The name meant nothing to Father Samson, though Christina felt some vague jangling of memory. De Roules continued, 'So what I need to do now is let de Beauchamp know what I have. Monks write, so which of you black sheep can wield a quill? Hands up.'

The brothers looked to Father Samson, who frowned, but nodded. Two brothers held up a hand. De Roules pointed to the elder, a mild-looking man with fluffy, greying hair that had once been ginger ringing his tonsure.

'You, the old one, come here.' He swept bowls from the small table in the room and nodded at Guy, who brought out vellum, quill and ink. He pressed the brother onto the narrow bench. 'Write just what I tell you.'

He set out his demand, which was simple enough, and carried the threat of the murder of the hostages, one by one. At the end, he picked up the vellum by one corner as if tainted, and handed it to Guy, who scanned it. The scribe went white. Guy

60

looked down at the monk, momentary respect in his eyes, and then struck him from the seat.

'My lord, this brother is guilty of the sin of disobedience. He has not written just what was said. He has rather told the sheriff who you are and how many men we are.'

Reynald de Roules looked at the brother sprawling on the dirt floor. When he spoke, his voice was very calm, and matter-of-fact.

'Oh yes, I did not say that Guy here could write, but nor did I say he could not read. Disobedience is a sin, Brother. You must do penance. It shall be not to write again.' He looked at Guy. 'The message would be best delivered by hand, so de Beauchamp knows we are serious, do you not think?'

They exchanged glances, and Guy grabbed the Benedictine by the scruff of the neck and hauled him outside into the dark. De Roules looked at the other brother who could write.

'You will be obedient, won't you, Brother?' The monk nodded, wide-eyed with fear, and jumped as there came a thud and a scream from outside. 'Then write exactly what I say.'

It was pure chance that the brother was found before he froze to death. A man walking back from the next village had turned aside to attend to the demands of nature, with some reluctance. Exposing his buttocks in the biting cold was less than appealing, but there was no help for it. He stepped from the track into the undergrowth and almost fell over the body, effectively camouflaged by the dark habit. The man bent down to draw back the cowl, his bowels forgotten, and crossed himself. There was blood, sticky to the touch, and with the smell that clung in the nostrils, from a wound that sliced into the tonsure above the left ear, but was mostly a mess at the top of his jaw. He assumed the man – not an old man either – was dead, and shook his head that any should strike down a man of God. He rolled the body onto its back, and only then noticed that there was breath and life within. The Good Samaritan sniffed, and wiped his sleeve under his nose. The man did not look huge, but it was not going to be easy, carrying him the half-mile home. Muttering to himself about wishing that he could guarantee regular meals that fed the cloistered, he shouldered his burden with a grunt, and then put him down again. It was no use, nature had to come first.

By the time he reached his home, the colour had gone from the world, and the grey of deep gloaming lay upon the way like a dark blanket. He opened the door clumsily, breathing heavily from his load. The man's wife, exclaiming at what he had found, was both pitying and worried. What if the brother died in their cottage? What if he didn't die and needed nursing and feeding for who knew how long? She bade her husband lay him on their palliasse and then go, as soon as he had the breath in his lungs, to fetch the priest, both in case the poor man needed final absolution, but more importantly so that he could assume control and responsibility for the situation.

Father Cuthbert arrived, wheezing, frowning, and mopping his brow with his sleeve. It was both a foul crime and, as far as he could see, a useless one, to rob a man who possessed nothing, and how could any man do such a thing to a holy brother? He looked at the unconscious monk. He was no physician, and had no more idea if the Benedictine would die than the cottagers.

'If the skull is full broken, he will most likely die. If the bone is but scored or slightly cracked, he may live. The wound must be bound and cleaned, and he must be kept warm.'

'Can he be moved, Father?'

The woman was not just trying to rid herself of a burden. There were four children in the one-roomed dwelling, and all huddled on the same straw-filled bed at night for warmth in the winter cold. If the wounded man took the bed, they either had to join him, a stranger, and potentially a dying man, or all lie upon the compacted dirt of the floor.

The priest stroked his chin and sighed. If the man was to die, it was the will of God, though the Almighty had had nothing to do with the getting of the wound. He had already been carried over a man's shoulder and survived, so another hundred paces or so should make little difference. He understood the woman's concerns. He sighed.

'Let him come to me, and I will keep vigil. You have many other duties. But I will fetch Wulfram, and that hurdle he was making today, on which to carry our poor brother. And in the morning, whatever has come to pass, I will go to the lord, and have him send word to the lord Sheriff at Warwick. A crime such as this must, of a surety, be laid before the law.'

Father Cuthbert's charge did not die, but nor did he awaken. He seemed to be in a deep sleep, but there was no hint of the changes in breathing that the good father, who had attended many deathbeds, had come to recognise. In the morning he did as he had said, and went to the lord of the manor to report the crime, leaving old Mother Hild to sit and watch the patient. The lord pulled a face.

'Where was he found, Father?'

'By the King's road, my lord, so there is no requirement for hue and cry in the village, not that it would avail us aught. An attack is a wicked thing, but upon a holy brother . . .' The priest shook his head at the evils men perpetrated. 'The lord Sheriff should be told, though whether it is a killing is yet to be seen.'

'I will send a man to inform him, and let me know if the brother wakens, or dies.'

Chapter Five

A man-at-arms crossed the bailey and made his way as inconspicuously as possible up to Serjeant Catchpoll, looking both embarrassed and a little shocked. Catchpoll's eyes widened for a second as the man whispered in his ear, and he frowned, the grizzled, grey brows beetling. The man-at-arms winced, expecting to be berated, but the serjeant ignored him and went straight to the sheriff and undersheriff, his face inscrutable.

'My lords, there is something you should see on the castle gate.'

'If it's at the gate, then bring it here, Serjeant.' De Beauchamp was only half attending.

'No, my lord, I said "on", not "at".'

The import of what Catchpoll had said sunk in. His superiors followed him and the man-at-arms, who was now considering whether he was going to be shouted at by even more important people or whether, if he was fortunate, he would now be forgotten.

The castle gate had been opened, and several of the castle inhabitants had drawn round in ghoulish interest. They now fell back. There was a stained piece of vellum attached to the door by an iron spike hammered into the solid oak, but what had attracted the attention was that the spike passed first through the palm of a smallish, dismembered hand. It was both repellent and magnetic, drawing the eye even as it turned the stomach. A woman crossed herself.

Catchpoll was not squeamish. He got as close as possible and peered at the hand.

'Hacked off cleanish in a couple of strokes I would say, my lords. May I remove it?'

'Yes, take it down, Catchpoll so we can see the message.'

Catchpoll pulled the cold metal from the equally cold flesh, and dropped the spike, holding the hand in place for a moment. There was no blood, what had remained having already stained the vellum. He took the writing in his free hand and passed it to Bradecote, since it meant nothing to him. Instead he studied the hand itself.

Bradecote could read, not as fast as a clerk, but well enough. His cheek paled and he took a sharp intake of breath.

'My lord, this comes from someone who wants the release of Geoffrey the Moneyer, to be set free at noon tomorrow in Upton, by the sheriff himself, and alone. In exchange for which they will free the Archbishop of Canterbury's envoy and his party, whom they took on the road north-east of Stratford. That must have been the day before yesterday.

Failure to comply will mean the deaths of the hostages, one by one. We will know when the envoy has met his Maker by the arrival of his head. As a token of the seriousness of their intent they deliver this demand "by hand".' He paused. 'My lord, they hold my Christina.'

He looked suddenly to Catchpoll, holding the hand, and the serjeant, as if reading his thoughts, put his first fear aside.

'This, I would say, was the hand of a man, and a religious. There are no calluses from heavy labour, but there are ink stains beneath the nails and a thickening of the skin at the tip joint of the middle finger. This was a clerk or scribe.'

He heard Bradecote's relieved exhalation. He ought to be able to tell the difference himself, but his mind was a tumble of thoughts.

'Bring these things where we can be private. I have no intention of discussing this before a load of gawping idiots.' The lord Sheriff sounded aggrieved. He had been envisaging a few days of feasting and relaxation still, and now this had arisen to spoil everything. 'Bradecote,' he jerked his head towards the hall and stalked away.

'I will be with you directly, my lords,' Catchpoll threw after them, turning to the man-at-arms, who had not been forgotten.

'I want whoever was on watch from the time these gates were closed last night, now.'

The last word was barked, and sent the man-at-arms scurrying away. He returned within a couple of minutes with four hangdog-looking men.

'So, you were on watch at the gate all night, but I suppose none of you happened to notice anyone come up to it? Admittedly, someone could do that on the quiet, and be missed, but tell me, do, just how in the name of Our Lady and all the saints of heaven, did you cloth-ears not hear some bastard hammering a dirty great spike into the door?'

'We might have been taking a turn on the battlement, Serjeant,' offered a man tentatively.

'The very battlement that overlooks the gate?'

'If we were on the stair—'

'Either you climb so slow your aged fathers – if you ever knew who they were – could still go faster, or the bastard with the spike hammered mighty fast and has the muscles of a blacksmith.'

'Then that is a clue, Serjeant. Should we go and make enquiries of the bla—'

'No, you dolt. I want to know what you think I am going to tell the lord Sheriff that will keep you from a flogging for being asleep on watch.'

'We wasn't none of us asleep, honest, Serjeant.'

'You might as well have been, for the use you are.' Catchpoll shook his head at their ineptitude and swore, long and smoothly, then sighed. 'You are dismissed, but you will be on double watch for the next week, and no Twelfth Night feasting for any of you. Now bugger off, before I think of any other punishments I care to mete out.'

The men dispersed, not daring to so much as grumble, and still hoping that the sheriff would not have them flogged as an example.

Catchpoll went to the sheriff's chamber, bearing the severed limb like a bizarre trophy, set it on the floor, and took position near the brazier where he could warm his chilled hands.

Bradecote sat leaning forward, staring at his own hands, which were clasped between his knees, almost as if in prayer. He felt sick, a clammy hand gripping his viscera, and his brain could not claw its way past the simple fact that Christina was in the hands of men who had no compunction in lopping off the limb of an innocent man of God. What might they not do to a woman? He should have remained resolute. He should have forbidden her to go and stuck to his resolve, not been weak and succumbed to her pleading and sulks. And yet he had had no right to stop her, nor the heart, when she was so determined that only this would give her the talisman that would see a child of her own at her knee. She had said it must not be easy or it would not be valid as a pilgrimage. He thought that was why she had been so keen to go without his escort, the pleasure of being together. Well, she could not have imagined it would be this hard. His hands clenched and he did pray, silently and fervently, that God would keep her safe. He barely registered that the sheriff and Catchpoll were now in discussion over the implications of the ransom.

'Their demand is simple enough.' William de Beauchamp was frowning, thinking out loud. 'Which makes me wonder just what our man Geoffrey is up to. They would not want a man simply because he can forge coin. All they would need to do is put pressure upon any who possess the dies. Even a good, honest man could be expected to comply if he or his family were at risk. So that means Geoffrey has, or knows, something special.'

'If what he knows means they just wanted him dead, because of what he could reveal, getting someone into the castle wouldn't be that difficult if nobody was expecting a problem, my lord.' Catchpoll rubbed his grizzled chin. 'We have folk in and out all day. One distraction, mayhap one bribe, and there would be access to the cells, and whether he was killed obvious or killed subtle, dead he would be, and the risk of him loosing his tongue would be gone. No, there is more, much more here.'

Bradecote, catching the end of the serjeant's comment, looked from one to the other. They were calmly discussing the man in their custody when Christina stood in fear of her life. He wanted to cry out that it did not matter what was special about Geoffrey, unless it was going to help them find her, get her back safely. He ran a hand that was not quite steady through his hair. His voice, when he got control of it, was edged with a fear that Catchpoll could almost touch.

'We have nothing. We don't know who they are, where they are, only that they have hostages and no compunction about killing them, only that they have Christina.' Bradecote's voice was barely above a whisper.

'My lord, it is natural enough that you should feel this way, but it ain't any use you thinking bleak.' Catchpoll sounded perfectly calm. 'Your lady needs you strong right now, thinking straight and clear. And you are wrong. There are things we know: we know what they want, for a start. Since Geoffrey the Moneyer is not honest, you can lay odds that he has some knowledge of the men who want to free him. Criminals know criminals. If any moneyer would do, these men could have simply taken any in the trade, and used them. No, they want Geoffrey for a reason, so sense says he knows about them, even if they have not worked together before or even met face to face, and what he knows, we shall know soon enough. Best leave him to me, my lord.'

Catchpoll knew his superior was not in favour of extracting information by force. He regarded it as both wrong and liable to provide merely the answers the prisoner thought would be acceptable. Bradecote's response surprised him.

'Do what you will, but do it fast, and if he holds back, call me.'

There was a cold ruthlessness in the voice that left the serjeant without words for a moment, and he simply nodded. Bradecote, whose gaze had been blank, looked at him; the eyes were hard, and a bitter half-smile twisted his mouth.

'You think me inconsistent. Well, I am. I don't care for torture, but if that is the way to get her back safely, then I care not what you do.'

'Not inconsistent, my lord, just normal, and I don't recall you offering Reginald, de Malfleur's man, soft words when he tried to keep knowledge of the lady's whereabouts from us in Wich. You offered him a fair choice: tell or suffer. And if he didn't believe you, he learnt his mistake fast enough.'

'That was heat of the moment, gut reaction.'

'Aye, my lord, and sometimes we needs to follow our gut reaction. I'll get what Geoffrey knows, have no doubt about it, and we already know something else as well.'

'What?' Bradecote sighed.

71

'They have someone with them who knows his letters, a scribbler, and—'

'Or simply compelling one of Father Samson's scribes under duress,' interjected Bradecote, dejectedly.

'Aye, that they could, but they'd be fools if they sent out any message unread. What would be to stop the message saying just where they were and what was toward? No, if that is so, they have someone at least lettered enough to read the message. And if they sent that message in during the night, then they are within a day of Worcester. I know it is perishing cold and that hand would not start to rot fast in such weather, but they are not going to want to wait for days while a message is delivered. My guess is that they have headed back towards Worcester, and are no more than half a night's ride away this dawning.'

'But will be sure to depart as soon as their messenger returns.' Bradecote sounded glum.

'Indeed, but haring off across the shire borders keeps them also from their prize. They cannot afford to go too far. If we were to release Geoffrey . . .'

Bradecote repeated the serjeant's words, suddenly considering their merit. He looked at William de Beauchamp, who had been lost in his own thoughts.

'Let the man go as they ask, and follow him to where they meet. You want them; this guarantees you get what you want, my lord Sheriff.'

William de Beauchamp shook his head, not without regret.

'No. I am sorry, but no.'

'Why not? It would—'

72

'—not guarantee either the safety of Father Samson, or your betrothed, but it would give the bastards the chance to show that holding to ransom works. What if they manage to elude us? Or fail to come up with their side of the bargain? They are criminals, when all is said and done. I'll not have that in my shire, for the sake of every free man in its bounds, though it goes hard now. No,' he held up a hand as Hugh Bradecote made to say more, 'I will not be swayed on this, Bradecote, there is an end to it. We find these men; we bring them to justice or kill them, and we do the best we can for those they have taken. Every man I possess can be turned to this, and if we do not sleep for a week, so be it.'

Bradecote knew further remonstrance was pointless, and there was, sadly, truth in what the lord Sheriff said. Had it been any other hostage he would have agreed with him, but this was personal.

Serjeant Catchpoll sent men about every street to proclaim that the lord Sheriff of Worcester would reward any person with useful information about whosoever had nailed the hand to the castle gate. Their best chances were near the castle itself and at the gates, and it took all Bradecote's self-control not to go to every dwelling before the castle in person to find out any scrap of information. William de Beauchamp watched him, saw the tumult within and kept his own counsel. His new undersheriff, drafted in, it must be said, upon a whim, had proved remarkably good, and had won the respect of Serjeant Catchpoll. That said a great deal about Hugh Bradecote, but if this all went to the bad, as it could, the sheriff wondered how much use he might be thereafter. Well, time would tell, but when Catchpoll met up with him again, he took him to one side.

'Oh aye, my lord. I'll watch him like a cat with one kitten. He'll need a mite of time to come to terms with the situation, but I don't think he'll crack under the strain.' He omitted to add the 'not quite' that echoed in his head. 'And once there is something to be done it will be a lot easier on him, as on us all. No man likes to feel helpless in the face of a threat upon his own.' He paused. 'What would you have us do first, my lord, since we are not handing Geoffrey the Forger over?'

De Beauchamp's eyes narrowed.

'Do I detect a hint that you would do so, Catchpoll?' His voice had an edge of sneer. 'I had not thought you soft, in the head or of heart.'

'No, my lord, you do not. You were right; we cannot be weak or there will be no law in the shire.'

'Well, it is my intent to go to Upton and cross with my prisoner, but I want you and Bradecote, and as many men as we can muster, to cross here at dawn and follow the far bank of the Severn to come into Upton from the north, just in case they have decided to do the least expected. They might be stupid enough to turn up for us if they have no experience.'

Catchpoll sucked his teeth, for that sounded unlikely.

The word had got around. Small wonder the undersheriff was in a foul mood, with his betrothed held captive by whoever had sent the severed hand, but they wished he would not take it out upon them. He had already bitten the head off a man-at-arms for merely mentioning that there had been no answer at three premises where he had knocked the door, so the residents were clearly not within. He had been cuffed about the ear, sent to break down the doors, if needs must, to prove that, and not to return until he had either spoken to the householders or proved their absence.

'Not our fault, is it,' mumbled one, 'if his wench gets taken.'

'It's having her "taken" that's like to be worrying him most.'

A man chortled, seeing the comment as a clever jest, but was spun round and sent sprawling on the ground. He had not realised the undersheriff had stopped around the corner and was still within earshot. Hugh Bradecote stared down at him with a face so thunderous, the man cowered, his arm protecting his head, fully expecting to hear the sound of steel being drawn.

'You'd best lie there in the dirt, like the foul-mouthed cur you are, for if you rise I will not vouch for my actions.'

Bradecote spoke softly, through gritted teeth, his hand now clenched upon the hilt of his sword. The other men, thanking Providence it had not been them who had laughed, stepped back and tried to be as inconspicuous as possible.

'And if I hear one word, one single word, insulting the honour of the lady I am to wed,' and his fierce glance now challenged them all, 'I will have the man flogged first, and then will deal with him personally. Understood?'

The men nodded, gazed at their feet, and mumbled their comprehension. Bradecote turned away swiftly, and headed off with a long stride. His breathing was laboured, though not from any exertion, and once away from the men he stopped, closed his eyes, and leant against the side wall of the kitchens. A young woman, emerging to cast the contents of a greasy pail into the dust, glanced at him in concern.

'If you are taken bad, my lord, I can offer you a stool and a beaker within.'

Her lilting voice was uncertain, her intent generous. He shook his head, and, mastering his voice at last, thanked her for the offer. She bobbed a curtsey, and he carried on to the great hall, where he could consult with the lord Sheriff.

He was shaken, mentally, though it had found physical expression. He was not a man with a temper on a short leash, not normally. This, he told himself, was not normal, but even as he acknowledged it, he was assailed by the fear that his ability to focus, his chance of doing everything that Christina needed of him now, was imperilled by his emotions. He made a conscious effort to get a grip upon himself, and put the nightmarish thoughts, so presciently voiced by the man-at-arms, firmly from his mind.

As he walked in upon de Beauchamp and Serjeant Catchpoll there was a sudden silence. It did not take a great intellect to gather that he had been in their minds and on their lips. His lips compressed together, lest he speak unwisely, but his eyes could not hide his anger. Catchpoll was not blind, and tried to ease the tension. A chilling of relations between his superiors would not help matters.

'We were discussing how much information we might gain from Geoffrey, my lord,' Catchpoll lied, unflinchingly. 'We do not know whether he had direct contact with these men, or only knew them via an intermediary. To my mind the latter might even be of greater use. He might have been out of Worcester and met them where they are wont to be, but it would be safer for both him and them if he stayed put and someone came to him, either a single member of the gang, or a middle man. If that person can be taken, well they will know details of how many there are, what they plan overall; they will have our vital answers.'

'Then we speak to Geoffrey, right away.' Bradecote's crisp tone implied he, for one, would not accept prevarication from the prisoner.

Catchpoll pulled a face, not one of his 'thinking' faces, but one where he knew he was about to give unpalatable information.

'That, my lord, is not possible. I went to the cells when you sent the men out to the Foregate. Truth is, the man must have had some coin about him, secret like, and bribed one of the guards to get him ale, ale enough to get him stone drunk. Either he wanted to blot out his captivity or ensure we could not get sense out of him a while longer.'

'He bribed one of my gaolers?' growled de Beauchamp, grinding his teeth. 'I'll have whoever it was flogged to within an inch of his life.'

'Indeed, my lord, I am going to spend the rest of the day finding out, since there is little more to be done until tomorrow upon the kidnapping.'

'We sluice the man down and sober him up,' muttered Bradecote.

'Aye, we could, my lord, but what credit could we give to his answers, and at the moment he is unconscious.'

Bradecote picked up a beaker that stood upon the trestle table, and threw it at the wall, vindictively. The other two men showed no reaction. After all, a man needed to work off his frustration, and Hugh Bradecote was a very frustrated man.

Chapter Six

He looked innocent enough, the man waiting for the blacksmith to shoe his horse, and the fact that he was a stranger mattered not. Travellers upon the road needed their horses shod, and so nobody paid him any attention. He stamped his feet and blew upon his chilled hands occasionally, and did not say much, but then, the blacksmith was plying his trade, and not making small-talk on a cold January morning, with the hoarfrost clinging silvery upon the bare branches of the trees, and the ground as hard as iron.

There was ice upon the Severn, near to the banks, although not enough to prevent the ferryman from breaking it with a stout pole, and taking a shawl-wrapped woman across to be with her daughter at her confinement up over the hill in Croome. He had no expectation of making the return with any passenger, and was only too pleased to be offered coin by the grand lord, dragging behind him a bound man, no doubt some villain guilty of absconding after some misdemeanour. The man's hood was dragged over his bowed head and his hands looked blue with cold. The ferryman could see why the man appeared so despondent. Looking at the scowling countenance of the fur-cloaked rider, he did not give much for his chances once he was got home.

On the far side, the prisoner was dragged unceremoniously up the bank behind the big bay horse as the ferryman tied up his craft. Villagers turned their heads, and the traveller did likewise, though none saw the narrowing of his eyes as he studied the figure of the stumbling prisoner. In the centre of the village the horseman halted, dismissing the lad who ran forward to take his horse as if he was swatting away an irksome fly. The horse stamped and blew down its nostrils, its opaque breath hanging in the air. A small child hid its head in its mother's skirts, and mumbled about a monster. Everyone stood as if waiting for something to happen, though only horseman and prisoner had any inkling what it might be. The blacksmith, having spared the novelty a glance, returned to his work, and the clang of hammer on iron and anvil rang clear in the air.

William de Beauchamp pursed his lips. His feet were getting cold and he disliked inaction. He waited. The scene remained frozen, like the ice at the Severn's banks, in anticipation of something unknown. After a while, however, the villagers shrugged and continued about their business. The blacksmith took up the horse's off hind between his knees, the nails clamped between his thin lips, and began to drive them home, but the horse shied and struggled, and he was forced to let the hoof down as a large number of horsemen clattered into the village, not just upon the road, but from between cottages. They arrived at the canter, purposefully, and with weapons drawn. Their leader trotted forward to the stationary lord, and engaged him in conversation, which none of the villagers would have understood, even had they overheard it, for it was conducted in Norman French.

'Nothing?'

'Nothing, my lord.' Bradecote shook his head. 'No sign that any group of horses have waited within a half-mile of here in the last day or so, for even if the ground is too hard for imprints of shoes, as Catchpoll says, horse dung is horse dung.'

'Bastards.' The lord Sheriff swore, not at Bradecote and his men, but at the faithless kidnappers. 'They never had any intention of letting the hostages free here. I knew as much.'

The undersheriff's face was pinched, and not just from the cold. He had told himself it was unlikely, but the glimmer of hope that they might resolve this now, today, and he could have Christina safe in his hold, had suffused his mind. That hope now lay cold as the lingering frost.

By the smithy, the final nail had been clenched, and the smith let the horse put hoof to ground and patted the haunch. The traveller paid him with thanks, mounted and trotted past the lord Sheriff, with a respectful nod in recognition of his obvious status, out on the westward road.

'It was worth the attempt, if only to prove the vermin we are dealing with,' de Beauchamp admitted, in a low grumble, 'but now we have to hunt as we hunt vermin, to the death, Bradecote.'

Hugh Bradecote's heart sank. De Beauchamp would try to keep so important a churchman as Father Samson alive, and Christina too, but his patience was thin, and if he thought there was even a glimmer of a chance, he would take the kidnappers on, man on man, and hope to Providence that he could rescue the important hostages before they were murdered. Bradecote had little faith in such a tactic.

Serjeant Catchpoll approached on foot, having dismounted and sought counsel of the village reeve.

'Nothing of note within the village these last two days, my lords, not that they would ride through, not the whole party. A group of armed horsemen and religious would set tongues wagging, sure enough. There haven't even been strangers, above the man who had his horse shod this . . .'

The sentence trailed off, as all three men saw the blindingly obvious.

'They did not specify an exchange here, just that Geoffrey be freed. My God, he was here to see if it was Geoffrey and if he was to be let go.' Bradecote shut his eyes in horror. 'And he saw the men-at-arms arrive. He knows we were not going to do as they demanded.'

'Before you start taking birch rods to your own back, Bradecote, remember we have no reason, whatsoever, to assume they were then going to release their hostages. If they have what they want, why let those go who could identify them?'

Catchpoll looked at the undersheriff's haggard face with some sympathy.

'The lord Sheriff has the right of it, my lord, though sorry I am to drive the point home. In doing what we have today we may have even kept your lady safe for longer. They may take retribution, but their only bargaining power is live hostages. They might not be so kind to the brethren, but the archbishop's man and a noble lady, well, they are valuable to them, as long as they still seek their man.'

Bradecote felt sick to his stomach, and his brain felt as sluggish as the half-frozen waters of the river. He tried hard to think, and the more he did, the more his fear took hold.

'The man with the shod horse took the westward road, my lords, towards the crossing of the Hills to Ledbury, past the Old Place.' Catchpoll pointed to where long, long ago men had made their mark upon the shire border, and terraced the top of the hill into a prominent gathering point. It still stuck above the treeline near the southern end of the Malvern Hills. There was a wooden palisade and raised motte upon it now, as the lord Waleran de Meulun, Earl of Worcester, had stamped his authority on the shire boundary in these troubled times, but Catchpoll still called it the 'Old Place' as his forefathers had done. He ignored his superior's pallor. 'It isn't much, but we know they are on this side of the river and getting back will be hard to do without us knowing, if we set a watch here, for there are no other regular crossings between here and Worcester, or towards Gloucester. They will not want to go beyond the Hills into Herefordshire or they are too far from Worcester. We hunt here. The rider is but a few minutes ahead of us. There must be signs and the gang cannot be so far away that the single rider could not reach them by mid-afternoon, as I would guess.' He went and untied the hooded man-at-arms who was standing patiently behind the sheriff's horse. 'Any man needs shelter in weather like this, and the lone rider probably only left the group this morning. They must have taken a barn somewhere as shelter. We ask. We check. We will find them.'

Catchpoll sounded determined, even quietly confident. It was enough for de Beauchamp, but Bradecote knew now that finding them was only half the battle, and his mind crowded with unwelcome thoughts, like spectres in a nightmare.

The villagers of Upton saw the imposing lord circle his horse, keen to be gone, whilst a grizzled man retrieved his mount. Then the horsemen were gone, even more quickly than they arrived, and the village shrank back to the peaceful normality of winter's noontide with barely a shrug. Whoever they were, whatever they had wanted, it had nothing to do with Upton folk.

The man on the newly shod horse took the first few miles quickly, always listening for hoof beats behind him, but steadied where he passed people. At a fork he took the south track that ran along a low ridge, but then dropped into slightly marshy ground and cut back to head north almost parallel to the east side of the Malvern Hills, sticking up like the spine of a sleeping dragon. The path was scarce more than a deer track. He skirted an assart, sweeping around the thatched dwellings of man and hog before joining the trackway beyond for another mile, and at a stricken oak swung east towards the river.

He arrived at the clearing, an abandoned assart with a dilapidated barn, if one could term so small a building a barn. There, kidnappers and hostages alike crowded round a fire of dead branches augmented by a couple of broken planks, the monks holding out bound hands as if still in prayer.

The rider dismounted, pleasantly warm from his exertions, handed the reins of the nondescript brown horse to another, and strode across to where Reynald de Roules leant against a tree, idly picking his teeth. He raised an eyebrow at his second in command.

'What news, Guy?'

Guy grinned.

'They thought we would turn up, like a crowd at a hanging, no doubt, and wait for them to take us.'

De Roules did not look surprised. He merely nodded.

'So. We show them we are not to be treated with contempt. They know we are this side of the river. They will be hunting. Let us give them something to sniff out. A corpse would be just the thing. Kill,' he paused and surveyed the huddle of prisoners, lengthening the tension, 'that one.'

He pointed to a wiry monk with a strongly aquiline nose and, for a man of God, remarkably fierce eyes. He wanted the choice to appear random, but he had watched his victims closely, if surreptitiously, and this was one he thought less sheep-like, and more likely to cause problems. The woman, she interested him, in more ways than one. She was of no value as a pawn. She was a widow of recent date, she said, and looked it. Most women looked at men, as men looked at women. They looked, they assessed, and marriage did not generally make a difference. The exceptions were nuns professed, for the most part at least, the newly wedded and bedded who were still lovesick, and the newly bereaved, who saw nobody outside their bubble of grief. Her voice was good, from what little she had said, so she was the relict of some wealthy merchant, or more likely worthy lord of the manor, but there would be nobody to raise a ransom for her, if he had wanted a little money on the side, nor plague de Beauchamp for her safe return. He would wait a while. She had a good figure, and should provide good sport when he chose. He wondered idly if he would take her in front of the brethren and make them watch. He gave a snorting laugh. It would show them what they were missing as well as his power.

The laugh was taken by both captors and hostages to indicate that he found the arbitrary murder of a monk entertaining. His men were impressed, the monks horrified. They had already witnessed the mutilation of Brother Augustine, who lay wrapped in Christina's second cloak. There was no reason that they would think this some evil jest. The wiry monk had gone a deathly white, and his eyes showed a blend of panic tempered with venom, which gave de Roules a twisted satisfaction.

'Tut-tut, Brother, you must not give in to the sin of anger. You would like me dead? Struck down by some godly vengeance? Such faith, and such a waste of effort.'

A man grabbed the monk from behind by the elbows, and the one who answered to the name of Mauger took the religious by the throat and looked toward his leader.

'How?'

'I take it you mean in what way, since even you are perfectly capable of killing a man, especially an unarmed man.' He sounded almost weary of the subject already. 'Well, I think we should make it clear it was not an accident. Actually, I have quite a nice idea.'

He approached the held man, whose dry lips were moving in prayer even as his eyes spat hatred, pushed Mauger to one side as he drew his dagger, and drove it up under the ribs in a single swift movement. The monk's eyes widened for a moment and then he was dead. Reynald de Roules stepped back, and wiped the blade on the dark habit.

'So generous of me to make it quick, almost merciful. Now, strip him and tie him to that tree bough with his own cord for one arm and the sick one's for the other.' He looked at the Benedictines, and spoke almost sweetly. 'Do you think he will get to heaven quicker if he mimics his Saviour? He even has the wound in the side.'

Father Samson was as pale as his inferiors, but with outrage as much as shock.

'Blasphemy,' he cried, pointing his bound hands at Reynald. 'Your soul is forfeit doubly for such a deed.'

The leader of the kidnappers smiled, though his eyes glittered.

'You think I care?' he sneered.

Some of the gang looked at each other, not comfortable with so open a disregard for religion, but none spoke. Mauger stripped the body as instructed, then he, and the man who had held the arms, dragged the corpse to the tree.

'How do we . . .'

'Send a man along the branch, you witless oaf, and offer up the body.' He sighed at the ineptitude of others. 'It is only a foot or two that he'll dangle from the ground.'

De Roules turned away as his instructions were obeyed and looked at Christina. She had lowered her eyes. He walked towards her, though she resolutely did not look up, and stood at her shoulder.

'No need to look, eh, lady? A widow like you knows what a man looks like. Not that you can call these miserable celibates men.' He lifted her chin. 'You wait, and I will remind you what a real man is like.'

Christina did not so much look at him as through him, which he found oddly unsettling. There was neither fear, nor disdain, nor even anger. It was as if she simply saw the trees in the background. He frowned. It was not the response he had expected. Had he known how she felt inside he would have felt far more at ease, but Christina had learnt long ago to mask things from a man who took without asking.

The Benedictine brothers were on their knees, regardless of the cold ground, their mouths working in prayer as if the very familiarity of the words could cocoon them from the ghastliness of what went on before them. Father Samson, emboldened by his outrage, began to dwell upon the fate of those who died excommunicate as those involved surely would, until de Roules silenced him by hitting him about the face.

'You forget, my godly friend, you are useful to me alive, but not necessarily unharmed. Now cease your scaremongering, or I myself shall cut out your tongue and send that to the noble sheriff, William de Beauchamp. Much use you will be as the archbishop's envoy then.'

The sheriff's men were too numerous to be ignored. The sight of so many soldiers riding past a couple of woodmen's cotts was enough to halt all activity and it was not difficult to find out if any had seen a man upon a brown horse riding through with purpose in the last ten minutes. De Beauchamp was impatient and wanted to gallop, but Catchpoll's advice prevailed.

'We would overshoot the mark, my lord, and waste time in the long run. It costs but a minute or two to ask, and if we works from the known to the unknown we won't get ourselves lost and chasing our tails. Once we reach a place where the rider was not seen, we know the distance we have to backtrack and search for the place he left the road, for leave it he will. And they are none so daft, these men. Both horse and rider were forgettable, ordinary, without distinguishing marks. Number of times I've hunted a man who took a fancy horse, or wore a silly cap,' he shook his head, 'you would not credit.'

They had news of the 'forgettable man' at four lowly assarts, but then the road forked, and it was a toss-up which to take. The sheriff was unwilling to split his forces without a guarantee of reuniting them, and with no knowledge of how many they would face. They took the left fork, following likely hoofprints but met with blank faces at the next habitation.

'Clever bastard,' mumbled Catchpoll, grudgingly admiring. 'My guess is he has gone down where the ground is soft, but too soft to retain the hoof prints. He could have backtracked towards Upton, gone west, or threaded through the woods of the Chase to the north. There's few enough folk to see him. It's a large area we have to cover, and the afternoon is so advanced we will lose the light within half an hour, light good enough to track by.'

'But . . .' Bradecote opened his mouth to remonstrate, but shut it again. He wanted to yell that they must try one route at least, but good sense told him that blundering about in the greying late afternoon would achieve nothing. It hurt, though, to know that at this moment they must be within five miles of the hostages, of his Christina. Catchpoll shook his head regretfully.

'Aye, my lord, it is tempting for sure, but it would be easy to make a mistake and mar all. If we are here at first light we will not lose much time on them, for they too will be stopping for the night in this cold.'

'Right, then.' De Beauchamp clapped his gauntlet-clad hands together decisively. 'We will keep along this ridge and "visit" Robert Folet at Mortun. I was wanting to see what he has put up there. Thrown up a motte, as I hear, for fear of "brigandry", as though this side of the Severn is full of outlaws. He's more afraid he will be asked to side with Empress or King and choose the wrong one. He will no doubt be delighted to give shelter to the sheriff of the shire who can "protect" him for a night.'

'And all his men too,' murmured Catchpoll, with a wry smile.

The sheriff's bark of laughter was the only response. Hugh Bradecote was beyond finding anything funny this day.

The 'castle' was neither large nor designed to hold off any large-scale force, but it impressed the peasantry, and would keep out 'casual thieves' muttered de Beauchamp, having far better defences of his own. There was a motte with a palisaded lookout atop it, and a moated bailey with a small but cosy hall, kitchen, barrack for the handful of men-at-arms the lord Folet had to his name, and stabling. To the north, a stone chapel stood rather more sturdily. It did not look large enough to take in the lord Sheriff and upward of thirty men-at-arms, at least not comfortably bestowed, but William de Beauchamp was not particularly concerned how his men fared, as long as they had food in their bellies and a roof over their heads, even if in the stable. He was content that the owner could provide him with enough comfort to give him a good night's rest and a decent meal.

Robert Folet himself was a man in middle age, inclining towards the rotund, who looked as if comfort and security were his own priority. He was politeness itself to the lord Sheriff, though he groaned inwardly at the amount of even the most meagre fare that such a number of men would eat. He bade his noble guest take his ease in his hall. De Beauchamp accepted as formally, following his clearly unwilling host, and Bradecote naturally accompanied him. Catchpoll tagged along, having decided that the disadvantages of being among the 'fancy folk' outweighed being crammed into whatever space was allotted to the men-at-arms and sharing their victuals. De Beauchamp cast him a glance and sly grin. He would go along with it, and if asked, would say the serjeant's presence was required to discuss the next day's plan. Catchpoll was a curmudgeonly and insubordinate old devil if made more than normally miserable, and he would need him fresh and alert to track on the morrow.

The lady of the manor was most unexpected, being youthful, pretty, and slim, that slimness only disrupted by the pronounced bulge that indicated her advanced state of pregnancy. Her natural inclination seemed to be to withdraw modestly, but her husband was obviously as keen to show her off, perhaps to flaunt that he possessed so attractive a woman or, as de Beauchamp whispered to Bradecote while the man's attention was distracted, to trumpet the fact that he could still sire a brat. Bradecote himself looked at the woman, scarcely more than a girl really, and thought of Christina's past. Was this man, who seemed indolent rather than unpleasant, at least a reasonable husband, or was he, within the privacy of the lordly bed, a monster? The lady did not seem nervous of her lord when she looked at him. Her voice was soft, her manner mouse-like, but that seemed her natural self. Christina, his Christina, was of an entirely different mettle, and being submissive must have come hard to her. As he later laid himself to sleep, and listened to de Beauchamp's even snoring, he whispered into the darkness, 'I will find you.'

Chapter Seven

It was on the second morning after his discovery that the wounded Benedictine stirred and moaned, muttering words the old woman could not understand. She dithered, and then went to find Father Cuthbert, who hurried back, only to find that the patient was asleep again, but in his view, more lightly so.

'I think this is true sleep, not unconsciousness, praise be. If he wakes again, come straight away to tell me of it.'

He made every effort to be close on hand for the rest of the day, and was rewarded in the afternoon when he was himself taking watch, with a sigh and flickering of the eyelids. Father Cuthbert laid a hand upon the brother's shoulder to speak calming words of reassurance, but the poor man flinched and began to speak in rushed half-phrases that old Mother Hild, who was setting a pease pottage over the hearth fire, thought mere gibberish.

'Ah, poor man's wits have gone, Father.'

'No, I think it was just he was not speaking English.'

It certainly sounded more like the Norman French used by the lordly class, but Father Cuthbert could understand a little of that and this man's accent was thicker and almost unintelligible. In an effort to communicate he therefore resorted to Latin. Father Cuthbert was a parish priest, more used to getting his hands dirty alongside his parishioners, and had forgotten most of the Latin he had learnt beyond the Offices, but it was enough to calm the sick man. He mumbled about Père Samson, and the priest wondered if that was his abbot. He knew none of the local religious houses were led by a Samson, so it aided him not at all, but he did manage to get the brother's name, which was Bernard, and this he passed on to the lord of the manor, Robert of Fulbrook.

'Let me speak to him, if he is awake, Father, and see what I can find out.'

It was an unimportant manor and the lord Robert was English born and more comfortable in the language of his tenants and peasants than he would have cared to admit, but he spoke the tongue of his forefathers, if not mothers, well enough. It took much concentration, because, in his opinion, Brother Bernard was not many years in England.

'You know, Father, I must send again to the sheriff, but this time to the sheriff in Worcester. I am not certain of everything, for his thoughts are still somewhat knotted, and his accent thick, but he was clearly part of the entourage of this unknown Father Samson, on their way from Worcester. Whither they have disappeared is anybody's guess, but it is most odd they did not return to find one of their number. William de Beauchamp may have a key to unlock all this. I shall go myself, and hope that he is currently at the castle. The poor brother is not fit to be moved, is he? If we took him by cart?' The lord asked the question in hope, for he would rather the monk faced the questions than himself, for he had little beyond what he would send via his messenger.

'The infirmary at the priory would be best placed to continue his treatment,' sighed Father Cuthbert. 'My skills are limited – in fact, I have done almost nothing but bind his head and ensure he has been watched lest he fit, and I am but one man, assisted by whosoever I can bring in to sit with him. Yet I am not sure that the jolting journey would not worsen his condition. Keep him in your prayers as he is in mine, ask me again in the morning, my lord, and we will see.'

Father Cuthbert's medicinal skills were perhaps better than he thought, for on the morrow, Brother Bernard was not slipping in and out of consciousness. Whilst his brain was still clouded and fuddled, and his expression the pained one of a man with an evil headache, he was able to answer, coherently, the simple day-to-day questions put to him, and Father Cuthbert declared him fit to travel, with the lord Robert's escort. He sent him upon his way with his benediction and the assurance of his being, with his missing companions, remembered in his orisons. The lord Robert brought the travelling cart his mother had always used, which was covered. A thoughtful and kind man, he also provided rugs and a bolster against which the injured man might recline. It would mean a slow pace, and two days of travelling, but the infirmary of the monks at

Alcester could care for the injured Benedictine overnight.

'What if the lord Sheriff is not in Worcester, my lord?' Father Cuthbert asked, as Brother Bernard was tucked tenderly beneath the furs.

'I thought of that, and sent one of my men, yesterday, after we spoke, with a message to the castle. It would be unfortunate if he was about to depart for some time and we just missed him. And if he is upon his own manorial business at Elmley, or one of his lesser holdings in the shire, they can send fast enough to him. Unless he is far distant, he will know that I am coming, and the poor brother also, if fit enough.'

The little priest smiled, and gave silent thanks yet again that the lord of this manor was both well-intentioned, and thoughtful. There were neighbouring villages that were far less fortunate.

Reynald roused the occupants of the dilapidated barn at dawn, dragging the timorous scribe outside as soon as it was possible to discern word on vellum, to add a line to the message he had dictated in the gloaming the previous afternoon. The nervous monk studiously avoided looking at the stiffened corpse of his Brother in Christ. Guy gave the message a cursory glance, but there was no fear that the scribe would have dared deviate by a letter from what was said. In fact, there was more danger that his trembling hand rendered the writing difficult to decipher. Reynald sneered at the nervous Benedictine.

'Afraid to meet your Maker, Brother? Tut-tut. What a sinful life you must have led.'

His laugh sent a chill through the monk that was far worse than that of the cold.

Within the barn, Christina, though she definitely thought the title flattered the structure, tried, surreptitiously, to rub some warmth into her chilled legs. They felt as cold as those of the poor dead brother must be, up in the tree. She had cooked the meagre meal, and tended the injured brother, Brother Augustine. The other Benedictines seemed to want to keep well away from her. She had even heard two in muttered conversation saying that it was her presence that had brought misfortunes upon them, for 'consorting' with a woman. She despised them, and pitied them also. They looked like men who had never genuinely 'consorted' with a woman in their entire lives, probably oblates who had entered the claustral world as children and had simply learnt that the Daughters of Eve were as dangerous as the Serpent itself. Seeing their kidnap as a 'Judgement from God' was risible. That Father Samson, whilst not sharing their view entirely, nevertheless was uncomfortable with her being in such close proximity with the brethren, and kept his speech with her to a minimum, did not help.

She had little enough experience of nursing, but none of the brothers had faced wounds before, and had proved remarkably squeamish. When Brother Augustine had been dragged back into the grange that first night, the bloody stump flailing, and the severed hand held like a trophy by Guy, one monk had fainted clean away, and another vomited in the corner. She had been the only one to go forward, with a linen coif from her small bag of possessions, and had attempted to staunch the bleeding. Instead of assisting her, the brothers had got on their knees to

97

pray. The poor man was in shock, which kept the pain at bay a short while, but had then felt it the more when it kicked in. She had nothing to give him ease, and it tore her heart to see how he tried so hard not to show his distress. It showed in his eyes, and he whispered, disjointedly, that he did not wish to upset his brothers. Christina's own eyes had misted. They were doing nothing for him, except praying, which she thought of limited use in a practical emergency, and yet he was lying there, biting his lip until it bled in an effort not to cry out. She had spoken soothingly, sought fresh binding to press over the reddened bandages, and wondered if he would die from loss of blood.

He had not, though he passed a bad night, and she had little rest. He had been sat upon a mule up before another brother for travelling, though the jolting was the last thing he needed, and by that evening she had seen the spots of colour that presaged the fever into which he then fell. Father Samson had sat with him then, and only then, and taken his confession. Now he was only lucid at times, and once took her hand in his good one and blessed her as an angel in his hour of trial, which brought a lump to her throat, but then as quickly slipped to tossing and muttering incoherently. One of the kidnappers had come over in the night and kicked him for disturbing his sleep with his ramblings.

Now, on the fourth day, her heart had sunk. The bandages had taken on a foul smell, and she had no fresh linen to apply to the wound. If the wound was festering she knew of nothing that she could do. She spoke to Father Samson when she could do so without everyone hearing her words. He had closed his eyes in an expression of pain, sighed, and said that it was

God's will, and that she should not blame herself too much. She dug her nails into her palms at that, and bit back the obvious retort.

She glanced behind her, as she trotted along, and saw the nodding tonsure of Brother Augustine, bumping along unsteadily in front of a brother who seemed offended by the, as yet faint, odour of putrefaction. His eyes were open but unfocussed, his cheeks flushed with a dry heat. At least, she thought bleakly, if he was delirious, he would not notice the discomfort of the bouncing around. If the wound should bleed heavily, well, the end might come a little quicker, that was all. Her throat tightened. Just at this moment Brother Augustine seemed her only friend in a grey world of cold and evil, and miserable suffering.

The sheriff and his men broke their fast even as the streaks of a winter dawn lightened the sky, and bade their host and his lady a polite farewell, conscious that it was met with patent relief. Their numbers had put a considerable strain upon the modest resources available, and the attempt of a man-at-arms to make free with a comely wench, whose father took strong exception to his advances upon his daughter, had left the atmosphere more than a little strained at the subordinate level.

Bradecote could barely disguise his impatience to depart beneath the formal civilities, which communicated itself to his big-boned grey and had it sidling and on the fret in the bailey. The undersheriff breathed an audible sigh of relief as they cantered back up the trackway to where Catchpoll had called off the search the previous night, and then back to the westward-leading trackway. Catchpoll was like a hound casting around for a scent, and de Beauchamp, watching from his horse, and alongside Bradecote, jestingly wondered if they would end up hunting boar. Bradecote managed a small smile, but his eyes were focussed upon Catchpoll's expressive face.

He was not in luck from the length turning back to the last sighting, and it was mid-morning and more towards the rising slope of wooded hills that there came a contented 'Aah' from the wily serjeant. Bradecote's horse was fidgeting in response to his agitation, and he sent it bounding forward at the touch of an unintended spur.

'You have something?' The undersheriff's excitement was clear.

'Aye, my lord, at last we do. He has cut across country, and this direction would suggest he was heading north towards the priory at Malvern, but he will have steered clear of it. So now we see where he leads us.'

Catchpoll set off, mounted, but frequently leaning to look down his horse's sloping shoulder at the ground and vegetation. Occasionally he halted, dismounted with a grumble, and peered more closely at a broken twig or imprinted mark. The pace was steady, however, and it was with the pallid sun only a little past its zenith that the sheriff and his entourage came upon the clearing and the deserted assart. The remnants of the fire and the signs of horses having lingered would have confirmed that their quarry had stopped here for some time, but neither of these things drew any attention. They stared instead at the corpse tied to the tree bough. As they approached, a crow flapped lazily away, cawing its disapproval at being disturbed. Even without its depredations, the sight would have been unpleasant. The lord Sheriff's lip curled in distaste. Catchpoll swore, long and hard, and at the conclusion sent two men to cut the body down.

'They knows we are following and this is to show us they do not care. It says, "follow and find us if you can, if you dare". It's a challenge, pox on them.'

'I take it the wound was fatal?' asked Bradecote, controlling his voice to sound calm and unemotional, and dismounting to stand beside Catchpoll as he inspected the body as it lay upon the hard ground. The corpse was stiff still, the now crow-pecked sockets dark and ghoulish. Catchpoll looked for other signs upon the body before studying the single wound under the ribcage.

'It was quick, there is that for it,' he muttered. He looked up at Bradecote, and beyond him to the sheriff. 'Killed the moment the knife entered the heart, my lords. There was little blood. Though a man could reach up, just, and drive a knife in like that, I am of the view he was killed face to face. What they did to the body was all for show, and after the deed was done.'

'But why go to such lengths? We would hardly fail to see it even had it been left on the ground?' Walkelin frowned. 'Unless they thought wild animals might drag it away.'

'Oh aye, and do the Malvern Hills boast giant foxes, or were you thinking these woods harbour wolves?' Catchpoll mocked, but smiled as he shook his head. 'No, this was to show us, and perhaps also to cow the hostages. Think what having one of their number displayed like that would do to the brothers.'

'They would see the blasphemy,' murmured Bradecote, thinking that Christina also had been a witness to this barbarity.

Catchpoll had finished his inspection of the body, and went to the wooden building. He emerged almost immediately, grunting contentedly and with a scrap of vellum in his hand.

'Thought as much. They knew we would follow them, knew we would find the body, so it follows they would leave us some message.'

He handed the roll to Bradecote, knowing the lord Sheriff knew the sight of his own name when he set his mark beside it, but was not a man for words.

'And it says?' William de Beauchamp spoke impatiently as Bradecote frowned over the scrawl and his lips moved silently. At length he looked up, his visage grim.

'What cause has this man to be at odds with you, my lord?'

'How do I know?' snapped de Beauchamp. 'Since you have yet to tell me what the scribble says.'

Bradecote moistened his lips and read slowly and carefully, his voice devoid of feeling.

'You do not take me seriously, de Beauchamp, which is a mistake. Only a fool would try the ruse you used at Upton, and I am no fool, whatever else you think me. The good brother who brings you this is the result of your folly. Add him to your conscience. I give you a second chance, because I am a generous man. Bring Geoffrey, and alive, not a hanged corpse, to the crossing of the Teme by Powick, on the third day after Upton. That should give you enough time, if you bestir yourself from here.' Bradecote paused, took a deep breath and continued. 'Do not disappoint me, for I am running out of dark-garbed figures, and who knows who will be next.'

It was running through Bradecote's mind, as the import of the words sunk in, that Christina was soberly clad, and the note said 'dark' not 'black'. The Benedictines' habit was not a deep black, but they were called the Black Monks, and to him at least, it seemed as if Christina was specifically included in the threat. The dread of what might happen to her, how he might find her, made the bile rise in his throat. He was silent, fighting his inner horrors.

Catchpoll ruminated, sucked his teeth, and looked at de Beauchamp, who was pensive but not troubled.

'What do you want done with the body, my lord?'

'What?' The question recalled the sheriff from his brown study. 'Oh, we take him to the priory at Malvern and get the monks to bury him, as soon as the ground is soft enough to dig. Let us see if this place gives us any more idea of numbers, or any indication at all of where next to hunt. Following your nose works well enough, but is not swift.'

While the corpse was laid over the withers of a horse, and covered with a blanket, and the rider prepared to mount up behind one of his fellows, Catchpoll touched the undersheriff lightly on the arm. He turned a face to the serjeant, which showed far more than he would have wished to divulge, but Catchpoll, however illiterate, could also put two and two together, and had a good idea of his superior's thoughts. He said nothing beyond repeating the instruction to ferret around the area. Dwelling on things would achieve nothing, so best he keep active.

Catchpoll, Walkelin and Bradecote looked closely about the fire, though it revealed nothing, and then within the ruined barn. There was little enough shelter, for half the roof was gone, boards missing from the walls, and there were no remnants of straw in which to have burrowed for warmth. The best that could be said for it was that it gave reasonable protection from the prevailing wind. There was an area of desiccated vegetation that had stood from the previous summer and had been flattened. This, then, was where everyone had huddled, probably captors and captives alike, through the long, cold night. Bradecote wondered, almost inconsequentially, whether Christina had had her second cloak about her. Even if she had, she would have spent a most miserable night, and it was probably the third she had endured. He thought guiltily of his place in the great hall, and the mulled wine he had enjoyed the previous evening, warming his chilled feet by the hearth.

William de Beauchamp wriggled cold toes within his boots, and wiped a dewdrop from the end of a reddened nose. The temperature was dropping rapidly and the sun had disappeared behind thick grey cloud. He almost wished he had not told Catchpoll to search the scene, for standing still let the ache into one's bones.

The trio emerged from the barn without any sign of having made any more useful discoveries. Catchpoll approached, shaking his head.

'Nothing to help us in there, my lord. It was slept in by a group of people, and we guessed that much anyway.'

'Back to tracking, then.' De Beauchamp sighed, pulling his horse's head round, and preparing to move off. A shout from a man-at-arms halted him. A horseman was approaching. 'Now what?' he grumbled.

The man was flushed and had clearly been riding hard that day. He bowed to the lord Sheriff, and made his report.

'My lord, I have a message from the lord Constable, requesting that you return at once to Worcester. There is news from a lord in Warwickshire, about an injured monk who was overlooked in the kidnap. The lord will bring the injured brother as soon as he is fit to travel.'

'So Furnaux is back in the castle. Well, on this occasion it is of use, I suppose.' De Beauchamp spoke almost to himself, then looked piercingly at the messenger. 'When did you set out, man?'

'Crack of dawn, my lord. It was known you were heading for Upton so I went first there, though the ferryman is cracking ice all the way across now, and I doubt not Severn will be frozen by dawn. I asked at places thereafter and was told which way you headed by a man a ways back. A group of nigh on thirty men is easy enough to follow.'

'Well done to you, anyway. Bradecote, I will return to Worcester immediately. If we make good speed we might be near home before dark.' He looked at the messenger. 'If you need a fresher horse, exchange with one of the men here. These beasts have not had to gallop today.'

Hugh Bradecote did not need to ask if de Beauchamp would obey the instruction on the vellum. He could only pray that this new lead might somehow help, although he could not see how it would mean catching the kidnappers.

'My lord,' Catchpoll spoke up, suddenly. 'Will you take young Walkelin with you? If you're going to be "talking" to our forger it would be well to have one who is learning the trade with you. He has seen the way I work a fair bit now, and the effect of two men loosing questions is far better than one, and who's tongue is English, only English.'

Walkelin's eyes widened, in part in disbelief at being put forward by his mentor, and also from the frightening thought of having to work alongside the lord Sheriff himself, who was a figure so elevated he had barely exchanged more than a dozen words with him before becoming Catchpoll's 'serjeanting apprentice'. Catchpoll saw the look, and grinned his best death's head grin at him.

'Fair enough, that's a good thought, Serjeant.'

De Beauchamp turned to give some instructions to Bradecote, and Catchpoll took Walkelin by the sleeve, whispering softly in his ear.

'Remember what you've learnt, lad, and try not to let the lord Sheriff charge about like a wounded boar. You've brain enough to get good information from Geoffrey. Speak respectful with the lord Sheriff, but think for yourself. Now, off you go, with my blessing, and if you muddy it all, remember the lord Sheriff may shout, but it's me that can make your life a misery.'

With which cheering words, he held Walkelin's shaggy-coated horse for him to mount, and slapped it jovially upon the hind quarters. As they watched the three horsemen canter away, their speed limited by the tortuous path to the trackway, Bradecote glanced at Catchpoll, speculatively.

'So, do you think young Walkelin will do all you want of him?'

'Well, my lord,' Catchpoll sniffed. 'He can but try when it comes to reining in the lord Sheriff once he gets the bit between his teeth, you might say, but I think once he gets into working on the prisoner, his natural instincts to follow a scent will take over and he will find out far more than the lord Sheriff alone might do. It all comes down, perhaps, to whom he most fears displeasing – William de Beauchamp or me.'

Bradecote did not need to see Serjeant Catchpoll's grin to know the answer to his unspoken question.

Chapter Eight

With William de Beauchamp's departure, Bradecote was now in command, but Catchpoll knew that at this moment he was in no condition to exercise authority. He realised, with some surprise, that six months ago he would have delighted in this situation, eager to show the fledgling undersheriff that he was but a lordly figurehead. Yet now he wanted to protect Bradecote from looking weak. He had known Drogo's jest that he wanted to adopt the undersheriff for what it was, and had laughed at the idea when Walkelin had asked if he 'liked' the man, only at Michaelmas. Was it that he had simply got used to a new way of working, or did he genuinely like the man, lord that he was?

The previous undersheriff, Fulk de Crespignac, had possessed a well-muscled sword arm, and as much muscle between the ears, in Catchpoll's opinion. He had expected to present the final culprit before the sheriff, had expected also the rare praise, though he knew that his superior was aware that Catchpoll did the vast majority of the work. He also let the serjeant have a free rein, which had suited Catchpoll very nicely.

Bradecote had no inclination to work that way, even from the first, which had taken Catchpoll by surprise. He was no fool, and had a 'ferreting brain', which had meant a far more even working relationship. Catchpoll had resented the intrusion in the beginning, but had swiftly come to realise that they worked well as a team. He lacked the experience and the cynicism, though he appeared to be learning fast enough, and he had an overdeveloped dislike of coercion, and a terrible weakness for feeling guilty over things no sensible man would think twice over, but he had humour, and a quick grasp of fact, and . . . Catchpoll sucked his teeth. He must be getting soft indeed, because he did like him, not just respect him.

He cast the undersheriff a covert glance. The dark brows were now knitted in a frown, the mouth tight shut beneath that long nose of his. He often said Catchpoll's face told him much, but in fact it only told that he was thinking hard. Bradecote's face showed more of the man beneath. He was worried, in fact more than worried; he was afraid. Not that his personal courage was in doubt, but that he was afraid for what might befall the lady Christina, and chafed by his inability to protect her. He was now clearly brooding upon the message, and its hinted threat. They were natural fears, but he would have to snap out of it.

'My lord?' Catchpoll had to repeat himself to get Bradecote's attention. 'My lord, what would you have us do now?'

Bradecote looked at him, owlishly.

'Do? We follow the trail.'

'Aye, my lord, but the temperature is dropping like a stone and we have at best two hours of usable daylight. We will have to find shelter and we are not an inconsiderable number. We were fortunate at the manor last night. Our best chance would be to go up the hill to Malvern and shelter at the priory, where we can leave the corpse also.'

'But the trail will be stone cold.'

'If we stay out overnight it is us who will be stone cold, my lord, and that's a fact.'

Catchpoll turned to order those who had dismounted to mount up and prepare to move, as if given a command from the undersheriff, then turned back as Bradecote spoke softly, 'They have half a day's advantage.'

'Maybe a little more, my lord, what with us checking here, as we had to do. But think. They have to be within range of the bridge over the Teme at Powick, two days from now. They are not going to range far west of Malvern, nor far north, either, in these conditions.'

'And if we do not find them before then? De Beauchamp will not bring Geoffrey to the meeting point.'

'No, my lord, he will not.'

'So then what? Another "example" like this?' Bradecote, wearied in spirit, ran his hand round the back of his neck, and immediately his mind was filled with the memory of Christina's hand there, soft and caressing. 'What if it is her, Catchpoll?' he whispered.

'My lord, think straight.' Catchpoll spoke slowly, carefully. 'The lady is too precious to waste, too good a bargaining point if pressed. And besides, knowing her to be yours, what man would harm her, since nothing could be more certain than the law going to the utmost lengths, and with a man with vengeance in his heart at its head. He would be a fool to harm the lady FitzPayne, and one thing he has shown us thus far is that he is no fool. He's cool, yes, and a cruel bastard, certainly, but he has a clear head. For all the threat, and I know what you read into that message to the lord Sheriff, he will keep your lady and Father Samson alive.'

He put foot to stirrup and mounted, and Bradecote followed his lead without question. They set off along the trail, now not of one horseman but a large party, and thus easy to follow. The undersheriff was silent, desperately trying to find some way to advance logically through the fog that clouded his brain. What Catchpoll said was true, he knew, but the dull ache of fear remained within him, even as logic told him to be calm. Eventually he spoke.

'Can you make any guess as to how many we follow, Catchpoll?'

'As I would estimate, about twenty, give or take a few, which means, since some are the hostages, we have the advantage of them in numbers, as long as they do not have somewhere to defend, and even then it seems they are swordsmen, so if cornered they would have to parley upon the lives of the captives, or come out and fight, losing the advantage.'

'How well do you know this area between the Severn and the Hills?'

'Not well enough, my lord, if I speak truth, but . . . Yes, we have a man from hereabouts.' Catchpoll turned in his saddle and shouted, 'Thomas Wood, come here.'

A man-at-arms cantered forward so that his horse was shoulder to shoulder with Serjeant Catchpoll's.

'Yes, Serjeant?'

'You're local here, aren't you?'

'Yes, Serjeant. Born and raised up in Malvern weald. My father was forester at Hanley.'

'Then you can be of use to us now. You answer the lord Bradecote's questions, and think carefully.'

Thomas eyed the undersheriff's stern face nervously, and Bradecote made a determined effort to smile, though it emerged as a twisted grimace.

'We know the kidnappers will be no further than the clearing was from Upton when they hope for an exchange at the Teme bridge by Powick, two days from now. Can you think of anywhere locally where they could find shelter, but not be likely to find people, between now and then?'

The man rubbed his chin, pensively.

'Nothing natural, my lord, not for such a number. A single man, or a couple, might hide in a cleft, or secluded dell with thick cover, but these men will need barns, sure enough.'

'And do you know of any broken down or disused ones hereabouts?' Bradecote needed something useful upon which to fix his thoughts.

'My lord, I have been in the lord Sheriff's service these four years past, and rarely back to home, and certainly not wandering about the country as a youth might be, messing about or whatever. I cannot recall any, and would not know any recently fallen into disrepair.'

Catchpoll wondered what minor crimes had been

encompassed within the 'whatever' but kept his mouth shut.

'Then barns on the edge of villages perhaps? In this weather, people are less likely to be abroad.'

'Then I'm thinking you'd be wanting tithe barns, best of all, my lord.'

'Ah, now that is a good thought, my lord.' Catchpoll nodded his head. 'Tithe barns or granges with just a brother or two to tend them, this season, would be ideal.'

'And do you know of any such, Wood?'

'Well, I knows there is none at Powick itself, my lord. The brothers at Malvern would be most likely to know all the granges hereabouts, of other houses as well as their own.'

The man-at-arms spoke without any prompting from Catchpoll, Bradecote knew, and gave another reason to head into Malvern. He made his decision.

'Then we track to the next pathway, which will give us a starting point to work from tomorrow, and thereafter go to Malvern for shelter and information.'

It was getting dark as the horses plodded up the hill from Newlands back towards where the squat stone tower of the priory church peeped above the green of the trees. The Benedictine priory nestled among the woods on the slopes beneath the high points of the Malvern Hills, its seclusion a reflection of its reclusive origins in the previous century. It was not designed to accommodate large numbers in its guest hall, and the arrival of the sheriff's men caused considerable disruption. Serjeant Catchpoll, with remarkable – and surprising – tact, ventured that the good brothers would offer refuge against the elements and that, since it was good enough for the Holy Family, their stable would provide adequate shelter for any that could not fit in the guest hall.

Bradecote hid a genuine smile at Catchpoll's pious demeanour. The wily old fox, he thought, was going to get the best he could from the situation. He watched as Catchpoll told the sorry tale of their quest and then, with a flourish, ended it by uncovering the body of the unnamed brother, which caused as great a gasp of shock and horror as even Reynald could have hoped to see.

Father Prior's eyes widened, and he crossed himself.

'We have no name to him, Father Prior, but know that you will bury him with all due rites.' Catchpoll spoke reverentially, as if they had brought the body especially to Malvern for this reason.

'His name is known to the Almighty, for certain, and the manner of his death, which is so damning to the perpetrator, has an element of martyrdom to it. This kidnapper clearly has no respect for the godly, and they suffer for it. We will offer up prayers for our poor Brother in Christ, and place his body in a chapel until the cloister garth is soft enough to dig. He will lie among us until Judgement.'

'We hope that you will pray for our success in capturing the evildoers, before they commit any more deeds of such depravity. The men have had a long, cold day, and have eaten but a crust since breaking their fast.'

The swift glance that Catchpoll cast Bradecote showed eyes that glittered. He was angling for as good a hot meal as the priory kitchen could produce, and Prior John took the bait.

'I will instruct the brothers in the kitchen to ensure there is plenty to assuage their hunger, a good thick pottage, fresh bread and perhaps baked apples.'

Bradecote's own stomach nearly rumbled out loud at the thought, and he realised he had eaten nothing since before dawn.

When he sat down at the prior's own table, however, and faced not only these delights, but a plump pigeon also, Hugh Bradecote's appetite dwindled, for in his mind he saw Christina, cold and hungry, living upon what little her captors spared her. Prior John noticed the reluctance, and pressed him, gently, both to eat and explain his loss of appetite. The prior was a man who listened well, and Bradecote found himself telling him about Christina FitzPayne. The Benedictine's advice was curiously similar to Catchpoll's. He recommended that he eat well to keep up his strength for the hunt, trust her current safety to God, who would surely watch over her, and focus all his mind on a successful resolution.

'What would she say to you, my son, if she saw you leave the sustenance you need, out of thinking of her lacking?'

'She would tell me to eat, Father,' he smiled sadly, 'as if I was a recalcitrant child.'

That was one of the things he loved about her, he thought. Ela, and he realised with a jolt he had not had his first wife in his thoughts once in the last few weeks, would have wrung her hands and worried if he did not eat, but Christina would be practical, and if she thought there was no reason that he should fast, she would chivvy and berate him. The smile lengthened. He actually wanted to be wed to a woman who would nag him;

she would nag him, though, from love, and her passionate nature, not as some shrew.

'Then do as she would tell you. I will mention her especially in our prayers. We will pray for all the captives, and for God to guide you to success in releasing them.' He paused and then, with sudden insight said, 'It must be very lonely for her as the only woman.'

'Indeed, Father.'

'But remember this also. The blessed saint to whom she is upon pilgrimage, will be sure to add her protection, and will assuredly grant her benison.'

Later, as he lay wakeful in his cot, Hugh Bradecote also prayed that St Eadgyth would protect his intended, and whispered his firm intent to find her into the cold darkness.

The sheriff's men woke to flurries of snow so thick as to be a blizzard, though Catchpoll promised an increasingly restless Bradecote that it would not last, and that it would hamper those they pursued as much as themselves. In the end they departed just after Sext, assured that they might return to the priory that evening, if their path had not taken them too far distant, and with repeated assurances of prayers for their success being offered at every office. The temperature had not risen with the dawn, and the wind now blew from the north-east, slicing through layers of clothing as if they were gossamer. Those men who had complained at being billeted in the priory stables now thought of them in a far more favourable way, and muttered about chasing about the shire when all sane folk were within doors by their hearth fires.

They retraced their route to the point where the trail crossed the track that had led them to the priory, though even in the woods the snow was deeper and hindered their progress, and set off once again across country. The woods were very quiet, except for the sound of the wind whipping between the bare branches. Once, a dog fox with some rodent in its jaws, slipped across their path, the orange-red coat standing out sharply in the colourless landscape, but otherwise it was a seemingly uninhabited world.

Prior John had told them that the Malvern brothers had no true tithe barn, but stored grain and straw at a small barn at Bransford, and that the monks of Worcester had an old grange a few miles further west, at Knightwick, but upon the southern bank of the Teme. The path they were now following certainly headed in the right direction, and Bradecote found himself wondering how best to tackle the situation if they found their quarry there. If there had been no hostages it would be simple, for, despite the loss to the priory, they would demand surrender or they would burn them out. The captives put a whole new complexion upon the matter. Starving them out would be nigh on impossible since the weather was so bad a besieging force could not camp outside more than a night or two at best, and the water they had should last that long at the least, if they had been sensible. The kidnappers would have no reason to throw down their arms at the first sign of being surrounded, and in fact were more likely to threaten the important hostages. The permutations made his head spin. He was brought back to the present by Catchpoll's sudden halt, and the raising of his hand. Ahead of them, crows were squabbling over something upon the ground. His heart sank. Not another death, he prayed. Catchpoll watched, waited a moment, and then trotted forward, dispersing the angry birds. Bradecote fought his unwillingness to view another body, and followed. He was amazed to see Catchpoll looking at him, grinning.

'Be eased, my lord. No monkish corpse this, just a roebuck as broke its leg and died. The crows haven't been at it long, so I would say it was fresh overnight, and there is good meat here. What say we butcher it now and take the meat back as an offering for our lodgings at the priory. Venison stew would go down well, even if it has not hung.'

'Are we on the King's land, Catchpoll?'

'Not sure, my lord,' he rubbed his thumb down the side of his nose, 'but if the King don't think it right to feed men upon his business, he's lacking in royal generosity. Besides,' he added pragmatically, 'he won't ever know and we won't tell.'

'Catchpoll, killing the King's deer . . .'

'And we never killed it, neither,' added Catchpoll as a clincher.

Bradecote realised that leaving the carcass to the crows would be seen, probably rightly, as a cruel waste by his men. On the other hand, he had no wish to be delayed.

'We'll take it, but I want to keep going. Sling it across a beast and it can be butchered when we reach our halt for the night, whether that is Malvern or elsewhere.'

Grinning, Catchpoll dismounted, hoisted the deer onto his shoulder and carried it to one of the men-at-arms to put across his horse's withers, with the reasoning that the man's horse looked the sturdiest for the added burden. Then they resumed the trail, with the men thinking of warmth and good meat.

There was no sun, but if it had been showing through the cloud it would have shown itself well into its descent when they reached Bransford. The village reeve shook his head and said they had seen no body of men, but Catchpoll knew that the kidnappers would not have ridden through habitation, but rather around it. They were shown to the barn, set back from the village, that was used by the Malvern monks to store tithes from the vicinity. It was small, and tired-looking, and had, declared the reeve proudly, been the village barn, until replaced by a newer and larger one. The Benedictines had negotiated with their brothers in Pershore, who held the manor, for the right to the old one. It had saved them building from fresh, and their tenants down by the Teme and Severn from trailing all their dues back to Malvern itself.

'You hear as how sometimes the houses of monks are not in charity with one another, but Abbot William and Prior John are good men, and fair. It has been a good arrangement. A lay brother comes out this way every so often to check the store, or brings a cart to take what is needed, and we sends in a dog, ratting, but otherwise it is their business and we leaves them to it.'

The barn showed evidence of having seen human habitation, and it was clear that this had been the gang's refuge the previous night.

'Well, we know where they were, but not where they have gone,' grumbled Catchpoll.

'If men, about twenty in number, wanted shelter near here, where would they be?' Bradecote wanted all options laid before them.

'They'd cross the Teme by Powick, and head for Cotheridge or Broadwas, or keep west and south of the river, cross the brook at Leigh and ask shelter of the brothers at Knightwick, for the grange is this side of the river loop. That would be some five miles west of here, and the closer. No, wait. The grange there has nobody living there at this moment, for one of the poor brothers slipped and broke his arm last week, and his companion brought him through here on the way back to Worcester. There is not much to be a doing there this season, and with the weather so bad I doubt the monks will send replacements this side of Candlemas.'

They thanked the reeve and took up the trail, which at first seemed clear enough. Bradecote was, however, turning over a problem in his mind.

'We are asking where there is shelter.'

'Aye, my lord, of course.'

'But the kidnappers do not wander into a village, asking for the best place to stay. Either they are in company with someone who knows this area well, or they are simply coming upon habitation, and scouting for anywhere that might suffice them. We are assuming they are heading for Knightwick because we know it is unoccupied, whereas they are very unlikely to have this information, and may not even know Knightwick exists. It is also heading away from Powick, and that they will know.'

'Well,' Catchpoll sucked his teeth. 'First off, my lord, we are taking this path because this is where their track leads us. Mind, I agree with what you say. We were being perhaps too clever in our leaping to conclusions. It is not beyond the bounds of likelihood, though, that they have a local man with them, for why else come this side of Severn. Perhaps their leader himself comes from these parts, and if they knew of the grange, well I doubt the presence of a couple of brothers would worry men like these.' He was frowning the more now. 'Trouble is, the path is less obvious here, the ground being so hard and a bit more open. There are fewer twigs to break, or briars to catch a hair from a horse's tail, and the light is bad, mortal bad for details.'

'You want us to go back to Malvern for the night, Catchpoll.'

'Aye, my lord. We would be best to do so. The trail is hard here, but almost certainly leads the way to Knightwick. If we make a good pace to Leigh . . .' He paused and called Thomas Wood to confirm his thought, then continued, 'As I thought, there is a good track back to skirt the Hills and to Malvern. We know they have to be about near Powick bridge tomorrow, so the worst case is we send a couple of men to look out for the man the kidnappers send to scout for them. Since they are almost certainly spending the night in,' he grinned, fleetingly, 'Knightwick, what we do is head out there just before dawn, when we can use the trackway, while going across country would be hard. We catches them after they leave their shelter, and we don't want them holed up in it. At Leigh, we should have a good chance of finding if they have crossed the brook coming back towards Powick, and if not then we wait in ambush.'

'There is a chance they will have crossed the Teme at Knightwick itself and come to Powick bridge from the north, though, isn't there?'

'A slim one, my lord, but it is hillier ground and they would have to make a far better pace than they have thus far to guarantee being near to their man at the bridge, so I doubt it.'

Bradecote saw the logic of Catchpoll's reasoning, and he certainly wanted to take the kidnappers in the open when, whatever the lord Sheriff's priorities, he would be looking out for Christina. Abandoning the hunt for the night was logical, but riding away from where she must be was hard.

'You are right, Catchpoll. Leigh it is, and then best pace to Malvern Priory, where we can present Prior John with your "findings".'

'Though our luck may mean it is too late to cook the venison, my lord, and I have this nasty fear that we will not go back to Malvern tomorrow, since we are like to make our capture. Pity.'

Chapter Nine

Walkelin was struck almost dumb with awe when he realised that he was to conduct the interview with Geoffrey, son of Herluin, the next morning, under the critical gaze of the lord Sheriff himself. Geoffrey initially looked blankly at both de Beauchamp and Serjeant Catchpoll's protégé. A certain amount of rough persuasion, and the threat of permanent damage to his person, did elicit the information that he had been approached by a man with a proposition he could not refuse, because if he did so, his life would be forfeit. He strenuously denied the drowning of Osbern's journeyman, saying that the poor man must have been observed by the shady emissary, and that it was the emissary who had committed the murder. He made much of being an honest man under duress, which made the sheriff's eyes narrow, as he pondered, but not for nothing had Walkelin attended to Serjeant Catchpoll over the months, and he regarded the plea with open scepticism.

'You see, my lord Sheriff,' Walkelin addressed William de Beauchamp whilst holding Geoffrey by the throat, 'this "man under duress" has just said he did not "drown" Edmund the Journeyman, which sounds fair enough, until you recall that we never told how the man died, and that we never actually called it murder.'

The sheriff growled at Geoffrey, angry that the man's lies might have left him looking foolish before a subordinate.

'It was known he drowned,' offered Geoffrey, his words in a rush.

'Liar.' De Beauchamp accompanied the word with a swipe with the back of his hand. Geoffrey licked the blood from his split lip. 'But I care not whether you dangle for murder or your other crimes, as long as you dangle.'

'Why did this other man come to you, if you are so honest, Master Moneyer?' Walkelin was now thinking upon a trail of his own.

'Chance, I suppose, or because I had no journeyman, nobody else to reveal what we were about, and I am good.'

'Depends at what,' snorted the sheriff.

'He made no mention of anyone, then, nor gave his own name?'

'No, most tight-lipped he was.'

'Then why did you believe him?' Walkelin sprang his question like a trap on a stoat. 'Why agree, honest man that you are, to this crime?'

Geoffrey stiffened, and de Beauchamp gave Catchpoll's 'Apprentice Serjeant' a look of approbation which, had he not been concentrating on the prisoner, would have done the young man's self-esteem the world of good.

'All right,' conceded Geoffrey, 'this man selected me because he had heard of me through my cousin, Mauger, the wheelwright's son out of Stoulton. He went to the bad, did Mauger, and was outlawed in '35, for sheep stealing. Any man he consorts with cannot be good, and is most like to slit your throat if you disagree. This man was one such.'

'Describe him, then.' De Beauchamp knew that they now had a trace to follow, but it would be unlikely to be anything but a cold trail.

'Careful, clever, the sort of man you forget easily because he wants you to do so. He has brown hair and a close-cropped beard, and acts like he commands, though he was not the leader of the gang I was to work for. He mentioned "my lord" several times.'

'And he had no name, nor gave a clue as to this lord?'

'He gave me no name, but once mentioned the "lord Reginald" or Raymond or Raybald – some such name. I cannot be sure.'

'So what I am left wondering,' commented Walkelin, almost conversationally, 'is why this "nasty lord beginning with R" has not, on hearing of your capture, simply sent in this crafty bearded fellow to slit your throat, nice and quiet, down here, and found himself another moneyer.'

Geoffrey paled, but made a recovery. He even managed a small smile.

'That would be because I know where the other dies are hid, and the hoard of silver. In fact, I would guess they will do everything to get me set free.'

The silence was all he could have wished. His interrogators stared at him for a full minute, taking in the import of what he had just said.

'The other dies? Have you taken copies of the other moneyers' dies in Worcester?' De Beauchamp found his voice first.

'Not all, my lord. They provided dies from shires as far away as Sussex. I could produce coin that covers half of the minting towns south of the Trent.'

'But why? You would need a huge amount of silver to make that worth doing, since it must have taken quite a time and risk to get them, and why not just use the silver to be coined as usual?'

'Why? Because he can, I think, and his silver is in foreign coin, which would have to be re-minted here, with a loss on each pound in weight. This way, stand fast my payment, he gets more than the weight of the silver, and makes mischief at the same time.'

Walkelin was thinking through this.

'Foreign coin? You mean from Normandy?'

'From Normandy, Anjou, France. From Outremer too, I doubt not. I think he had, shall we say, a profitable time abroad.'

'A man does not go to Outremer to make profit, if he went that far. It is for the good of his soul.' De Beauchamp frowned.

'Well, whatever his motive for going, that is how he returned. Now I think of it, the bearded man still had that touch of weathering to the face that you see on men who have seen a deal of sun, day in, day out.'

'And if he wanted the money minted here, is it because he knows this area, has manors here?' Walkelin wondered, half to himself.

'I know the manorial lords of this shire who have been on pilgrimage, aye or with the Templars and Hospitallers,' William de Beauchamp shook his head, 'and none recently returned have a name beginning with "R", nor sound like this man. He must be some renegade, cast from a high-ranking retinue for misdeeds.'

'The next question, then, is where have you hidden the dies, and where is this hoard?' Walkelin smiled at Geoffrey, in what he hoped was a fair imitation of Catchpoll's death's head grin, though the lord Sheriff wondered if he was suffering from indigestion.

Geoffrey eyed the lord Sheriff and his minion, considering the risks of revelation against the risks of keeping quiet. He had little doubt that the lord who was commanding this 'enterprise' would be already making plans for his release, and if the man found out that he had revealed everything to the sheriff of the shire, his life would not be worth a single coin of his own forging. Yet at the same time, the immediate threat to life and limb stood before him. They were unlikely to kill him out of hand, however much they intended to see him hang, but he remembered the words of Serjeant Catchpoll as he brought him in. That miserable old bastard had told him there were worse things than dying, and he said it as if he knew just what they were. For some reason he was not involved today. With luck, thought Geoffrey, malevolently, he had the bloody flux.

Perhaps the best course was to reveal just enough to keep the lord Sheriff from hanging him by his thumbs, but not so much that he could not find an excuse for it to the man who would be seeking his release. He therefore, with a suitable show of reluctance, gave up the details of the two places where he had secreted dies. He omitted telling them there were two other sites as well. Let them feel pleased with themselves over their success. The hoard was a more difficult problem. He had boasted that he knew where it lay hidden, so that denying it was impossible, and yet if it were discovered, there would be no mercy from the lord who had accumulated it. Geoffrey began to sweat, and de Beauchamp eyed him with grim satisfaction. He could almost read the dilemma in the prisoner's head. He did not see the moment of revelation when the man realised his way out of the coil. Geoffrey sighed, apparently with resignation and defeat, though in fact it was with massive relief. He moistened his lips, and described a place off the road to Evesham, with a dead tree between whose roots the silver was buried.

William de Beauchamp smiled, slowly. He had supreme confidence that no man would actually lie to him, not in the situation Geoffrey found himself. He and Walkelin left the prisoner to commune with the walls of his cell, and returned to the seeming glare of pale winter sunlight in the bailey.

'According to the message from Warwickshire, Fulbrook, who has hopefully got the injured brother with him, should arrive by late afternoon. You are therefore to take two men and fetch the dies back here. It will be interesting to see whence they come. I may have to send to sheriffs elsewhere to discover whether these were obtained by deception, and copied, or whether there is a trail of dead moneyers through the realm.'

'Would that not have been noticed before, my lord?' queried Walkelin, cautiously. He had no wish to be seen as challenging the lord Sheriff's judgement.

'No,' de Beauchamp shook his head, 'particularly not as things stand. England is broken, in some ways. It is seen in the loss of authority even within the King's Exchequer. A sheriff keeps his shire, and I have good contact with my neighbours, but I would not vouch for having seen the Sheriff of Kent, for example, these two years past. He would investigate a murder in Thanet, but have no reason to send to the Sheriff of Berkshire to mention it. No, if done without a trail, town to neighbouring town, and no more than one in each shire, this would be undetected.'

Walkelin nodded in understanding. With his instructions and men 'under his command', a secretly proud Walkelin set off to find the stolen dies. William de Beauchamp was left waiting, which did not improve his mood. This was made even worse when he was waylaid by the constable, though he tried not to look as irritated as he felt. Simon Furnaux had sent the message calling him back to Worcester, for which he was grateful, but not when Furnaux made so much of his action. After a couple of minutes he was desperate to escape, and when, rather later than he would possibly have wanted, a servant came to inform him of the arrival of a lord from Fulbrook to have speech with him, he absented himself with speed.

Robert of Fulbrook was alone, which made de Beauchamp frown, but he explained that he had taken the ailing brother straight to the infirmary in the priory, and thought that they could speak to him there.

'He is far from well, my lord Sheriff. Very weak still, and possessed of a fearful headache.'

'But is he lucid?'

'Oh yes. You need not fear that his thoughts wander now. He will answer your questions well enough, though he is much fatigued by the journey. I thought that the infirmarer might give him some draught to make him feel better before you spoke with him.'

'I do not suppose you have slaked your own thirst. How about some ale and cold meat before we go to see the monk? You can tell me the background as you know it.'

De Beauchamp, made convivial by the thought of food and the absence of the castellan, clapped the surprised but flattered Robert of Fulbrook upon the back, and led him to the hall. His guest, much junior in both years and status, and having heard of William de Beauchamp as a gruff and unapproachable sort of man, launched into what he knew with more speed than clarity.

De Beauchamp had, however, learnt all about the discovery of Brother Bernard, and the monk's early ramblings, by the time a messenger from the Sheriff of Warwickshire was announced. The man handed over a vellum roll, and de Beauchamp sent for a scribe. Waving away Fulbrook's offer to withdraw, he listened as the clerk relayed to him, in a dry monotone, that having been informed of the assault upon a monk, the lord Sheriff of Warwickshire had now discovered the brutal killing of two lay brothers in a grange some five miles from the initial attack.

'He informs me of this?' de Beauchamp wondered. 'Why does he think he ought to do so?'

'I sent to tell the lord Sheriff of my shire that I was bringing the brother to you, my lord, because of his meanderings.' Robert of Fulbrook explained, and then blinked. 'Do you think these attacks are connected?'

'As I was telling you, the kidnap of Father Samson has been marked by brutality. How can this not be another instance of it? No doubt they used the grange as shelter.'

'But it is an even more heinous crime, treating godly men so, and in cold blood, as it must have been.'

De Beauchamp raised his thick eyebrows at the younger man's naive innocence.

'You lead a sheltered life, my friend, if you do not realise that there are men who care not one used horse nail for that.'

The lord Sheriff dismissed the clerk, finished his ale, and 'suggested' that they go to see Brother Bernard. Fulbrook gulped and choked upon the last of his drink, and followed obediently in his wake.

The infirmary of the Priory of St Mary was warmed by the heat from braziers glowing red at each end of the chamber. Most of those within were elderly monks, rheumy of eye, and congested of chest. A novice was rubbing goose grease upon the bony, white chest of one old man, who wheezed loudly. There was a smell of herbs and embrocation. In a cot at the end of the room lay a much younger Benedictine, his head bound, and his face pale.

Brother Hubert, the infirmarer, recognising Robert of Fulbrook as the man who had brought the brother to him, came towards them, and smiled beatifically upon them.

'My lords, our brother is rested a little, and can answer your questions, but not for long, since he has been severely concussed, and his head broken.'

He ushered them to Brother Bernard's bedside, nodded encouragingly at the invalid, introduced the lord Sheriff to him in Latin, and went about his tasks. The hard winter weather made this the busiest season of the year for him.

'You feel a little restored?' asked Fulbrook, smiling down, reassuringly, at the injured religious.

Brother Bernard inclined his head, slowly.

'Good,' remarked de Beauchamp, rather bracingly, the Warwickshire lord thought. 'Now, Brother, what can you tell me about the attack upon Father Samson's party?'

The monk's voice was thready, but not uncertain, his Norman French, so difficult for Robert of Fulbrook, easy enough for de Beauchamp to comprehend.

'I recall but little, mon seigneur. We were still some miles short of Warwick. At first, we thought these men were simply going to pass us upon some important journey, then they surrounded us on three sides, against the thick undergrowth.'

'How many would you say?'

'A dozen, mon seigneur, as I would guess, but I was struck down early, when a man threatened violence upon Father Samson. Certainly, there were not many more.'

'Were they like thieves or soldiers?'

'They were no rabble, mon seigneur. They carried swords, as my head will vouch, though they wore little mail, excepting the one I glimpsed and saw as a leader, a close-bearded man.'

'Ah, our close-bearded "friend" again. I wonder if he is the lord's minion, or the lord himself, then, pretending to a lesser role to our forger?'

The monk frowned, and grimaced at the ensuing pain.

'I do not understand you. I saw this man but for a few

moments and he seemed in a position of some power. That is all that I can tell you.'

'You heard no names?' The chances were small that the brother would have done so, but de Beauchamp asked anyway. 'Nothing that would tell us an identity?'

Brother Bernard shut his eyes and sighed. After a minute he shook his head, gingerly. Brother Hubert, catching sight of this, glided back down his domain, and informed the lord Sheriff that the patient could do no more today. Brother Bernard opened his eyes briefly, and took my lord Fulbrook's hand, thanking him for his care. Fulbrook blushed and demurred. De Beauchamp thought the lord pleasant enough but too soft, and for a moment imagined how Catchpoll would react to having such a man as his superior. A sly smile crossed the sheriff's features. There would be much foul language, at the very least, and Catchpoll would grind his teeth to stumps in short order.

Walkelin was enjoying himself. He had picked two men-at-arms junior to himself in service, who accepted his leadership without any grumbling or joshing him at his elevation. Whilst in the lord Sheriff's presence, Walkelin had been nervous, but now out on de Beauchamp's business, and reporting direct to that august personage, he even imagined what it would be like to wield the power of Serjeant Catchpoll.

The details of the hiding places had been clear enough; Geoffrey did not want the sheriff's men to return entirely empty-handed or he would surely suffer for it. The first was, not entirely surprisingly, in the dwelling of his leman. Walkelin was a young man whose dealings with the weaker sex had been more anticipatory than real, and limited to giggling clandestine encounters with young women who were nearly as inexperienced as he was himself. He found the lank-haired whore, with her hard eyes and casual manner, intimidating.

Mald, for her part, knew men well enough to see the nervousness in the sheriff's man, and was in no good humour, since the trio's arrival ended what had looked a promising negotiation of terms with a man whose purse, if as well filled as his fat belly, must have provided her with two days' food at the least. He had suddenly thanked her, very loudly, for 'her directions', and bustled away.

She stood, arms folded, lips pursed, and then, very deliberately, raised one foot onto the stool that she had placed before her doorway, drawing up the grubby kirtle over her knee as both a challenge and a tease. Walkelin blushed, one man-at-arms blinked, and the other's jaw dropped.

'Well, lads, I'm not above a frolic, but if you think I can manage all three of you at once . . .' She laughed out loud at their horrified and embarrassed faces. They scarce had mother's milk dry on their lips, to her mind. The smile turned to a sneer. 'Besides, I'd as likely have to teach you what to do.'

Walkelin, desperate to assert his authority over the situation, scowled at the woman.

'We are here upon the lord Sheriff's business.'

'Really? I thought the noble lord would do that sort of thing for himself. Not that he's had the pleasure of me before. Perhaps my fame has spread. Let's say one at a time. Who's first?'

Mald was enjoying this. One of the men-at-arms was now opening and closing his mouth like a landed fish.

Walkelin stepped forward, took her by the elbow, and moved her to one side.

'We are here to search for things hidden by Geoffrey, son of Herluin.' He pointedly ignored her last remark, and stepped over the threshold into the dimness beyond. The state of Mald's abode, he thought, would have horrified his mother, who swept her dirt floor so often he was surprised there was any surface left, and kept what possessions she had neat and tidy. Mald was clearly no housewife. The front chamber was tiny, with a plank table on which the remnants of food and ale remained, and behind a ragged curtain the rear chamber contained little more than a wide box bed and lumpy palliasse, over which a grimy blanket was half drawn. He lifted the corner of the palliasse with distaste. A nest of mice scattered, but in one corner was a small sack that was heavy when he lifted it. He peered inside, and even in the gloom could recognise the piles and trussels, the two dies that were struck to form the patterns on a coin. He smiled, and went out to where Mald now watched the men-at-arms with undisguised dislike.

'Thank you, Mistress,' grinned Walkelin, giving the stress of the word a far less polite meaning than normal, 'you can resume your trade now, but know that whatever you earn in that bed of yours will never match what Geoffrey, son of Herluin, hid beneath it.'

The angry glint in her eyes seemed a sweet revenge for the embarrassment she had caused him. He jerked his head at the two men-at-arms, and they went on their way to hunt the second cache. For this they went to Geoffrey's workshop in Meal Cheaping. He certainly knew how to keep his precious items from prying eyes. Even though he had departed in a hurry, he had placed his supply of silver, already prepared as blanks, and his dies, both his own and the stolen ones, beneath the stone threshold between workshop and living area. It was scuffed over with dirt so as to be hardly visible, but yielded up its treasures once the men-at-arms levered it up with the aid of a wood axe they found in a corner.

It was a highly satisfied Walkelin who returned to the castle to report his success to the lord Sheriff.

Chapter Ten

Only dire necessity had sent the man out into the January cold. The store of wood, which he had planned to augment as soon as the weather improved, had been raided sometime after he had shut himself up with his family the afternoon before, and at this rate there would be nothing left in a day or two. The skies again did not bode well, and he feared being snowed in without means to keep his wife and children warm, or a fire on which to cook. He wrapped sacking round his legs, put on as many layers of clothing as he could, topped with a grimy fleece about his shoulders, and set out into the woodland proper with a small sled on which to pile his gatherings. He saw nobody, which was what he would have expected, and kept his eyes groundward, hunting the dry, fallen limbs and twigs that would provide his heat. His mind wandered, and he looked forward to spring, when his sow would farrow, and his own family would increase by one. Well, there would be more mouths to feed, but his eldest lad was strong and, at eleven, fit to take his mother's place when she was too full-bellied to work the land, and by the time the child was weaned, if the Almighty was gracious, would be able to take on a man's work.

He bent to take up an ash stick, and as his hand grasped it, heard horses' hooves. He stayed very still, some sixth sense making his hackles rise. There was no track here, and why should decent folk be out riding through the woods with an iron ground and bone-freezing wind? They were certainly not hunting, not that it was the weather for it. He turned his head very cautiously to the sound, and saw, from his sideways view, a large number of heavily cloaked figures on horseback. The wind whipped back the hood of a man upon a mule, and the peasant saw the pale tonsure of a priest. Then his heart missed a beat, for he would have sworn a gaze was turned upon him, and he expected to hear a shout as he was discovered. For no reason beyond instinct, he knew this would be a bad thing. The figure, smaller than most of the others, inclined their head, but so subtly that he wondered if the acknowledgement was his imagining, and looked away. He held his breath until the beat of his heart was pounding in his ears, and the party were beyond him and all with their backs to him. Then he breathed, very slowly, and only resumed his foraging when they were lost to his sight among the skeletal trees.

That the grange at Knightwick was empty only made the difference that Reynald did not get the pleasure of killing. Kenelm had hoped for praise for remembering its location and leading them to it unerringly, but felt that his leader did not appreciate his efforts. Safely out of earshot he grumbled at his companion. He could not be said to be grumbling 'to' him, since 'Pigface' was French, and so dull-witted he seemed to have little comprehension of even his native tongue, let alone good solid English. Reynald de Roules had added him to his entourage as he made his way back across France from the southern coast, where he had been employed in other people's feuds. He was in no rush to return to England, and felt the rest of France would offer 'opportunities' that a swifter sea voyage would not. He had been right, but then he often was. Attaching himself to whoever paid the best as a soldier of fortune, and with men who held other human life as cheaply as he did, had added to the considerable sum he had 'acquired' in Cyprus, though he did it as much for entertainment as remuneration. They had been travelling from a siege, which had become boring, so they had left, when they came across a crowd about to enjoy a good hanging. For some perverse reason, that day de Roules considered watching a hanging boring too. The man, big, bemused, and with very small eyes that looked confused, just stood with the noose about his neck, waiting. He did not look like he would rant or struggle.

De Roules asked his crime. He did not look a vengeful man, indeed he looked unnaturally placid. The answer was that a neighbour had thrown a stone at him, because he was 'in the way, as usual'. This act, which the villagers considered perfectly acceptable, had resulted in him grabbing the neighbour by the throat, lifting him off the ground and shaking him so that his neck broke.

Reynald de Roules had no interest in justice, and even less in the law, but he saw a large battering ram that could be manipulated until it had no further use. He made it clear to the villagers that there would be no deaths that day except their own, had cut down the condemned man and told Kenelm he was in charge of him, rather as if he was in charge of a hound.

Kenelm spoke nothing but English and a few words, mostly obscene, picked up on his travels. His method of communication with his charge was largely visual. He had no idea of his name, and, since the man would not understand him anyway, christened him 'Pigface', to which he learnt to respond with a nod and grin. The man's intellect was weak, but he did what he was told, without question, as long as it was made clear, and his strength had come in useful. He had come to follow Kenelm about, like a dumb beast, thought his 'keeper' savagely, when he proved very off-putting during Kenelm's forays into wenching.

It was not a large grange. The accommodation for the brothers was merely a lean-to at the end of the barn, and there was no chance of everyone fitting within it. Their humble dwelling would serve for de Roules himself to sleep in, in lordly isolation. The rest would find what rest they could within the barn itself.

Mauger, who was in charge of the wood they had stolen the day before, requested permission to get a fire going out of the wind, not just a cook fire but one to warm them all for the evening. The grange was not close enough to the few homes that made up the hamlet that a fire on the far side of the river would be noticed if anyone should set foot outside their door tonight, not that it was likely. Once it was got going, Christina was set to make what she could of the rations remaining, which were dwindling. There were handfuls of barley, a few onions, and a wood pigeon that an enterprising man had knocked from a bough with a sling. She had never plucked a bird herself, and gripping the tough quills hurt her chapped hands. She had seen it done often enough to make a decent job of it, whilst dreading the task of drawing it, but Guy appeared, out of the gloaming, and took it from her unexpectedly, saying he would not trust her with a larger knife, and removed head, feet and entrails, before tossing it into the pot. Christina glanced at him, but it was too gloomy to make out his expression, and she could not decide whether it had been a charitable act or simply that he really did not trust her. There was stale bread, not enough for more than a chunk the size of Christina's palm for each of them, which they soaked in the thin soupy stew, in which the flavour of pigeon was more apparent than its meat. Those that got a morsel to chew counted themselves fortunate.

Brother Augustine, laid within the barn, near to the door, did not eat, though Christina tried to get a little nutrition into him, filling a beaker with just the warm liquid and pressing it to his lips. He took but little. His eyes, which seemed to focus most of the time upon the far distance, rested for a minute upon her worried face.

'I never thought an angel would worry over me,' he whispered, his voice dreamy.

'No angel, Brother, just another lost soul,' she replied, and there was a catch in her voice.

'You will be found.'

There was an assurance in his tone, a confidence that for a moment gave her a spark of hope, before it faltered and failed. After all, these were but the words of a fevered brain, a dying man.

The soup trickled down his chin. She laid him back down, and wiped the residue away with her sleeve, which was all she had to hand. The monk sighed, and the remaining hand grew agitated, thumb and index finger rubbing together in some half-remembered gesture. He spoke in mumbles, half-words that made no sense, but she sat with him, hoping he knew of another's presence, even in his delirium. Silently, in her own head, she told him of herself, of old things put away, of hopes that now seemed impossible. She talked of Hugh Bradecote, and even as her heart ached, and she felt she would never know what it was to be his, a calm washed over her. There was another voice in her head, and it told her he would not abandon her, would not rest until she was safe, that all would be well, that she would be found.

With a start, she looked down into Brother Augustine's weak blue eyes, though the dimness made them just darkness in the pale face, and thought he regarded her intently. Had he 'heard' her thoughts, by some divine communication? It was fanciful, but felt true.

'May you be blessed.' His words were faint.

'Brother, I . . .'

His good hand fumbled for hers.

'Thank you. By their deeds shall you know them. God sees your kindness. He will bless you.'

Words choked in her throat.

'I am not afraid,' he said, quite strongly, then drifted into muttering again.

Dimly, she wondered why it was she and not one of his own brothers that was close to him now, when his life was ebbing. The smell from the stump was almost enough to make her gag, but if she could bear it, had half got used to it, could they not do so also?

Father Samson sat some way away, an upright figure in the gloom, hands folded as if he sat in contemplation within the claustral walls of Bec, not some cold and draughty barn in Worcestershire. He seemed to regard the events of which he was now a part as divorced from him, happening to another. The remaining monks looked at his austere aloofness, and saw it as a sign that he was truly spiritual.

Reynald de Roules entered the barn, speaking with Guy. At the sound of his voice, the Benedictine looked up. He pursed his lips, and frowned, not in anger, but as if perplexed.

'Why do you not just let us go, my son?' he asked, gently.

De Roules spun round towards the sound.

'I am no son of your siring, monk. I told you before, and you'll be pleased to remember that.'

'What have I – we – done to raise such anger within you, m—' wisely, Father Samson halted.

'What have I done, that you think you can treat me like a fool who will listen to your sanctimonious lies?' de Roules threw back at him.

'Lies?'

143

'You sit there, with your oh-so-reasonable tone, so calm, so sure, so . . . holy,' he spat the word as if it were an insult, 'but it is nothing but an illusion to give you power over weak and fearful minds. You hide behind the trappings, the tonsure, the habit, and use them to make you seem strong, bigger than the men you really are.'

'It is faith that makes us strong,' Father Samson averred, his voice less measured than usual. 'God gives us—'

'Oh yes, if all else fails, hide behind God, then nobody can assail you. But you see, I have seen through it, the deception, the Great Lie. The god you prate about is strong by being honest and humble, so you pretend such things are "virtues", you preach them to the masses whilst you are dishonest and vain beneath the cowl, using your god as a talisman, the throw of the dice against which even kings cannot win. And you denounce "the sins of the flesh" so loudly, so often, you pretend you are above thinking about such things, and "blame" women for "tempting". I see it here, where you try and pretend the woman is invisible, try and avoid looking, or even thinking about her, huddle together as if you were sheep and she the slavering wolf. Some of you even believe it and emasculate yourselves by thought, cease to be men, actually fear the frailer sex, and I promise you, they break so easily.' His voice became a hiss. 'And then there are the other sort, who just pretend in public, and in private enjoy the very thing they declaim in others. Does that give it an extra spice, I wonder? Which are you, eunuch or secret lecher?'

'I will pray for you.'

'Cannot decide, or unwilling to confess? And confession is so good for the soul, too.' Reynald drew so close his eyes glittered

144

into the Benedictine's. 'You will confess before the end.'

Father Samson's eyes widened, just a fraction, just enough for Reynald to at last detect fear in him.

'But the lord Sheriff may—'

'You do not know William de Beauchamp. I do. I think you had best pray very hard to your god for deliverance, don't you?'

'He is your God also, if you would but accept . . .'

'He is no god of mine. I believe in nothing but myself.'

'Your soul . . .'

'Don't waste your breath.' Reynald made a sound between a growl and a laugh. 'Oh, and do not think to frighten me with excommunication, should a prelate hear of my deeds, for I am excommunicate already.'

Christina watched him turn away and shivered, not just from the cold. If Father Samson had not met a man like Reynald de Roules before, then she, in her misfortune, had. She hoped that his focus upon his dislike of the Benedictines would keep him from any interest in her, but her head told her she remained at risk, and her only protection was her knife, which she used to cut onions. 'They break so easily' he had said, as if he had broken women before. It was not a comforting thought with which to curl up and attempt to sleep, and she felt as if her prayers were as lost in the cold dark as her body.

'Pigface' shivered. The warmth of the fire outside had been just enough to keep misery at bay, but here in the barn the chill had got to him once more, though he had burrowed as best he could in the hay, and tried to creep closer to Kenelm, who had kicked him away, drowsily. He had trodden in a fox's fouling, and the smell was pungent, but taking off his boots would have meant frozen feet for sure. That fire, it glowed in his mind. He wanted to be warm again. He could be warm again. In the darkness he crawled towards the barn door, stood, and eased it open. If any stirred, they thought it the wind in the wooden structure, or someone going outside to relieve themselves of more than could soak into the dirt in some corner. Behind the barn the last red glow remained, but it was disappointing. The flames had shrunk to nervous red tongues licking up through the charring twigs. The fire was warm but the wind was bitter cold. 'Pigface' had an idea. He would clear a small space and make himself a little hearth. After all, people had hearths in their homes. He took some twigs and sticks from the edge of the fire and went back into the barn, cautiously, pleased with himself and keen that this should be his very own fire. He pushed the hay aside on the dirt floor, and made a little pyre, then crept outside and, risking his fingers, took the end of a stick, the farthest end of which glowed scarlet. Cosseting it, protecting it from the wind, he returned and coaxed it into life with his kindling. For a few minutes his success looked in doubt, but then the little redness spread. 'Pigface' smiled in innocent delight. The amount of heat he would gain was actually meagre, but he felt he was warmer, and curled up, watching it until his eyelids drooped and slumber took him.

Christina was dreaming. It was a nightmare of the sort where everything was confused. She was cooking again, but with orders to produce a feast for the King, and yet had two cabbages, a string of onions and a bag of flour. She was stirring a distinctly unappetising-looking 'glue' over the fire, and it

146

smelt of cabbage water and onions and was likely to have her flogged for incompetence or worse, executed for trying to poison King Stephen. Now the attendants were stamping their feet, tired of waiting, and the fire was smoking and making her cough. She coughed, and the unreal and the real met, and parted with her on the side of wakefulness, still smelling smoke. She opened her eyes, coughed again, and, without thinking, screamed 'Fire!', stumbling to her feet as she did so, and almost falling over Brother Augustine.

Her cry alerted others, more deeply asleep. The smoke had been joined by a crackle, and the sight of hungry flame lipping at the straw. Everything was confused. In the darkness men swore, and stumbled about, trying to calm and grab the increasingly agitated horses. Christina was near the door. Her thoughts were of herself and Brother Augustine, who was incapable. She grabbed him by the shoulders and heaved, dragging him nearer the door, pushing it open, taking a breath of pure air so sharp with cold her lungs pained her.

The opening of the door sucked in the air the fire craved, and suddenly it was not licking but ravaging. She was outside, hauling the injured monk so that he was not about to be trampled by man or horse. There was mayhem. Figures came out with horses in tow, the brethren, their hands bound, were tripping over their habits as they made their escape from the increasing heat. For a brief, liberating moment, Christina saw her chance. She did not know where she was, or which direction she might head, but if she slipped away now, unseen, there was a chance she might be considered unworthy of following. Leaving the brother would be a sorrow, but the man was dying. It was only a matter of time, she was sure, for all her care of him. She made her decision, stood, and felt the hand on her arm. It was Guy.

'Just in case you had any ideas of leaving us, Mistress,' he said, softly, 'think again. I am watching you. Watching you is the best job on this miserable meandering, so don't think I am going to abandon it, or you.'

He felt her sag. She would do nothing. He returned to chivvying the men to get the beasts out.

Reynald stood with his own horse, as if deep in thought. For a man of action he could be remarkably still. Then he shouted, and everyone attended.

'All men out? All beasts? Guy, count 'em.'

There was silence, then Guy's response.

'All prisoners, all men, one mule short.'

'Which of you stupid bastards lit a fire?' He could see the blaze had started from within, and had not been some spark from the near-dead fire outside. His eyes, demonic in the fire glow, ran over his men. No prisoner could have set a fire. They looked scared, and confused, like panicked sheep. His men were little better. He watched, judged. Then he stared at 'Pigface'.

'*Le feu?*'

The man's little eyes stared back at him. He said but one word.

'*Froid.*'

So he had been cold. Well, now he would not be. Reynald shoved the big man to the door of the barn, now well alight.

'*Allez chercher la mule.*'

He pushed him inside.

'He'll not manage—' Kenelm began to speak, but stopped, and his jaw dropped, as Reynald put the bar across the door.

148

'Mount up and let us be gone before the locals notice the sky is all red. Come on.'

Without so much as looking again at the barn, he swung up into the saddle and trotted away, confident of being followed. Part of the barn roof fell in, and the departing figures heard a high-pitched scream, which might have been the mule.

Chapter Eleven

William de Beauchamp had never had any intention of complying with the demand to appear at the bridge over the Teme with Geoffrey. Indeed, he had not considered it even worth stating to his undersheriff and serjeant before leaving them. As far as he was concerned, he had left them hunting on the west bank of the Severn, and he had taken the precaution of ensuring he was informed of any body of men crossing at the ferry points, both at Upton and Worcester ford itself. He was tackling the situation from the other end. The information that this morning the river was frozen so that no ferry could cross, played into his own hands. The kidnappers would not know whether he had been going to give in or not, and might just decide not to kill another hostage. With the exception of Christina FitzPayne, who was a comely woman, and whose death would possibly ruin Bradecote, and the likely reaction of the Archbishop of Canterbury to the loss of his envoy, de Beauchamp was not particularly concerned whether other hostages were killed, except that it taunted his authority. He hoped Bradecote and Catchpoll might have success, but could do nothing practical to aid them. He therefore concentrated his efforts on the things he could work upon, and sent Walkelin to find the hoard of silver, which would deny it to the enemy, and perhaps give a solid clue to who these criminals were, or at least whence they had come.

With his previous day's success boosting his confidence, Walkelin set off early next morning, through the Sutheburi Gate and onto the Evesham road. 'His' men-at-arms were only really required so that they could assist in carrying the silver back to Worcester if it was too heavy, and as a nominal protection. It was a task without risk, and had the weather been kinder, all three would have considered it as good as a Holy Day, with none to order them about for the morning. The January weather, however, chose to chastise them. A north-easterly wind bit deep through the layers of cloak, cotte and undershirt, for they wore as many layers as possible, and carried flurries of snow that settled upon ground already iron-hard. They held to a brisk trot, which kept the horses warm enough, but failed to assist the extremities of the riders. They muffled their faces in an effort to prevent frost-nip, but their breath condensed to an icy wetness on the woollen cloth. It was not a day to be abroad.

They saw but three souls upon their journey, and those only upon the outskirts of Worcester itself. About halfway between Whittington and Stoulton they slowed to a walk, keeping an eye out to the left of the road for the blasted elm that had been given as the sign for them to halt.

Geoffrey had not told them to look beneath this gaunt ghost of a tree. It was, he said, too obvious a place of itself. Instead, they were to hunt between the roots of a holly tree, some ten paces eastward and out of direct sight from the road. The undergrowth was certainly a good concealment, out of which the holly protruded, glossy amidst the winter dullness. The trio tethered their mounts to a sturdy branch, and grubbed about beneath the holly – like hogs in the forest, complained one of the men-at-arms. There was meant to be a large flat stone, disguised by a dusting of earth and vegetation, so there would be no need to dig properly. With bare hands, that had been chilled even within gauntlets and now hurt in the freezing air, they scrabbled, swearing, at the unforgiving soil. It was one of the men-at-arms who raised the shout of success as his broken fingernails contacted a clear stony edge.

Three pairs of eyes were focussed upon the slab as it was lifted, to reveal a chamber the size of a horse's head, and two feet deep, the sides slabbed like a small kist, but totally empty. Walkelin's disappointment was vented in a long exhalation.

'The bastard sent us out for nothing. I'll . . .' he paused, trying to think of something suitable and Catchpoll-like to suggest doing to Geoffrey upon his return, but nothing came, and he merely growled menacingly. The men-at-arms were less aggrieved, and shrugged. Life was full of disappointments.

Walkelin seethed all the way back to Worcester, his anger on the boil, and was even tempted to go direct to the cells before reporting to de Beauchamp, but sense won over ire.

The lord Sheriff was equally annoyed, though he had enjoyed the proximity of a good fire all forenoon, and had not experienced the perishing cold. He swore in words Walkelin did not understand, but which were clearly vengeful. Walkelin hoped they were not directed at him, and this showed upon his face. Seeing his uncertainty, de Beauchamp smiled, grimly.

'Not your fault. The other information was true enough, what reason had we to doubt this? None. No, it is our creator of false coin and false words we have to blame, and he will not like the penalties.'

With which he strode off towards the cells, with Walkelin trailing in his wake. The gaoler had scarcely time to fumble the key in the lock and open the door, before the lord Sheriff thrust him out of the way and advanced into the dank cell, grabbed Geoffrey by the throat, even as he tried to stand, and shook him as a dog shakes a rat. Walkelin actually wondered if the man's neck might snap with the force. Geoffrey's eyes bulged, and his teeth rattled.

'Play games with me, would you, cur?' de Beauchamp yelled, but then dropped his voice to a dangerous purr. 'Well, the games I play are far rougher than you would like.'

He dropped the forger, gasping for air, to lie crumpled on the dirt floor, and sneered down at him.

'No breath for lies now, eh?'

De Beauchamp watched the heaving chest, saw the fearful look in the face that was eventually upturned to him. The hard eyes met the wide, terrified ones, and locked. Without blinking, or losing contact, the sheriff moved a booted foot, and stood upon the hand which braced Geoffrey from lying face down in the dirt. William de Beauchamp was a big man, and he let his weight balance shift so that the vast majority was on that foot, crushing that hand. Geoffrey's mouth opened in a cry of pain.

'What lies?' he screamed, realising they had now found the empty hiding place.

'The hoard of foreign silver that has vanished into thin air.'

'Gone?' Geoffrey whimpered, tremulously.

'Or was never there,' growled de Beauchamp.

'No, no, he must have come and removed it, the bearded man, when he heard I was taken.'

It was possible, but de Beauchamp was not entirely convinced. Better to let the man stew and ask again later. He watched the pain and fear in the prisoner's eyes, and then spoke calmly, almost silkily.

'As I said, you won't like my games, and down here, there are so many to play. The best bit is that I know when, and you do not. Anticipation is half the pleasure, don't you think?'

He ground his boot, very slightly, just to increase the agony, and then turned away, telling the gaoler that the prisoner had lost his appetite and would need no more food that day. He did not look back at Geoffrey, and spared only a glance at Walkelin, until they were outside again. Walkelin, who had himself been in a mood to strike Geoffrey, was divided between admiration and horror. If that was just the start of things, what would the lord Sheriff order next? Walkelin did not think he had a weak stomach, but torture in cold blood was not an easy thing to face.

De Beauchamp smiled.

'I feel a lot better for that. Now, I wonder if the chicken I was promised has finished upon the spit.'

Walkelin's jaw dropped, as de Beauchamp guessed it would, and he laughed out loud.

'Not been at this long enough, have you? I'd lay you odds Serjeant Catchpoll has told you before now that a man's fearful imaginings are worth twice what you can achieve by simple violence. I hurt him for sure; I enjoyed it and he deserved it, but think how much worse he feels now, wondering what is next.'

'And what is next, my lord?'

'No idea yet,' shrugged the sheriff, 'but I would wager it is not half as bad as he thinks it will be.'

Walkelin had to admit that was just what Serjeant Catchpoll would have said.

William de Beauchamp did enjoy a noontide meal, though Walkelin was not, of course, privy to it. Instead, Catchpoll's apprentice made his way to the kitchens, not so much for sustenance as warmth, and company. There was a new kitchen maid with dark tresses and a way of glancing under her long lashes that made him think thoughts for which, had she known of them, his mother would beat him with her broom, and then lecture him on how things were when she was young and maids were modest. The girl's name was Eluned, which would also have caused mutterings, since his mother never failed to denunciate all Welsh females as loose in morals. Walkelin once asked her why she thought this, and had his ears boxed for impertinence.

He would certainly have defended this particular Welsh maid as demure. Her glances were shy, and not enticing, and in his more depressed moments, Walkelin wondered if she was just bemused by his red hair. There was much talk of her in the guardroom, but anticipatory rather than from knowledge. She was some distant relative of Nesta, erstwhile widow and baker in the castle foregate, and now wife to Drogo, who commanded in the kitchens.

Walkelin was interested, but not about to risk being snubbed, so he undertook what Serjeant Catchpoll described as 'becoming a wall', the fine art of being forgotten by the people around you. He found himself a spot that was warm, not going to have him berated for being underfoot, and gave a good view of all that went on in the busy castle kitchen. Then he watched, and he listened. It was true; after a few minutes he was no more considered than the spits and spoons.

He had gone to watch the shapely Eluned, but what he heard took more of his mind. The hand nailed to the castle door was still a major topic of conversation, and he could almost have laughed out loud at the wildness of the speculation that it produced. There were those who said the kidnappers were Welsh, and not really interested in Geoffrey, but in forcing the archbishop's man to concede to the Bishop of St David's. This drew a snort and angry shake of the head from Eluned, though she was too junior to dare speak out. When another, with good reason, asked why Welsh churchmen should mutilate their non-Celtic brothers, one man shrugged and simply said the Welsh were heathen at heart. This did draw a response, and she clattered a platter onto the trestle table, declaring, in her lilting voice, that the Welsh had been Christians when the English were wicked pagans with more gods than days of the week. There then ensued a loud interchange between those with Celtic ancestry and those purely Anglo-Saxon, and which was only halted by Drogo's bellowing reprimand to everyone, which was so colourful in its language that several girls covered their ears.

Having had a good helping of watching Eluned, and a reasonable hunk of fresh bread and some ale, Walkelin, mindful of his mentor's absence, did what he thought Catchpoll would do in the circumstances. He checked with the men at the gate that no messengers had come for the lord Sheriff, and nothing untoward had been seen. Judging that by this time his superior would have finished his repast, he then reported back to the sheriff, who was picking meat from his teeth. Together, they ambled back to the cells, knowing Geoffrey had had nothing at all. While the gaoler unlocked the door, de Beauchamp described a delicious pigeon patty in loud and glowing detail to Walkelin, with an accompanying wink and broad smile.

'And I thought you was having chicken, my lord,' murmured Walkelin, forgetting himself, then colouring to the roots of his red hair and garbling a humble apology.

'You have, for certain, been learning from Serjeant Catchpoll,' de Beauchamp drawled, raising an eyebrow. Fortunately, he was in a mellow mood. 'But you would be wise to remember that he has been in my service as serjeant these twenty years, and is thus, sometimes, permitted . . . a jest.'

As set-downs went, it was positively benign, but Walkelin

gulped and looked distinctly chastened. The sheriff gave him a sideways glance as the gaoler opened the cell.

'But now you play your part in this, so do not present that face before the prisoner. We are confident, remember. Swagger counts for much.'

As if to confirm this, he entered the cell and belched contentedly, looking down at Geoffrey, who cringed, unsure whether he should struggle to his feet out of respect, or remain on the floor where there was not so far to fall.

'I decided you might be missing us, be feeling lonely, perhaps,' William de Beauchamp's voice was mockingly solicitous, 'so we came back.'

Geoffrey's expression was all that his captors could have wanted, blending loathing, distrust, and, most of all, abject fear. The Geoffrey that Catchpoll had brought in, cocky and in control, as he thought, was no more. The combination of miserable conditions, mistreatment, and the fear of worse, which even haunted his fitful sleeping, had broken him. He had expected the bearded man, or whoever commanded him, to have made a push to have him freed, but nothing had happened. He had been abandoned to his fate, which looked increasingly grim. The relief he had initially felt over the absence of Catchpoll had been replaced by the realisation that the lord Sheriff was of a similar disposition, and had as many unpleasant things in store for him. He also appeared to get a remarkable amount of entertainment from the process. Geoffrey, son of Herluin, had never seen much more to the sheriff than the office itself, with whom he came into contact for taxation, but had no more inkling about William de Beauchamp than any other artisan or tradesman in Worcester. He was powerful, tough, and worked way above their level. Now, far too late, he saw that he was indeed a man to fear, which was just what de Beauchamp wanted him to do.

'Now, this time we are going to ask you questions, and you are going to tell us the truth, not some "clever" little story. You see, you made a mistake, being clever. Me, I do not pretend to be clever, because I do not need to. I am simply brutal. It serves me very well and,' he leant down close enough for Geoffrey to feel his breath, 'is very satisfying.'

Geoffrey shuddered. He had thought himself clever; too clever to use all the silver hoard in the forgeries; too clever to be caught; too clever not to have made himself valuable in case of the worst befalling him; but now he was doomed. He was going to die, that was for certain, for the death of the aspiring journeyman let alone his moneying deceits. The noose seemed an almost welcome prospect in comparison with the unthinkable penalties he might face for those, and all after this monster of a sheriff had finished 'playing' with him as a cat would toss a helpless mouse.

'I will tell no lie, will confess all, my lord,' he whimpered, abject and defeated.

'The silver was never in that hiding hole you have on the Evesham road, was it?' Walkelin grumbled, for it rankled that he had been sent on such a fool's errand in the cold.

Geoffrey shook his head, and looked from Walkelin to the sheriff.

'No, my lord. The silver is beneath the henhouse of

my neighbour, the Widow Thatcher. She is innocent of all knowledge, my lord, being old and three-parts blind. She has kept her chickens more years than I can recall, and I offered to repair her henhouse two summers back, and to double-check for any eggs once or twice a week, if I could have what I found. She misses quite a few, of course, but it also means I have regular access, and I thought it an even safer spot than within my workshop. I always keep some silver blanks there, and old good coin, in case I should ever be robbed in my own home. It was the obvious place to put the hoard.'

Walkelin looked to de Beauchamp, wondering whether he would be sent straightaway to find the cache, and rather hoping he might stay to see what else the prisoner revealed. The sheriff's response saved him asking.

'We will relieve the fowls of their shiny lodgers in good time. Now . . .'

'Are there any more hidden dies?' Walkelin blurted out, suddenly wondering if dividing his precious possessions was usual for the man. 'I am sorry, my lord, but if he splits his silver . . .'

De Beauchamp's instant scowl eased.

'Aye, it is a fair enough question. You might as well tell us, anyway, Moneyer, since you will never strike another coin.'

There was a truth and finality to the statement that crushed Geoffrey completely. He gulped, and there were tears in his voice as he named the two other secret places, and gave directions to find them.

'Now, we proceed to the other side of this affair, the man or men for whom you work.'

'I told truth, my lord, about the bearded man.'

'Perhaps you did,' agreed Walkelin, 'but we may learn more yet that you do not know you know.'

Geoffrey had a sudden image of foul torture and went from white to sickly green of cheek. The sheriff laughed.

'The idea of "extracting" information might appeal, but pain may cloud your memories. We shall reserve that in case you are not totally forthcoming.'

'Please, my lord, I will keep nothing back.'

'Hmmm, like you did not keep the other dies back,' murmured Walkelin, keeping up the pressure, and earning an approving nod from his superior. 'Tell us every scrap of information, however small. When were you approached? Was it by the bearded man? Tell us exactly how he looked, how he acted, what he said at your meetings.'

De Beauchamp, realising that he had no need to look more than normally threatening, leant against the stone wall of the cell, and folded his arms, casually, waiting, and also watching Walkelin. Catchpoll had said good things about his protégé, and the sheriff could see he was right. There was a dogged focus within him that worked through a problem, even if he was not one to make leaps of thought. That concentration was upon the slightly freckled face now, as he listened carefully to Geoffrey's tale.

He had been approached just before Advent, by this man with the close-cropped beard, who introduced himself as one who knew his kinsman Mauger, the Stoulton sheep-stealer. The proposal he made was one of mutual advantage. He would bring Geoffrey a supply of dies from about the country, so diverse as not to have caused flutterings in the King's Exchequer, at least in such uncertain times, and also a good weight of high-quality silver. From this, and with whatever dross a coiner would use, Geoffrey was to produce forged coin that could be put into circulation easily. For his work he would get a portion of the coin and make a tidy fortune in the process. The aim was to keep the silver content as low as possible without easy detection. The silver pennies that had come to light were from the first minting, which Geoffrey said had been pitifully poor, but he wanted to see if the population were as easily fooled as he thought. He had made no more than forty such pennies, some already cut to halfpennies, and got Roger the alehouse keeper to use them. The burgesses of Worcester, he admitted, were more astute than he gave them credit for, and so the next minting, made but not distributed, was of a higher content, though he said, with some pride, that it had a quarter less silver than it should. Walkelin had not interrupted to enquire why Mauger might have thought his cousin would be open to such an offer, if his probity had always been good, but he did halt the tale to ask why the bearded man was happy to trust Geoffrey with dies and silver.

'It was uncanny.' Geoffrey actually crossed himself. 'He said I could not deceive them nor run, for everything about me was known, and in truth, he was right. He knew about Mald . . .'

'I should think all those who supped in the Moon alehouse knew about her,' Walkelin snorted.

'Yes, but . . . He could even tell me the side of the bed I used, as if he had been there, watched us sleeping.'

'You pay to actually sleep there?' It was de Beauchamp's turn to sound incredulous. 'I would have thought . . .' He shrugged. 'Continue.'

'He knew how I spent my day from the moment I rose to the moment I slumbered, knew those whom I counted acquaintance, or friend – knew I disliked raw onions, even. He said every move I made would be watched and if I betrayed the trust put in me, his lord would personally rip out my guts and feed them to the curs of Worcester. He meant it, I know he did.'

'Then describe again this man, who could be so forgettable,' challenged Walkelin. 'What manner of speech had he. You said before that his face was weathered, so were there also marks? What sort of boots did he wear?'

'His boots?' queried de Beauchamp.

'Aye, my lord. A man may have several changes of clothes, but if he is not wealthy, or if he moves about without a permanent home, he is unlikely to possess more than one pair of boots.'

'Fair point. Then yes, tell us about his boots too.'

'I . . . er . . . well, his boots were brown. Well used, but good boots. I can say no more about them.'

'A very "brown" man all told, our bearded friend,' remarked de Beauchamp, casually.

'Yes indeed, my lord. His face was swarthy, bronzed as I said before. His clothes had seen good wear but were not from your common sort of man, and his eyes too were brown.'

'Was there anything about him that was not?' sighed the sheriff.

'What did he say about his lord?' Walkelin was not giving up.

'Mentioned him but rarely, he did. But there was a pride in him, I'd vouch for that. He knew his lord to be a very hard man, but did not seem afraid of him, as though he knew him many years and was more a companion than mere servant. He was not a servile sort of man at all.'

'And the name? Can you recall better the name of the lord?'

'No, only that it began with an "R", and was not Rannulph or Robert. I am fairly certain it ended in "D", but might be wrong. He mentioned it in passing, once only.'

'Did he have a horse, the brown-bearded man? And please do not say it was brown.'

'He arrived on foot, my lord. I never saw any horse. In fact, he sort of appeared, and disappeared.'

'Hmmm.' De Beauchamp pulled a face. 'Not very helpful.'

'I am sorry, my lord,' stammered Geoffrey, instantly.

'If,' wondered Walkelin slowly, 'the man knew so much about your private life, how come he did not know about your hideaways?'

'The one in my own workshop, beneath the threshold, I have only ever used when the place is shut and safe. Nobody could know of that one.'

'But Mald's? And the henhouse?'

'Perhaps he did not watch me that particular visit.'

'The henhouse was more regular, so it is possible he knew.' Walkelin frowned. 'My lord, I think it best I go and find out what Widow Thatcher's hens are brooding.'

'Yes.' De Beauchamp stretched. 'We have finished here.'

He called for the gaoler, and Geoffrey heard the man ask whether he might now feed the prisoner. The sheriff looked surprised.

'Feed him? Did I say so? No. Then do not. He can wait until tomorrow and digest his own failings.'

On which depressing note, he stalked out.

Chapter Twelve

During the night it snowed again, even more heavily. Bradecote swore in frustration when he stepped out and discovered it, but Catchpoll reminded him yet again that if it hampered them then it hampered the kidnappers also. They made their farewells to Father Prior, with Catchpoll resigned to the fact that the venison, which had filled his dreams, would never pass his lips. He hoped the monks appreciated it.

The horses had to plough through snow that came halfway up to their hocks, and snow flurries remained upon the wind as the dismal dawn reluctantly gave up what light it possessed. Two men were sent upon the road to Powick to conceal themselves within view of the bridge, to see whether there were any others watching the crossing of the Teme, while the remainder crossed the bridge of its tributary at Leigh. They had no need to ask whether any riders had been sighted, for the snow was a pristine white blanket on the far side, marred only by the footprints of deer and fox.

'There, my lord, none have passed through here this morning. We make our dispositions as we wish and wait for them to walk into our arms, nice and snug. Our only real concern is keeping the horses warm enough while we stand about, for what might be an hour or even two if we are unlucky.'

Bradecote was conscious now of excitement, an anticipation of action, though also of a peak of risk for his Christina. Well, it was up to him to make sure she was unharmed. The snow now worked against them, for concealment among the trees and undergrowth would mean urging their mounts from perhaps fifty paces from their targets, and if the hostages were close bound, there might be time to either slaughter them or use them as shields with which to bargain. He regretted having so few archers among the men-at-arms. Thomas Wood had a bow, and perhaps five others. Kidnappers and captives alike would be wrapped up as best they could, hooded and indistinguishable, but those upon mules would almost certainly be Benedictines. Father Samson had been upon a horse, he recalled, but it had not been a beast he would recognise again. Christina ought to be easiest to spot, thank God, smaller, upon a white-blazed chestnut, though she might not be as obvious as he would like. He detailed Wood and another archer, one on each side, to concentrate upon identifying her, and bringing down any threat that existed before he himself could reach her.

Deployment of his men was easy, since the enemy was effectively funnelled into the bottleneck of the little bridge. All they had to do was get into the closest cover either side, with

167

a couple of men left to prevent any who reached the bridge passing beyond, and to do so without churning up so much snow that it would be obvious there had been many horsemen here, from a distance. He made good use of every holly bush and evergreen for concealment, and hoped that the kidnappers would not be on the alert, since some men had simply to keep still among the bare trees. At least the archers could be placed well, their mounts kept back on the eastern side of the bridge.

They waited. They grew numb of foot and finger, and a worm of worry began to eat at Bradecote's brain. Could Catchpoll have misread the signs last night? A single horseman came over the horizon. Catchpoll and Bradecote exchanged glances. A man would need a very good reason to be riding out today.

'Perhaps they were delayed, my lord, and their scout is only a little way ahead of them. Shall I take him, far side of the bridge, where there will be less fuss?'

'Yes, and unharmed. We need all the information we can get from him.'

The rider was not well mounted, but upon a shaggy beast that looked best suited to pulling a cart, and as he passed by, Bradecote had to admit he did not look at all like a man of quick wits and actions. He frowned. There came the sound of hooves upon the wooden planks of the bridge, then a muffled cry from beyond. A minute or so later, Catchpoll appeared, grim-faced, and with the rider, trailing miserably behind him.

'Well?' Bradecote's tone was peremptory, for he guessed whatever news the serjeant brought was not good.

'My lord, this is the reeve from Knightwick, on his way to Worcester to tell the prior he no longer has a grange, and the lord Sheriff that there is a corpse, a burnt corpse, in the ashes.'

Bradecote went white. For a moment no words came. He wiped his hand across his mouth and swallowed hard.

'When was this fire? At dawn?' He wondered whether it had been set upon the kidnappers' departure, to lure them away from Powick. He looked at the reeve. 'Go on, man, tell me,' he barked.

'My lord,' the reeve looked unhappy, 'the fire was some time about midnight, we think. A cottager heard a screaming noise and peered out to see the sky lit by fire. The grange was all aflame when we reached it, and nothing could be done but let it burn itself out. Some poor pedlar, or traveller of some sort, since he had a pony, must have gone there, hoping for shelter and food from the brothers, found the place empty, and—'

'Set himself on fire inside?' Bradecote's voice was incredulous.

'I cannot explain that, my lord, but what other cause could there be for a man to be within the barn?'

'It was a man, for sure?' the undersheriff was suddenly eager.

'Well, I assumed . . .' The reeve pulled a face. 'I can only say for certain it was once a poor soul, and what woman would be abroad alone?'

Bradecote bit his lip, to hold back his retort. It was unfair. What could this man be expected to know? He tried to think clearly.

'Serjeant Catchpoll, it looks unlikely the kidnappers will come this way now, but it will be our quickest route back to Powick. Send half the men into Leigh, and have them warm themselves at any hearths they may, to exchange later with those here. You and I will make best pace with Master Reeve here, and see what remains of Knightwick grange. Tell Thomas Wood he has command in our absence, and if, by some strange occurrence, the gang appears, my orders stand, to the word, and, whatever the lord Sheriff might want, their priority is to save the lady Christina, is that understood?'

'Aye, my lord, it is.'

Catchpoll went to pass this order, while the reeve of Knightwick stood, looking worried, confused, and uncomfortable. The latter was caused by the trickle of melting snow within his cotte that was coursing down between his shoulder blades. He had spent a disturbed night, begun a miserable morning in foul weather, and was now at the beck and call of a very morose undersheriff. Within a couple of minutes Serjeant Catchpoll returned, mounted and leading the shaggy pony. Bradecote swung himself into his own saddle and the three horsemen urged their mounts back towards Knightwick, and the burnt-out grange.

The remains of Knightwick grange were a pathetic black and grey smudge in the near pristine whiteness of the snow. The wind picked up handfuls of ash, tossed them and then discarded them, so that the little ash flakes mixed with the snowflakes, and the smell of burning remained in the air. The reeve was not keen to go back to within where the barn itself had stood, for he had never seen a charred corpse before this morning, and never wished to again. Catchpoll had seen his fair share, and Bradecote also, in the course of his recent shrieval duties, though he still loathed the sweet smell of cooked flesh.

They stood where the doors of the barn would have hung. One doorpost still stood, a black finger pointing upwards, as if showing whence the flames had gone, with vestiges of a door hanging from it at a drunken angle. Catchpoll pointed to the dark, charred plank on the ground before it, remnants of the bar that had once secured it shut.

'What do you say to the bar having been across the doors, my lord?' Catchpoll muttered.

Bradecote nodded, and stepped over the threshold, the ash making a soft whispering sound beneath his boots. The reeve, from a 'safe' distance, offered the information that a horse had been in the far corner.

'Horse, or mule,' confirmed Catchpoll, sparing a brief glance at the remains. 'Mule, I would guess, from the hooves and what remains.' His interest, however, was at their feet. 'Poor bastard.'

Bradecote nodded again, trying not to let his gorge rise. He found something vaguely obscene in the contorted, blackened remains of what had so recently been a human being. Catchpoll pulled a face, but then knelt down beside the body. A blackened timber had fallen across it, pinning it at hip level.

'He was not dead when they shut him in.'

It was the gender that Bradecote pounced upon first.

'Definitely a man, Catchpoll?'

'Aye, my lord, from size alone. Look at it. A big man this, once.'

It was obvious, really, but the undersheriff had not trusted his own assessment, clouded as it was by his hopes and fears. The features were indiscernible, but the head was large, the jaw inclined to square. The burnt lips revealed the teeth as if in a grisly grin. The body was on its side, knees drawn up, the upper torso part twisted to face upwards, the fists clenched, half protecting the face, as if fighting the flames that had ravaged it, or berating an Almighty that had abandoned him to the heat of hell. Bradecote focussed upon the detail, now that his first fear was assuaged.

'Could there not have been a blow or wound? We would not be able to tell very easily from what is left.'

'A wound, perhaps, a blow that stunned long enough for the doors to be shut upon him? That might be so, my lord, but it was assuredly not fatal. If he had been dead already, he would lie like one dead, flat out or just crumpled. You see this position when the person lived. The body is often curled like this – defensive, I would say. The babe in the womb curls up, perhaps it is a reaction without thinking, in the face of death. A person avoiding blows will do it, but to more effect. It is a foolish response in a way, since you cannot defend yourself against flame as you would a blow, but,' he shrugged, 'I can give no other reason why it is so.'

'But why? Why kill a man this way when it must have meant they lost their refuge for the night and risked discovery? It makes no sense, and they have shown sense.'

'I doubt as it was planned, my lord, more – er – heat of the moment,' replied Catchpoll, with one of his death's head grins and Bradecote raised an eyebrow. 'To be serious, I would say the fire was clearly an accident.'

'But how did it spread here? There are signs over there,' Bradecote pointed to the circle of ash, 'of a fire as you would expect, outside and away from the building, and in its lee so that no local would see it. But you would have to be unbelievably stupid to try and light a fire in a barn, now, wouldn't you?'

'That I would not deny, my lord, but who is to say whether this great brute of a man was stupid or not? Now there might be some mighty clever big men, but when I consider Hammon, the lord Sheriff's man-at-arms who is built like a pillar in the cathedral church, and not an awful lot more intelligent than your horse over there, I am inclined to wonder. Add to that what we know of the man who commands this gang; he is not the charitable and forgiving sort. Losing their shelter, and the ensuing risk of discovery would have been inevitable by the time this man was shut inside to die. How do you imagine the leader reacted to finding his rest disturbed, his plans disrupted?'

'Fair enough,' Bradecote agreed. 'He would have been angry enough to shut the man within, and the others would not have risked their lives going in to save him. Not a man to cross, is he.'

'Not unless you have a sword in your hand and he doesn't, and even then you'd need to be fast, I would guess.'

'Do I detect admiration in your tone, Serjeant Catchpoll?' Bradecote feigned shock.

'Not admiration as such, my lord. He's an evil-minded bastard, no doubt about it, and I'll be the first to raise a cheer when we see him wriggle at the end of a rope, for he has caused us a tidy amount of trouble and worry, but I'd have to say he has qualities about him, a crafty mind, and a clear sense of purpose. Now if a man like that was on your side in a fight, you'd be offering up prayers of rejoicing, don't tell me you wouldn't.'

Bradecote, who considered the term 'a tidy amount of trouble and worry' a massive understatement, was forced to admit this was true, but frowned nonetheless.

'He kills without compunction, though, as if swatting flies. In fact, he would pull their wings off first. You say this deed was done in anger, but it is of one with his acts of cruelty. I

173

find such men hard to comprehend and impossible to like.'

'Now, I didn't say I like him, not that it would matter if I did. The law is the law and he has no time for it. When we get to him, he is going to find out that it does have the time for him, long enough to arraign him, try him, and hang him.'

'Which brings us to our main problem.' Bradecote's frown deepened, and his voice suddenly wearied. The confidence with which he had begun the morning had disappeared entirely. 'We don't know where he is, is order for us to catch him. They obviously left before it snowed, so we have no trail to follow, no trail at all. They might well have crossed the Leigh brook, or gone the route over the Teme to the north.'

'I still doubt that one, my lord. It would be just too far, and they would have not wanted to travel across unknown terrain. No, my best guess is that they headed back towards Powick, to the barn at Bransford, or the villagers' barn in Powick.'

In the chill darkness, the ill-assorted party had made its way back towards Leigh. Shock, the cold, and the aftermath of the adrenalin rush of escaping a fiery death made teeth chatter, but nobody spoke. It had begun to snow; flakes that the wind drove into faces and settled upon cloaks and turned the group into 'ghosts' in the night. Guy moved from the rear to ride beside Reynald.

'Where do we make for now? We cannot keep going all night and tomorrow also, not in this. This snow conceals all behind us now, but if we take shelter, any tracks as we leave will be too deep to be covered quickly.'

'You only just thought of this, my friend?' Reynald grinned, though his hood hid his expression. 'We return to where we know there is shelter, to Bransford. It is not too hard to find in the dark and this white blanket.'

'Our pursuers will have looked there. It was an obvious place.'

'Oh yes, and found we had departed many hours since. And yes, they will come to the same logical conclusion we have, once they are told of Pigface's little pyre.'

'Then I am not sure—'

'No, Guy, that is why I command and you follow. You are clever, but not clever enough. You see, Bransford has people, and people, so often an inconvenience, can be used.'

'Your plan, my lord, is to take the village hostage?' Guy was confused.

'The cold has got to your brain, assuredly. No, that would be too large a company to control with the men we have. We take a house, and we hold hostages, or rather you do. The head of the family, and I do so hope we do not just find some old crone on her own at our first knocking, we take to the barn and keep. With his loved ones held he will do as I say, act out the charade I demand. Meanwhile, you, I am afraid, will have to spend the rest of the night with the peasants, though you might actually be warmer. We keep your mount so you have a snowy trudge to the bridge at dawn. Your tracks from the dwelling will be one man on foot, as anyone would expect. How you disguise yourself is up to you, of course. You go to Powick, then you watch the bridge. If de Beauchamp comes, it will be by just after noon at the latest. If he brings our man, make sure you let him linger alone, and only then bring him back here. I trust you not to be followed. You return to the bosom of your new "family" and wait until dark before coming to the barn.'

Guy assimilated this information, amazed at the speed with which Reynald could concoct such a plan in the middle of the night and in a snowstorm, as if he sat before his hearth with a goblet of wine and hours to pass in idle contemplation. It was certainly sound enough. He nodded, for there was nothing more to be said.

By the time they reached Bransford, few cared what befell them, captive or captor. Reynald sent the hostages and three men into the barn, and took the rest on to the first dwelling that loomed out of the whiteness.

'You know, this is our friend who was so generous with his wood the other day. He also has a clamp of turnips, I see. Mauger,' he turned and called Mauger forward with a low growl, 'take what we can carry for a day or two, no more. Oh, how I will be glad to stop living like a serf. Good food, good wine, a woman – hmmm I could enjoy an English winter from within my own thick walls.'

With which happy image, he dismounted, and indicated his men were to follow suit. They did not of course knock on the door, but just entered. The door was not barred within, for why should anyone want to steal from a man who had almost nothing. In the total darkness Reynald worked by smell, turning to the left to where the family lived and slept, not to the right where the sow resided. It took but to grab something that lived and squirmed, and to threaten death for silence to replace alarm. There was a demand for light, a scraping of flint, a spark, and a sliver of flame from a rush light, just enough, when Guy shone it round, to discern a man, a woman, and five children, from a lad who awaited puberty down to a crawling infant. The woman's swollen belly indicated a sixth on the way. Reynald smiled. It was so easy.

'We,' he announced, 'are poor, cold travellers seeking shelter. Now, we can see you good people have not room here to accommodate us, so we are going to the tithe barn for the night. However, we might get lonely in the dark, so you, my friend,' he pointed at the father, 'are coming with us, and in the morning will do as we say, since Guy here is staying in your place here, to "look after" your family.' The voice was silkily persuasive, and yet very unpleasant. 'If you do not choose to accede to our very reasonable request,' and here he drew a knife that glinted in the light, and pulled the woman to him, resting the blade against the taut roundness of her pregnancy, 'you will see your next child rather earlier than you expected.'

The man nodded, whispered he would be glad to help, and was pushed outside. A small child grizzled, confused and afraid, and the mother tried to whisper comfort that she herself needed. As Reynald walked out, he spoke softly to Guy.

'You have your orders. Do nothing final, for we may yet have need of them tomorrow night also, if the weather deteriorates further. I am tired of wandering about in the snow to no good purpose. When they are of no further use . . .' He shrugged, and did not see the frown between Guy's brows.

Chapter Thirteen

Walkelin took men-at-arms with him to the first places of concealment, but left them loitering before he reached Widow Thatcher's dwelling. If he needed them to help carry what he found, if he found it, all well and good, but he did not want to worry the old woman more than was necessary. He knocked upon her door, firmly but not insistently, and there was no response. A woman shaking a blanket in front of the building next door shook her head.

'Mother Thatcher won't hear that. Who are you, and what business have you with her?'

The woman sounded protective rather than nosey.

'I am the lord Sheriff's man. The Widow Thatcher has done nothing wrong, but we think there are stolen items hidden beneath her henhouse.'

The woman eyed him suspiciously, but clearly decided he spoke the truth. She nodded.

'Well, you follow me, then.' She opened the door and entered the gloom. On such a winter's day many folk would already have a rush light at least, but this dwelling was in nothing more than half-light.

'No point in lights for her, poor dame. She would as like knock one over and burn us all in our beds,' explained the neighbour, who then shouted, 'Mother, 'tis Estrith.'

A frail voice answered her, bidding her come close. They advanced in the gloom, Walkelin barking his shins on a low chest and earning a word of reproach for his clumsiness. The old woman sat wrapped in all she possessed to keep warm.

'Have you brought my supper, girl?'

The voice tried to be imperious but was more in need of reassurance.

'Not yet, Mother. The broth is bubbling away nicely, though. I have here a man from the lord Sheriff as says he must look under your henhouse, for something hid.'

'What? He wants my hens? They're mine, I tell you.'

'No, Mother, your hens are yours, we know. It seems your neighbour, Geoffrey, hid something under their coop,' bellowed Walkelin, trying to be loud but unthreatening.

'Oh him,' grunted the neighbour, hunching a shoulder. 'Should've guessed it would be to do with him.'

'Geoffrey is hiding under my henhouse?' The voice was querulous and confused.

'Look, you go and do what you must, Sheriff's man, and let me settle her. No point worrying her more than needs be.'

The neighbour almost shooed him out the back. The little yard had a distinct odour of chicken excrement, and Walkelin could already imagine his mother's reaction when he got home. The chickens were settling, perching close together ready for the long, winter's night, their feathers fluffed up against the cold. They objected noisily and with much flapping to Walkelin's arrival as he poked his head within. Picking a feather from his mouth he looked at the floor of the henhouse. He judged it some two feet from the ground, yet on the outside it looked barely more than a foot. Well, a blind old woman would not query why it was built oddly. He scrabbled about in the thin straw, swearing as his hands made contact with something soft and wet, but then found an edge with his fingertips. Amidst much clucking, he lifted the hatch to the void below and felt inside with his hand, which came upon something hard and wrapped in cloth. He sighed in relief. The 'brown' man had not beaten him to it. Fumbling, he lifted the sack, which must once have contained flour. Now it was as heavy but more lumpy. One-handed lifting it was a strain, but he dragged it out and placed it upon the ground. Then he rummaged around again. By the end he had four bags. Geoffrey must have secreted it in several trips. Walkelin shut the henhouse and took a long breath of slightly less foetid air and gathered up the bags in his arms. It was as much as he could do to carry them without dropping one, and he feared spilling the contents for all to see. Indoors he called out gently, and the neighbour came to him.

'My, what have you there?'

'Things that should not be under the Widow's henhouse, for sure. Would you shut the back door, my arms are full, and the front door also, after me?'

'Yes. There's nothing against Mother Thatcher, surely?'

'No, nothing. She need never even be told if you do not think it can be explained.'

'That might be best.'

'Thank you. I hope you settled her. I am sorry if she was confused.'

'Well, I think so. I doubt she'll last the winter, frail as she is, but she helped me when I was but a bride, and I reckon as it is least I can do to help her now. Now, off with you afore nosey folk ask what it is has been found and cause trouble.'

Thus sent about his business, Walkelin whistled up the men-at-arms, and they carried their treasure back to the castle, the men-at-arms standing downwind of Walkelin whenever possible.

The knowledge that Geoffrey's forging materials were in his own hands pleased William de Beauchamp, since he could tell the representatives of the burgesses that there was no longer a threat from the man or his false dies, which might possibly have found their way into unsafe hands. However, the agitation of the good burgesses of Worcester was no longer his prime concern, and in the hunt for Archbishop Theobald's friend and envoy he had made little progress. The sheriff, without any great hope of anything revelatory, took Walkelin with him to Stoulton, a few miles from Worcester, to find out what he could about the errant Mauger, wheelwright's son and sheep-stealer. The manor was one of de Beauchamp's own holdings, and so they went first to the village reeve, to find out what they could about the local wheelwright. The first thing they discovered was that the old wheelwright had been dead some years past, and the business had passed to a nephew. The name of Mauger produced a look of distaste, and a shaking of the head. He had been, said the reeve, a bad lot almost since the day he entered the world, and the village was a happier – and safer – place since his ignominious departure eight years previously.

They found the wheelwright's, now worked by the cousin of Mauger, who was initially reticent about his reprobate relative.

'He's been gone a good many years, and good riddance, says I. You won't find any with a good word for him hereabouts. He brought shame on the whole village, and bad blood with our neighbours, whose sheep he stole, and it killed his poor mother as good as if he smote her with an axe.'

'But it has done you no harm, if you now have the business, Wheelwright. Was his father already dead?'

'No, my lord, but a long time ailing. Mauger' – and the wheelwright spat on the frozen dirt as he spoke the name – 'was taught the trade, of course, but was ham-fisted and not cut out for it. His father took me on when my own father died, and treated me as good as a son, even though the business would go to Mauger and I would work for him.'

'Did you resent that?' asked Walkelin, not unsympathetically. 'After all, you would be the craftsman.'

'What point was there?' The wheelwright shrugged. 'To be honest, I thought that when I ceased to be a journeyman I might leave Stoulton, and find a place with some older man who lacked kin to take over the work when he became too aged. But before that happened, Mauger got took for stealing sheep, and I fell for a village maid, and well . . . Here I am.'

De Beauchamp, who saw no point in this line of questioning, and had no interest in the wheelwright, returned the conversation to Mauger.

'He was declared outlaw. So he claimed sanctuary.'

'Aye, my lord, but not here. He took sanctuary away south in Bushlea.'

'In '35, yes?' De Beauchamp's eyes had narrowed. 'I wonder.'

'My lord?' Walkelin was in the dark, and the wheelwright just stood blinking. De Beauchamp did not seem to notice them, rather he was lost in some meditation of his own. He emerged, shaking himself like a wet dog, and looked at the wheelwright. 'Why Bushlea?'

'It was as far as he got before thinking he would be caught?' The man frowned. 'Though now I think about it, there was something.'

'Think harder, man. This may be important.'

The wheelwright rolled his eyes, under pressure. Walkelin did not think the sheriff was wise to fluster the man.

'I . . . I am not sure. His mother, my aunt, had kin there, I think.' The wheelwright pulled a face. 'He had been there before, when his "tricks" put him out of favour here at home, yes, that must have been it.' He sounded relieved, as if anything less would attract the lord Sheriff's wrath. 'There, my lord.'

De Beauchamp did not respond immediately, and the wheelwright's relief turned to disappointment. He had hoped for at least a word of praise for his effort of memory. He frowned, and there was silence for a minute.

'Reynald de Roules,' William de Beauchamp murmured, almost to himself.

The wheelwright's frown deepened.

'My lord?'

'It was that year that Picot de Roules sent his son abroad.'

Walkelin was as confused as the wheelwright.

'But, how does that . . .'

'Picot de Roules was a good man, a fair man. Always said there was bad blood on the wife's side, though. She was of the family of Bellême, and we all know their blood.'

Whatever was known among the landed classes, Walkelin and the wheelwright were no better off, and still looked mystified.

'Reynald was the second son, and his mother's favourite. There were rumours, but perhaps he really was Picot's. She encouraged Reynald, I would swear to it.' He was still talking more to himself than the other two. 'There was nothing he would not think within his rights, as he proved.'

He might not be talking to them, but he had their attention.

'Picot would never have asked for the heiress to such estates for a younger son, not without pressure from his wife and Reynald himself. It was foolish, and so I told him. I recommended that the King refuse his request, and King Henry agreed. I do not think Picot was surprised either. The next thing was that the girl disappeared. Reynald clearly hoped that possession, in every sense, would change minds. Perhaps it might, but the maid, though maid she was no more, took her own life. Reynald said he was just a "little rough" with her, but she was a fool, panicked, and slit her own wrists. Well, I saw the corpse. The state she was in I would doubt she would have had the strength left.' He shook his head, the memory revolting him. 'There's

184

force, and there's *force*. I dare say many a nervous virgin has jibbed like an unbacked filly, and submitted to a mixture of seduction and strength, but those bruises, aye and broken skin also, were not simply indications of a reluctant "bride" not yet blessed by church or given by the secular authority. I think she died under his foul mistreatment and as soon as she ceased to breathe, he slit her wrists. Catchpoll agreed, but we could not prove it, and would never have got a confession from him. Picot was ashamed, mightily and rightly so, and did the only thing he could. He sent Reynald on pilgrimage to atone for his sins, and said he never wanted to see him on his lands again.'

De Beauchamp blinked, and appeared to bring himself back to the present. His audience were respectful and silent for a moment, then Walkelin, who was frowning in concentration, spoke up.

'You said Picot de Roules "was" a good man, my lord. He is dead now?'

'Yes. Though I hardly see how it helps or hinders us.' The sheriff scowled disapprovingly, thinking Walkelin was too slow and had not taken note of what he had been saying.

In fact, Walkelin had listened very carefully, but his mind was thorough, rather than one which made great leaps of imagination. It was a trait Serjeant Catchpoll actively encouraged. He had commended him for it, saying that a good serjeant had to keep much in mind, and that letting it all jumble like a basket of eels was the path to madness, and failure.

'Reynald de Roules was exiled by his father, not the law, my lord. If his mother were still alive,' Walkelin speculated, hoping he was right, 'would not a favourite son visit his mother if he returned to England? Should we not visit Bushlea?'

De Beauchamp sniffed, considering the idea.

'I cannot say whether the lady Sybilla is alive or dead. Her name has not been mentioned by Henry, who succeeded his father. But then, what reason would he have to do so? He knows my thoughts on her. I even made enquiry when Picot died . . . But there was no suggestion his death was not natural.' The sheriff paused. 'We could get there and back in the daylight, and it would be thorough. Is that something Catchpoll has been teaching you?'

Walkelin nodded, and thanked the wheelwright, in whom de Beauchamp had patently lost interest. Then they left, he was just relieved to have passed from under shrieval scrutiny.

It was something over a dozen miles to Bushlea, but most of the journey was on the old Roman road that ran south to north, and the sheriff and his acolyte took the better part of it at a canter, both to keep warm and to give them the chance to get back to Worcester before full dark. Henry de Roules was not an old man, by any means, but he had a careworn look about him, and his lady likewise, though it was possible that some of her tiredness came from the three small children about her skirts. De Roules greeted his sheriff with due deference, and offered mulled wine in refreshment, but his eyes grew nervous when his brother's name was mentioned.

'My lord, I beg you, speak softly. If my lady mother were to hear . . . It is bad enough—'

'Hear what?'

The voice was acidic, and jangling sharp in tone. Henry de Roules shut his eyes in misery, and Walkelin looked to the doorway of the solar, where a diminutive woman stood, with one bony, claw-like hand upon the amber knob of a blackthorn stick. The atmosphere seemed to have chilled in a moment, and Walkelin actually repressed a shudder.

'Well?'

De Beauchamp vouchsafed the lady a nod, but no more, and spoke, since de Roules did not seem to have any words in him.

'I am come to ask if your son,' and he stressed the possessive, 'has shown his face here these last few months, my lady de Roules.'

The lady's hard eyes, dark as jet, narrowed, and her lip curled in disdain.

'Since my son was never sent from the shire by the law, I do not see it is the law's business whether he comes to his own home or not, de Beauchamp.'

She made no pretence of politeness, and Henry de Roules, seeing the sheriff's expression, interjected to placate him.

'My lady mother does not mean—'

'Silence, fool. What gives you the right to say what I do, or do not, mean? In fact, get out,' she pointed the stick at her unhappy son, and then, to his own horror, at Walkelin, 'and take that red-mopped peasant with you. Since when have you "entertained" peasants in my hall? What I have to say to de Beauchamp, if anything, I will say in private.'

She had said 'my hall', and Walkelin now understood the demeanour of Henry de Roules and his wife. This bird-like woman, more a crow to peck out eyes than a dove to coo lovingly, clearly ruled the roost. Part of him was shocked, for de Roules would otherwise have looked a very ordinary sort of lord, not one to be downtrodden, but this terrible crone who

187

had such power she might well be a witch, as far as Walkelin could see, had the place under a spell. He withdrew thankfully, with the lord de Roules murmuring how it was just like his brother to harass him, even when dead.

'Dead, my lord? You know this?'

'No, but it leaps to the mind. If he lived, he would have come as the lord Sheriff suggested, and I have, thankfully, neither heard nor seen sign of him from the day my father cast him off.'

'But the lady . . . ?'

'She will have it that he lives, and bides his time to return, though I have two healthy sons, and . . .' De Roules paled as the unthinkable was thought.

Walkelin, still uncomfortable getting information from his social superiors, effaced himself and went where he felt he might do more good. He went to the stables, ostensibly to check the sheriff's horse had been receiving good care.

In the hall, William de Beauchamp faced Sybilla de Roules. Somehow, he knew she would swear black was white, just to annoy him.

'So, why do you come here now, after all these years, to torment an old woman?'

She made it sound as if she were some enfeebled dame, although her twisted hands, and the stick, were the only indications of any infirmity of body, and her mind seemed as sharp as her tongue.

'Because most crimes are simple crimes, based on greed, on fear, on lust. There are crimes being committed in this shire that are done for pleasure also, and by one who knows me. There are few who combine coolness with malice, and I do not know that Reynald de Roules is dead. So . . .'

'You do him that justice, at least,' she murmured, smiling. 'He was always so very clever. Too clever for you, de Beauchamp, and if Picot de Roules had not been a mewling, weak-headed fool like his son and heir, he would be here now. I actually wonder sometimes if I ever gave birth to Henry or he was a changeling, a bastard-brat of Picot's, swapped while I was too wearied by the process to notice.'

Thus she calmly cast aspersions on both blameless son and spouse. De Beauchamp again wondered if old gossip spoke true. She had not mentioned her husband as Reynald's sire, but it was not pertinent to what he needed to know.

'Has Reynald come to you in these last months?' He knew she was delaying, keeping him from his question. 'Has he?'

'Many times,' she paused as his eyes widened, 'in my dreams.' Then she laughed. 'I would not tell you, and you know it, de Beauchamp. Why did you come? Because you thought Henry would tell you? You are a bigger fool than he is.'

William de Beauchamp would gladly have broken her thin neck, judging by the look on his face, and it made her laugh the louder.

'Ah yes, I am protected by both age and sex, am I not? Get you back to Worcester and hunt chicken thieves. Leave me and mine alone.'

De Beauchamp knew he was wasting his time. He withdrew with as much dignity as possible, and in a foul temper, which was only assuaged by the information that had been gleaned by Walkelin.

'My lord, I guessed the lady Sybilla is feared, but not loved, by all in the manor. Nobody would dare disobey her, but nor would they seek to protect her. The stable lad was happy to talk about how their lives are made misery by the old dame, though I doubt he sees her direct, but rather suffers from the misery filtering down. I said she must have little reason to come to the stables, since she is old and looks infirm. He said she had not ridden in a long while, but took it up again before Christmas, despite the weather, and would not ride attended, for all the lord begged her to do so. Mind, if I were him, I would encourage her and hope she broke her neck.'

'You liked her too, then.' De Beauchamp gave a sour smile, and kicked his horse to a canter.

'My lord, in truth, I think I saw a witch today.'

Walkelin crossed himself devoutly. De Beauchamp secretly agreed with him, but then they said a Bellême ancestor had made a pact with the Devil.

'So, the lady Sybilla takes to the saddle again, though she cannot find it comfortable, and at a strange time of year for enjoying the fresh air, and just before all this mayhem commences. Hmmmm. Does this all make sense to you, Walkelin?'

'It makes sense, and the more so if there is a connection between Mauger and this Reynald. The hoard, which we have not looked at closely, was said to be of foreign silver from France and eastward, and the leader of the gang had a name like "Reginald", according to Geoffrey. Add that to all this and what my lord Bradecote said when he read the last message, about how the man was at odds with you, my lord, personally . . . Yes, it fits.'

'If Mauger was outlawed and had to make for the nearest port, he would go to Bristow. What would be more likely than him to fall in with de Roules's "outlawed" son, for it was as good as an outlawing.'

'We do not know it was the same time, my lord,' Walkelin cautioned.

'No, but the coincidence seems too good. I think we work upon the idea that he is our man, until proven otherwise.'

Walkelin pursed his mouth, placing all the information in order in his head, methodically, as Serjeant Catchpoll had taught him. At the conclusion of this process he looked his sheriff in the eye.

'If all this is true, my lord, then may all the saints of heaven protect the lady FitzPayne.'

Chapter Fourteen

The sheriff's men-at-arms managed to find an evergreen thicket in which to secrete both themselves and their mounts, and approached it from an angle which they considered best hid their hoof prints. The only problem that they foresaw was that it was the only such thicket with a good view of the Powick bridge from the southern side, and they thereby risked finding the kidnapper's man being wishful of sharing their cover. One of the men-at-arms regarded this as an advantage, since the man would 'drop like a ripe apple in their lap', but his companion, less sanguine, was not convinced that two-to-one was safe enough odds against the dangerous criminals they faced.

'Besides, what if we have to kill him to protect ourselves? We was told to see where he went, and one of us to return here to meet the lord Undersheriff. Neither he nor Serjeant Catchpoll will be pleased if we present them with a corpse.'

'Well, if you can think of anywhere better to hide, just tell me and we'll go there,' mumbled his practical partner, blowing on his hands, and stamping his feet.

Guy left the occupants of the low-eaved dwelling huddled together, not just for warmth, but from fear. He told them that any attempt to go outside or alert anyone to what was going on would assuredly lead to the death of the head of the house, followed by their own. The woman did not, thankfully, try to hang about his feet and plead. Guy found such things histrionic and time-wasting. She nodded, promised, in hushed tones, to do as he commanded, and offered him the slightly stale bread that was to have been her meal. He pushed it away, gruffly. He was a man, after all, and would not take the food from a woman in her state.

What he did take was her husband's spare cotte and cloak, and the greasy fleece that the peasant had used to keep himself warm when scavenging in the woods. He also wrapped sacking about his legs, which further concealed his boots and gave a little extra warmth, and muffled his face as best he could. Today, Guy would be on foot, and his disguise was also a practical way to keep him from freezing. He saw the little sled beside the turnip clamp, and went off, dragging it behind him, a poor peasant whose supplies of kindling had been insufficient in the cold snap. None who saw him gave him a second thought.

He skirted round Powick itself, for a man seeking wood would not need to go through a village, and, as he descended the hill, began to collect dead wood from among the trees that bordered the Teme. There was mistletoe among the skeletal branches, and it gave him cause to grimace. He had been a midwinter babe, and his mother had jokingly said he had been named Guy after the mistletoe rather than his grandsire, since the French for the plant was 'gui', like his name. He tried to cast the memory aside, for the Guy that had been her son, her pride, was no more.

He made no attempt to conceal himself, indeed he even whistled a tune, one remembered from long ago and fully English. No fool was Guy, to ruin all with a song from beyond English shores. Nor did he fail to notice the best hiding place near the bridge. He smiled to himself, though his feet ached with cold, and his earlier noble impulse had left his stomach growling with hunger. If he was a man sent to spy upon a spy at the bridge, and just an average man, he would hide there for sure. Let them hide. He continued his quest for wood, and a wood pigeon, fluffed up against the cold on a branch above him, watched until he was almost below it, and then took off with a flapping sound that seemed extraordinarily loud in the white silence. It did not go far, in fact almost adjacent to the evergreens. Guy's smile grew wider. Why not? He could outwit a man who thought hiding meant standing in a bush.

He took a wandering course, adding branches he pulled from the snow to his load, and selecting a stone or two that he found as he scrabbled beneath the cold white blanket. He drew close, heard a faint whisper in the bushes, and lobbed the stone, full force, at the wood pigeon on its perch. Without a sling, his chances of hitting it were minimal, but it flapped off and the stone came to earth with a plonk, right next to the greenery, frightening the horses. There came swearing, and, in character of the wood gatherer, Guy cried out in a nervous English voice, 'Who's there? I have nothing worth stealing!'

The larger of the men-at-arms stepped from his cover, hand raised placatingly.

'No fear, friend. We mean you no harm.'

Guy stood his ground as if unsure whether to stand or run.

'Then why are you hid?'

'We are sheriff's men,' declared the man-at-arms, puffing out his chest a little, 'upon the lord Sheriff's business. And why are you out?'

'Collecting wood. Some bastard stole the best part of what I had remaining two days past.' Why not tell the truth, thought Guy, and give them something to tell their superior? 'And the pigeon, well, if I hit it there would be meat tonight, and me with five brats and another due.'

The second man-at-arms peered out between the leaves.

'You'd need a sling to have much chance of that.'

'Aye, but empty bellies mean you'll try anything.'

The first man looked at the peasant.

'Your wood, where did it go from?' he asked.

'Beside my home.' Guy was having fun.

'But that is where?'

'A ways off, beyond Bransford. I scoured nearer home yesterday.'

'And you saw no group of riders, with Black Monks among them?'

'No, surely I did not. Why do you seek such?'

Without any further prompting, the men told him of their hunt for dangerous monk murderers and kidnappers, the gang growing in size and viciousness in the telling. Guy learnt much about his pursuers and little truth about his fellow gang members. At the conclusion of their amicable chat, they requested he keep his eyes and ears open, and report anything unusual back to them, since they would be remaining until past the middle of the day.

Guy readily agreed, and passed beyond them, crossing the track to the bridge itself, and foraging along the riverbank beyond, keeping an eye out himself for any sign of activity from the north, and the Worcester road. After a while a cart rumbled into view. One man-at-arms had gone to stand upon the bridge and ask the carter if he had seen anything. The man was muffled up to the eyes and miserable. Guy, pricking up his ears, heard that he was headed for Worcester, but the Severn was frozen so hard no ferry could cross, and so he was coming southward to see if there was any way over still by Upton or even, at a push, Tewkesbury.

So the river was frozen. Guy sighed. Well, no point him waiting for the sheriff, who had been unlikely to make an appearance anyway. He would report back to Reynald, after waiting a decent interval. There came a sound among the undergrowth by the river, and three mallard waddled onto the ice. Guy wondered if the prayers of sinners were answered when they benefited the innocent. He had two more stones in the wrappings round his boots. He took one, crossed himself, and threw it with such force he lost his footing and fell forward in the snow. There was a loud quacking, and flapping, and he swore under his breath, but when he looked up, there was a drake flat out upon the ice. Elated, Guy took up the longest stick he could find and gingerly trod upon the ice at the edge of the river, reaching to pull his prize back to shore. Grinning, he held it up proudly towards the bushes, knowing the sheriff's men would have seen his exploit. What better reason to return 'home'? He passed them on his way back, with a cheery wave that was not mere pretence, and began the cold trudge back to Bransford. There was wood for a fire, and meat for a meal. One duck between twenty was not much, but split between two adults and five small children would be the nearest thing to a feast he had enjoyed in weeks.

Bradecote and Catchpoll returned to the waiting men-at-arms by the Leigh brook, with Bradecote near silent all the way. Catchpoll was more worried about him than the absence of a trail to follow. He remained hopeful that their quarry would turn up nearer the bridge, and that the men sent to watch there had had some success. There was no sign of any large number of horses having passed from Leigh to Bransford, but if they had set out before the snowfall was established, there would be nothing to indicate their path. The snow would work both ways, however, since wherever they went from this morning, their passage would be easy to see. The barns at Bransford should have been a good bet, but proved a disappointment. As they approached the Malvern tithe barn, there were no signs of hoof prints in front of it, and a man emerged, a little furtively, pulling straw from his hair. He looked scared, and when accosted mumbled about a tumble in the straw with a willing wench who was a lot more accommodating than his shrew-wife. Asking him if he had seen twenty men within was a pointless question. However consumed by lusting loins, he could not have failed to have noticed them and been noticed also, which might well have proved fatal, judging by recent events.

Bradecote looked at the man, trying not to be judgemental, though his opinion of those who strayed was not high. Yet he himself had known the stirrings of temptation, so who was he to cast the first stone at an adulterous tryst.

The village barn was devoid of any life bigger than a scrabbling rat, and there was still no evidence of horsemen. Catchpoll grew more uncomfortable, and muttered silent prayers, which remained unanswered. Powick had seen no horsemen even passing through, and it was there that they met up with the two men-at-arms, numb with cold, heading back. They vouched for the fact that the lord Sheriff had not appeared, which was expected, but not that it would have been impossible for him to have done so, with the Severn frozen and as yet impassable.

'And you saw nobody?' Bradecote was desperate now.

'None my lord, but the carter heading south to try and cross the river lower down if not solid, and the man who killed the duck.'

'The man who . . .' Bradecote looked, stupefied, at Catchpoll, who shrugged.

'Go on, surprise us with the tale of the man who killed the duck,' demanded the serjeant. 'I haven't heard that one.'

'He was just a peasant, collecting wood.'

'In this weather?' Bradecote was suspicious.

'Ah, but there was a reason for that, my lord. He said his wood store was raided two days ago, and him from beyond Bransford. He said he had been out foraging yesterday nearer home. Today he came along the riverbank.'

198

'He has a wife and five children, and another due, poor man. That's a lot of mouths to feed in a winter like this. He threw stones at a pigeon, thinking with luck he might strike it dead, but it flew off. We chatted a short while and then he went on, along the bank. We saw him throw a stone at some ducks on the ice. Fell right on his face, and it was hard not to laugh.'

'Aye, but it was worth the cold face, for he must have caught one right hard, for he killed it, and got it in with a stick and went home rejoicing.'

'Did this wood gatherer actually gather wood?' asked Catchpoll, quietly.

'Oh yes, we thought of that, Serjeant. He was certainly collecting wood, and putting it on his little sled.'

'What did he look like?' Bradecote was thinking along the same lines as Catchpoll.

'Average sort of fellow, not that we saw a lot of him, wrapped up against the cold as he was, my lord.'

'Was he bearded?'

'That we couldn't say, for his face was muffled, as you would be on a day like today, my lord. We did not think it suspicious, considering.'

Catchpoll was pulling a thinking face.

'The carter. What was he carrying?'

'We didn't look, and did not ask, Serjeant.'

'Did it not seem odd that a man should be taking a cartload of anything out in this weather?'

'Well . . .' The second man-at-arms frowned, but then his brow cleared. 'But the carter came, crossed the bridge, and passed on his way. He was only here for a few minutes.'

'You are sure he did not pass from view and then come back and watch you?'

'Cannot be certain, but if he did, we did not see him and we was in the best cover by the bridge.'

Catchpoll sighed and rubbed the side of his nose.

'In the end, my lord, we are probably looking at the wood gatherer as the kidnappers' man, though it is possible they too could not get anyone to the meeting point.'

The undersheriff looked as if he had not heard him.

'My lord?'

Bradecote frowned, and only after a pause did he respond.

'We do not know where the man came from, or where he went. We do not know if the kidnappers believe the sheriff ignored them, or was stopped from acceding to their demand. We—'

'My lord,' volunteered the larger man-at-arms, trying to be positive, 'we do know he did not cross the Teme bridge, for if he came early, we would have seen tracks in the snow beyond the bridge, with the sled marks, and there were none.'

'Then where in God's own name are they?' yelled Bradecote.

The men-at-arms had no answer, and just looked wooden, as subordinates found it safest to be when authority shouted at them.

'My lord,' Catchpoll's voice was even, almost gentle, 'we can only start again tomorrow. Perhaps they found shelter where we are unaware any exists.'

'Why do we not know?' Bradecote rounded upon him. 'Are there secret barns? Have villages appeared out of the earth without paying taxes, without someone having lordship over them?'

'No, my lord, but—'

'How can you sound so calm?'

'Because,' and Catchpoll's voice was raised now, 'it does no good ranting when what we need is thinking.'

'So I do not think?'

'At this moment, my lord, no.'

'You do not know how much I want to think, Catchpoll,' Bradecote managed, through gritted teeth, and running his hand through his hair so that it began to stand upright as if surprised.

'Oh, I do, my lord. Tonight we must return to Malvern. A night's rest and food in your belly will settle you, and us all. Tomorrow we start again. And what the men say is true. The kidnappers are not north of the Teme. Come, my lord.'

He touched Bradecote on the arm but was brushed aside, though the undersheriff did wheel his horse about to take the Malvern track. The men-at-arms, unsettled by arguments between their seniors, were at least heartened by the thought of Malvern Priory, and wondered if the priory kitchen had decided not to let the venison hang for long.

Guy returned to the barn a little after sunset, with the news that, even had he wanted to, William de Beauchamp could not have complied with the demand to bring his prisoner to the bridge over the Teme. This news was greeted with a non-committal sound from de Roules. Anger would have been pointless, but Guy had expected it. Cooping Reynald de Roules up in a gloomy barn all day was going to do nothing for his temper, and he seemed to be permanently on the edge now, like a leashed dog that had not been fed for days. He told him something of the numbers hunting them, how he had duped them with such ease. Some things, however, remained undisclosed, especially the fact that he was going back to enjoy a duck currently roasting upon a spit. It would be, he decided, cruel to divulge what his meal would be, when, from the look of things, the others would be chewing raw turnip. There was neither wood for a fire, nor a place to make one, since they could afford no sign outside that would advertise their presence.

The unwilling travelling companions had formed distinct groups within the barn, as might be expected. The kidnappers kept together, and the Benedictines did the same, with the exception of the injured monk, who lay apart, nearer the door, with the dark-haired woman in close attendance. Her coif was gone now, the thick plait of her hair lying on her shoulder. The brothers had looked offended when she had removed it; the captors just looked. The dictates of decency had ceased to matter, Christina had thought, when there was an ailing man to tend. The old bandages were so offensive now, she had used her last comparatively clean linen to redress the stump. It had proved almost impossible to do without retching, and it brought tears to her eyes, since it distressed the poor brother so. He whimpered, and tried to cry out, would have done so had Reynald not clamped his hand over the man's mouth. She and her charge were placed by the door, in the draught, where perhaps the stench might be dissipated. At first she feared for him chilling, but his fever seemed now much increased, and he burned, dry to the touch, in the dim chill of the barn. He had not been lucid since the previous night, and she thought perhaps he would not rouse to consciousness again.

She looked up from deep in her own thoughts, and saw Guy standing over her. She could not be sure, but she thought his face solemn.

'He is dying.' His inflexion made it less than a question.

'Oh yes.'

Guy gave no answer, and turned away. He spoke quietly to a couple of the men, went briefly to the peasant who was tied in a corner, and then, given leave by Reynald, returned to his own prisoners in the village.

Reynald de Roules looked at the piece of turnip in his hand, and spat out the mouthful of the unappetising vegetable which he had been chewing. It was only fit to feed kine, and peasants, and he would rather go hungry a little longer. It was time that now dominated his thoughts. Being trapped within this wooden prison for the best part of twenty-four hours had, as Guy had suspected, tried his patience and his temper. He could not endure another day of it, so tomorrow they moved. They were all cold, and hungry, and even the men were starting to snap at each other. Reynald began to wonder if it was not better to cast this whole plan aside, and think again, perhaps back across the Channel.

A monk began muttering, reciting prayers. It seemed to him they did it without even knowing. Mutter, mutter, their whining entreaties and self-abnegation were too much to bear. Without warning, he crossed the floor in a couple of strides, treading on the hand of one of his men, who yelled in pain. His hand went out to the praying religious, and hauled him to his feet. Angry, granite-hard eyes, stared into hazel ones, wide with fear.

'Cease your bleating,' he commanded, and ensured compliance by striking the monk hard across the face. He let him go, to fall, whimpering, to the ground.

Father Samson looked up from what might have been contemplation of his own folded hands.

'Does prayer frighten you?' His voice was very even.

'Frighten me?' Reynald was stunned for a moment, then his lip curled. 'Why should your mewling Latin frighten me? It is but a waste of breath. And I am not a man to be frightened. I do not fear death, and I do not fear life either, and you do both, whatever you say about your Faith and the Hereafter.'

'We do not fear death, for it is but a passing from the imperfect towards the perfect, but perhaps some fear the manner of it,' conceded Father Samson.

'Words, nothing more,' jeered Reynald. 'You fear life even more. Everything that a man does by nature you condemn as a sin, every pleasure, be it in drinking, eating, killing, wenching.'

The word seemed to remind him of Christina's presence. He had promised himself the taking of her, and if, as he intended, the end of this 'game' was in sight, he might not have much more opportunity. Besides, satisfying his needs elsewhere would take his mind off his empty stomach. He went and grabbed her by the plait of her hair, from where she knelt over the ailing monk, dragging her backwards, off balance, to the middle of the floor. Her cry of surprise and pain pleased him.

'Wenching. Now there is something you all need reminding of, my black eunuchs. Just think how it will stir you to watch, how much penance you will have to do for secretly wishing it was you, not me.' He looked to his own men. 'You are to make sure they do not close their eyes or look away. If they do, take out their eyes.'

Christina was trying to think, trying to fumble for the little knife within its sheath at her girdle. It was unlikely, in the gloom, that she could strike and kill him, but if all else failed, afterwards . . .

He straddled her, his weight heavy across her hips, and though the face was barely more than a paleness in the gloom, the eyes glittered. She had seen a look like that before often enough. He would not want it easy; the humiliation was part of his 'pleasure'. He was laughing, though for a moment he wondered at the emptiness in her eyes. Then he turned to the brethren.

'Forgotten what it is you are missing? Let me remind you.'

He yanked at the neck of her gown, and the fabric gave way before his violence, tearing down from one shoulder to expose pale flesh in the dimness. His hand touched her warmth, and an involuntary shudder ran through her. She saw the flash of his teeth as he smiled, and hated her own weakness. She was not strong enough, she was pinned. Physically there was nothing she could do. Blotting it all out in her mind had worked, a little, in the old days, but no more. She concentrated, tried to think lucidly, ignoring his boasts to the unwilling voyeurs of his depravity. What he said was alone enough to make one brother tremble with revulsion and yet fascination.

He shifted his weight slightly, and she felt the threat of him through her gown.

'Have you forgotten, too, Mistress?' Reynald whispered,

leaning forward, his face drawing close to hers. He wanted her fear as much as he now wanted her flesh.

'I cannot forget, my lord.' The sound was a soft hiss in his ear. 'For my loving husband gave me a "gift" to remind me of him always, gave me what killed him. I took this pilgrimage to pray for deliverance from its ravages. Take me if you must, but remember me when it destroys you. It is indeed "better to give than to receive".' Christina managed a smile, though there was a scream of animal loathing within her.

Reynald paused, paled a little. She might be lying, but if she was not? He wavered, and in that moment of wavering, Brother Augustine sat up, wild-eyed, and pointed a trembling finger at the figures on the floor.

'The wages of sin is death!' he cried out. 'Cursed be the fornicator.'

Christina felt Reynald tense. He stared at the monk, who seemed almost to have come from beyond death himself, and then down at her, with her cold smile. He struck that smile from her lips with his hand, and rolled away. She gasped, controlled the sob of pain and relief, and licked the blood from her lip.

Deprived of his prey, and shaken, Reynald struck out in words.

'I would say you must wait for another time, Brothers, but you have so little of it, it would be unfair of me to get your "hopes" up. I did not perhaps tell you that William de Beauchamp was unable to come to hand over my man, but then, he was never very likely to do so. We will try perhaps once more, for my forger is a valuable asset, but in truth I grow bored of this chasing about. To alleviate the boredom I am already thinking how you will end, one by one.' He turned again to Father Samson. 'And for you, being the most senior, I shall reserve the death I gave to my father. It was . . .' he paused for effect, 'appropriate.'

There was silence.

Chapter Fifteen

Guy woke early, and lay wakeful in the malodorous dark, his mind reviewing the past and contemplating the future. He was a man who enjoyed the life he had led with Reynald de Roules for the last four years, for the most part, though physical discomforts had been commonplace. There was a dangerous immediacy to it, a daring frisson, and, if he did not hold the same views upon religion as his adopted leader, he knew himself so far beyond saving that he might as well get all the excitement he could from this life, since the next would not be as pleasant, for all the Church claimed repentance could absolve all sin. Killing, once you got used to it, did not seem so hard, though he still recalled turning aside to vomit after his first battle, seeing the life leave the first man he killed in the Holy Land. Strange that of all the men he had killed since, it was that first face that haunted him, though it had been in fair fight and his enemy's life or his own. In the deepest hours of night, brown eyes bored into the remnants of his soul, perplexed, disbelieving, and then the blood issued from the mouth, and he felt it wet upon his cheeks as if red and real, not the product of the mind. Such foolishness it was, to be haunted by that, when those were the days he had not strayed beyond the bounds of what was accounted noble. Killing the enemy in battle, his proud ancestors would not object to that, would indeed applaud it. His service with the knights protecting pilgrims in the Holy Land had been pure enough, but on the way home he had fallen. Those same ancestors would not have approved killing a Gascon knight in jealousy over a woman, a woman who was the man's wife, and with a knife in the back. That she had played him as false as the husband in the end was perhaps justice, had driven him also to drink and distraction, which was where Reynald de Roules found him, impoverished, incoherent with wine, brandishing his sword at shadows.

Why Reynald, who never showed an ounce of compassion for anybody, should have taken it upon himself to sober him up and add him to his retinue, he would never know, but he was grateful for it. These last four years they had been soldiers of fortune to whoever paid them, no deed too low, no deed too dangerous, and then Reynald had taken it into his head to come home to England, where none of them ought to be, though it felt good to have arrived. Killing here felt different, though Guy told himself it was the same. He was glad they had never strayed north to where he might have been known. Better he remain a scion of a noble house, lost upon his returning from noble deeds, mourned proudly, than found to be a common criminal.

Reynald talked of making his fortune with the melted silver, talked of ruining the Sheriff of Worcestershire's reputation, of 'buying' an heiress from the King and holding land in England, but Guy could not see it happening. They had made trouble, which they were good at, but there was no ending he saw but blackness. He thought Reynald was tiring of this escapade, hoped they would make an escape to Anjou or Normandy. This was too cold, too grim, and Reynald's near obsessive hatred of the Black Monks was getting out of control.

When Reynald had sent him outside with the scribe, the day of the kidnap, he had taken the Benedictine's hand almost without thinking. It had even seemed a 'just' punishment, though he did not feel now it was his finest deed, and Reynald was getting into one of his darkest and most dangerous moods.

So here he was now, in a peasant's hovel, and expected to commit murder on a large scale. Whilst Reynald had not given an express command, he clearly intended that there should be no witnesses to their presence in Bransford, just a trail of cold bodies. Reynald was quite capable of killing a pregnant woman and five children in cold blood, but in truth, Guy was not. He realised that, even after all this time, there really were some things he would not stoop to do, as though the name he once bore would be too sullied by them.

He therefore had to persuade the woman and her brood to keep silent within their dark chamber, and hope that if he went to the barn, Reynald would not think to send any to check. In truth, de Roules had no reason to, since he had never before disobeyed him, but you never could tell with Reynald. Guy sighed, arose and went to explain, very clearly and slowly, to a frightened woman that he was not going to commit murder, not in this house at least.

Christina also awoke before a cold dawn, though her conscience was clear enough. The straw, in which she had formed a sort of nest, kept her from freezing, and, sporadically, she had dozed, but only exhaustion had given her that respite. She was cold, so cold in the extremities that it veered between numbness and pain. It seemed as if she could not remember what being truly warm and comfortable was like, and thought longingly of the fur-lined cloak she had eschewed in her show of humility. It was a natural step thereafter to think of Hugh Bradecote, whom she knew would be doing everything in his power to find her. For the umpteenth time she wondered if she would die, fated never to have enjoyed the happiness that at last seemed within her grasp. It chilled her the more, and it was only by a great effort of will that she arose to see how Brother Augustine fared. After his timely, if unknowing, intervention the previous evening, the fever had kept him unaware, keeping him trapped in a world of febrile dreams, and she hoped he had not felt the cold.

He had not, for neither heat nor cold would concern him again, and the cold flesh owed nothing to the temperature in the barn. The eyes were closed as restfully as in sleep, the jaw relaxed as if he had been about to sing Matins, the single hand that had picked and plucked at his coverings these last three days, lay stilled forever. The body was stiffening, but not yet quite so far gone that she could not lay the right arm to cross the left upon the chest, though the infected, bandaged stump made it a grotesque imitation of the norm. She prayed, blowing on her blue-white hands as she did so, but not just for the repose of a godly, gentle soul. Tears pricked her eyes, not for the Benedictine brother, whom she knew had not feared his death, and on whom the Almighty would assuredly have mercy, but for her loneliness and isolation. She prayed for justice, and she prayed for rescue. She crossed herself and shuddered, then moved, stiffly, under the watchful gaze of the malodorous individual that de Roules called Mauger, to where the Samson of Bec lay wrapped in his fine cloak. He was huddled about by the brothers, who had at least each other for warmth in this situation. As the lone woman she had nothing, bar the uncouth suggestions of those among her captors of ways they would warm her.

'Father Samson,' she called softly, unable to get close enough to shake him. He did not stir. His sleep, at least, was sound enough. She was guilty of the sin of jealousy, and as she called his name again, there was an edge to her tone. This time he opened his eyes, frowning as he focussed, and from displeasure at being dragged from the easing stupor of sleep.

'What is it, my la—daughter?'

'Brother Augustine is dead, Father. He died in the night. I am sorry.'

Father Samson sighed.

'We will pray for him.'

'I thought,' remarked Christina, with a degree of acerbity, 'that you might request a delay whilst you consecrate a patch of earth and bury him.'

'With what? I did not see that our captors possess shovels or picks, and the ground is frozen. Besides,' he sounded as if

212

explaining to a slow-witted child, 'I hardly think they would accede to such a request. Indeed, they would be inclined to treat the dead with even less respect.'

Christina bit her lip. Irritatingly, the churchman spoke sense. Her brain was working as fast as it could, made sluggish as it was by cold and hunger. If the good brother's corpse was left, and the kidnappers did not care, thinking they would be far away by the time the sheriff's men were alerted to it, she might have the chance to leave something that they could find. It would, at the very least, let Hugh know she was alive, and if only she had some indication of their intent, she might even give him the opportunity to make the leap that would bring him within striking range of a rescue attempt. She wished thoughts alone could travel through the winter air.

The cleric was speaking, though she did not pay him full attention. It was the sonorous and solemn tone of the religious declaring that man was born to die, and that it was a natural thing that should not be feared by the godly. She wanted to rail at that. What was natural about having one's hand hacked off by criminals and dying from the festering wound?

The other brothers assimilated the information as the threads of half waking, half sleeping, left them. One by one they crossed themselves and went down upon their knees. Christina joined them, but her prayers for the departed were done, and she was desperately trying to work out how best she could alert her betrothed. She could leave, if all else failed, a lock of her own hair, even if she had to pull it from her scalp and place it under the dead hand, but that was so little. It would tell Hugh Bradecote merely that she had been here. She made a decision.

It might well have been Father Samson's place to announce the death of one of his entourage to Reynald, but it had been she who had nursed the poor brother, as best as she was able, and so she brushed herself down and went to where the kidnappers rested, between the captives and the barn doors. They too were close packed for warmth, like piglets round a sow, she thought disdainfully.

'The man of God you disfigured, Brother Augustine, died in the night.' She kept her voice even, though she wanted to spit the news at him. 'I thought that you would want to know.'

Reynald de Roules yawned, sniffed, and wiped a dewdrop from the end of his nose.

'We'll travel the quicker for it. I had wondered whether to kill him anyway. He was holding us up, but nobody thought of trying to escape and abandon an injured companion, so he had his uses.' He paused. 'Indeed, he has still. Kenelm, wake up, you mangy cur. I have a task for you.'

He kicked at a man curled just beyond his feet, who grumbled and opened his eyes reluctantly, whilst scratching his groin.

'What?' He became fully awake, and added, 'My lord.'

'The monk died. Cut off an ear, and get the Scribbler over here. I am sending you to Worcester to deliver the final message, since they could not take action upon the last.' De Roules's voice had a trace of boredom in it. 'The river should be frozen enough by now.'

Christina feigned disinterest and even stood back, but listened intently, even as she was revolted by the thought of such desecration of the dead. The scribe was dragged from his

214

prayers for the departed, and hauled, shaking, before Reynald.

He dictated his demand in an emotionless tone, though it contained also a threat which made Christina bite her lip. This, he said, was his final offering to release the captives. His patience had worn thin. If Geoffrey was not released, at Tibberton church, by noon on the day the sheriff received the note, which was accompanied by the token of Reynald's 'esteem', then he would kill all the hostages in such manner as he thought appropriate and leave their corpses for de Beauchamp to discover about the shire.

Christina shuddered. What 'manner' would he think appropriate for her? She felt sick.

De Roules snatched the vellum from the scribe as he finished, and thrust it at Kenelm. Guy was not there to read it, but he had no fear whatsoever that the Benedictine would not have written exactly what he had been told.

'You take this to Worcester, but I want you to send another to the castle with the message. Get across the Severn today, where it is easier, north of Worcester itself. Go in by daylight first thing tomorrow, just an ordinary man about his business. Leave the horse somewhere outside the gate, for a man on foot is less conspicuous. They will be watching the castle gates. Use a child, or an old woman, from choice. A little bribery, or a simple threat, will see it done right. You leave once you see them get to the gate itself, mind. Even a dull wit like you should manage that.'

'And where do I meet you, then, my lord?'

Kenelm was suspicious, not a little convinced he was being abandoned. After all, as Pigface's 'keeper' he had already incurred Reynald's displeasure.

'We will be back at Evesham's tithe barn, the one near Bradecote we used the second night, tomorrow, at sunset. I am sure you can find it. Be there, for we will not linger in the morning.'

Christina clenched her fists within the long sleeves of her gown, and hoped none could hear the pounding of her heart, which thumped in her ears. She knew where they would be, tomorrow night. Her fate might, at last, not depend wholly upon others. This would be just what the sheriff's men needed, and almost certainly her only remaining chance of survival, but how could she convey the information? She could not write, and the brother who was deputed to write the demands was a pusillanimous fellow who would almost certainly reveal her plan, and see her suffer for it. Stealing any spare vellum or ink would be almost impossible, since it was kept by Reynald or Guy. She gasped as the thought hit her. Even a scratched sign might help, and if needs be a drop of blood would provide 'ink'. So what could be used to write upon? The linen of her shift, now doubtless begrimed and fraying, might just serve, though the marks would spread and be difficult to read. She went to a corner, ostensibly to be private and relieve herself. It occasioned nothing more than a lewd glance from one of her captors. Out of sight, she did the obvious and also tore a small strip from the linen, though it pained her chapped hands to do so. She thought carefully about what marks should go upon it, and then smiled. She took a sharp end of straw, and prised the chapped skin apart so that it oozed red. Dipping the end of the straw in the drop of blood, she made two vertical marks, and grimaced as she had to widen the cut for more blood. She drew a horizon line with the semicircle of a sun over it and an arrow indicating that it was setting. They had a time. That was easy, but the place? Her hand hurt, and her brain was spinning. She bit her lip, as much for the discomfort to counter the pain in her hand as in concentration. Her nerves jangled lest she be discovered, and the tiniest scratching sounded so loud it must give her away, but with a few more bloody strokes it was done.

She closed her eyes, and sent up a devout prayer that the message would be found, and found by those for whom it was intended. She wondered if Hugh Bradecote would realise it was directly from her, and then remembered the inspiration to use the lock of her hair. After all, what was a little more discomfort. She yanked enough strands for it to be clear it was intentionally left, and tied the thin lock round the strip of cloth. The body of Brother Augustine, though further brutalised, had thus far been otherwise ignored. She hoped they would not move him, at least his hand. She knelt beside him, placing her hands over it and tucking the cloth under the hand, with just a few hairs protruding. These men would not think to see them, but wily old Catchpoll would, or her Hugh. She prayed that whoever found the body would call the sheriff before burying it, and leave it be.

'I tried to help you, Brother. Now you do this last good deed for me, please, my friend,' she whispered, and pulled the edges of her cloak to half shroud the body, while the pale, restful face was left to draw the attention of any who entered the barn.

Guy now appeared, sidling into the barn cautiously. Reynald had stiffened at the sound of the door scraping open, and slid sword from scabbard, but relaxed as he spoke, and fired the important question at him.

'All tidy?'

'You will have no trouble, my lord.' Guy sounded casual.

'Good. The monk died. I am sending Kenelm to Worcester with a last note, and an ear.' Reynald laughed, softly. 'Might as well use him as much as we can, even if dead.'

Guy had an urge to cross himself, but fought it, for Reynald would sneer at any show of religion. Besides, why should Heaven forgive him this death, after all the others, even if he knew contrition?

'We cross the Severn today, to the north where it is narrower. The ice should be thick enough. If not . . . well, I am not going first.' Reynald smiled. 'I will tell you the current plan as we go along.' He stopped, and seemed to remember the lonely peasant, tied to a wooden upright in the corner. 'I must just finish our business here, and—'

'Let me, my lord.' Guy interrupted. 'It is nothing worth wiping your blade for. After all, I "tidied" the rest. I will catch you up in in the first few hundred paces.'

'As you will.' Reynald seemed to have lost interest, and turned to the rest of the company, who were in various states of readiness. 'Come on, you miserable apologies for men, up with you all. We have a river to cross. Has anyone got skates?' He laughed, but it was not a pleasant laugh.

The news was greeted with gruntings and grumbles, especially as there was nothing, yet again, with which to break their fast. Nobody, however, wanted to be the last ready, and come under Reynald's increasingly vicious displeasure. They bestirred themselves, Benedictine and criminal alike.

A few minutes later the barn was empty except for the stiffening corpse of Brother Augustine, Guy, and the tethered peasant. The man had few illusions as to why someone had hung back, but his thoughts at the last were of his family.

'My wife?' he murmured, eyes pleading. 'My children?'

'Be at ease on that, my friend. Your family are safe, upon that I give my oath, which once meant much. But you, I am sorry, cannot simply go free.'

Guy drew his knife.

The brown horse caught up before the riders were indeed more than a few hundred yards distant. Reynald smiled, and Guy managed to smile back. He held up a bloodied knife.

'I cut his throat,' he said, truthfully.

Chapter Sixteen

Hugh Bradecote stared upwards into the darkness. Sleep had claimed him whilst his body demanded it, but long before dawn he was awake, tossing in a nightmare from which he could not awaken. He had failed. He had failed William de Beauchamp, who had expected him to keep up the hunt, and capture the kidnappers whilst saving the precious hostage. Perhaps the sheriff had thought Christina important too, but he had not been specific. Well today he would head back to report that he had achieved nothing; the trail was as cold as the snowy ground, and he had no more idea where the kidnappers were than de Beauchamp himself. The sheriff would probably dismiss him ignominiously, and he really did not care. Failing his overlord was as nothing to failing her, his betrothed, his Christina. Each night, with his prayers, he had told her that he was coming, that he would find her, though only in his dreams did she hear him. Well, last night he could not say that; last night he could say nothing, for 'sorry' was too inadequate a word when he had lost her. He had failed to do what he had sworn to do, find her, save her, protect her from harm. Now she was lost, at the mercy of a man whose barbarity had been proven over and again, a cruel bastard who would think nothing of—Bradecote dug his nails into his palms. She deserved so much care, and he had proved dismally unworthy. He would go back to his manor, where baby Gilbert's infant gurgles would accuse him of depriving him of a mother to love him. And it was true. He covered his face with his hands, and in the blackness, both physical and mental, he wept silently.

It was a pensive-looking Serjeant Catchpoll who met him when they rose. Bradecote eschewed food, though he had barely touched the venison stew last night, and sat staring into the beaker of small beer as if it was as deep as the sea. Catchpoll had seen the sea a couple of times, down beyond Gloucester, in the grey-flecked, wintry Severn Estuary, and did not think much to it. Last night Bradecote had been a beaten man, and Catchpoll could understand it as a fleeting emotion. He was more concerned that it remained with the new day. For his own part he saw the situation as bad, yes, and would rather not have to face de Beauchamp's wrath when they returned empty-handed, but if the Severn had been frozen he would still lay odds on the kidnappers trying for another meeting. Whoever led them had put a lot of time and effort chasing about the shire, trying to get Geoffrey the Forger freed, and to give up now seemed, somehow, out of character. If he had, then Catchpoll expected to find a trail of bodies left for them to find, but best not tell the undersheriff that.

He watched him, and feared he had failed the sheriff twofold. He had said he would try and keep the undersheriff from crumbling under the strain, and it looked as if he had not just crumbled, but cracked. Grief, self-loathing, they could do that to a man, and pity it was they looked like ruining Hugh Bradecote.

'We had best be off, my lord,' said Catchpoll, touching his arm.

'Where? Back to tell the lord Sheriff I failed?' Bradecote's voice was listless.

'Not directly, no. Yesterday we lost 'em, and it was a blow, but in all truth, my lord, they cannot be that far away, and the river could not be crossed yesterday so they are still this side of Severn as we speak. Sitting here, gazing at nothing, achieves nothing. Doing nothing is failing. Acting is still working on the problem, so shift your lordly arse before I kick the bench from under you, and let's be about our duty.'

Catchpoll's tone and language were intentionally brusque, offensive. There was no point letting the man wallow, offering sympathy, for sympathy would do no good. Only action would help him, and only success, please God, would cure him. Normally, Hugh Bradecote would have reacted sharply, but he simply did as he was bid, in silence.

With Catchpoll in command, the sheriff's men trotted out from Malvern for the final time, Prior John watching the retreating figures with a frowning countenance, and a head full of prayer.

They headed towards Powick, Catchpoll working on the principle that if the kidnappers were not south of the Teme then they were not far to the north. There had been little sign of snow overnight, but the cold had made what lay icier and crunchy beneath the horses' hooves. In places it was clear enough to jog along, and in others they had to revert to walking pace.

They came once again to Bransford, and, out of habit, enquired of a woman carrying a pail to the midden if she had seen anything unusual.

'You'll be the lord Sheriff's men, then. Master Reeve, he's been going round like a chicken with its head off, and wondering how to find you.' The woman shook her head. 'A bad business, and for Godwin too, with his wife in her condition.'

With which cryptic comment, the woman tossed the contents of the pail onto the midden and turned to retrace her steps. Catchpoll looked at Bradecote, who was frowning, and raised an eyebrow.

'Perhaps Malvern Priory's prayers are heard in heaven,' he muttered, and turned his horse's head. 'Where is the reeve now?' he called after the woman.

'Up at the monks' barn, of course,' she replied, not turning round.

Bradecote touched spur to horse's flank, though more from instinct than it getting him to the barn faster. Catchpoll kept pace, thinking how best to deal with things if there was a woman's body involved, and the men-at-arms followed behind. Knowing the kidnappers had used the tithe barn before, they headed naturally to it rather than the newer structure.

* * *

The village reeve was pacing up and down, wringing his hands like a nervous father awaiting the cry of a newborn babe. He looked up at the sound of horses, momentarily fearful, and then flooded with relief. He had known he must do something, but had been unsure how to achieve it. He greeted them with a mixture of self-exculpation, exclamation and explanation, from which Catchpoll managed to gather there was a corpse in the barn, and then heard Bradecote's hiss of relief as it became clear the body was of a religious. The reeve let them into the barn, watched by the more curious villagers, some of whom already feared their spring would be cursed, tainted by the unnatural death of a holy brother among them.

Their eyes adjusted from the silvered brightness outside to the dimness within. Bradecote gave up silent thanks, for the body did not look as if it had been moved. They approached, the smell of death present even in the chill, and overlaid with the lingering odour of infection from the stump. The reeve stood a few feet from the corpse, but the sheriff's men came to stand either side of the mortal remains of Brother Augustine.

'Hello, Brother, we meet again,' murmured Catchpoll, kneeling down and surveying the bloodied head where the ear had been hacked off.

'Again? You knew . . .' Bradecote was not really thinking any more, his mind a numb void.

'Well, we've met a part of him, for sure. He was the owner of the hand. That stump was far from fresh, and the infected wound probably killed him.' His tone was matter of fact. 'They took the ear afterwards; there is very little blood, considering.' Catchpoll grinned his death's head grin, which the reeve thankfully did not see. 'Looks like the lord Sheriff will be receiving another body part to add to his collection.'

The serjeant chuckled, and this time the reeve gasped at the irreverence in the face of untimely death. Catchpoll ignored him, intent upon learning all that the dead could tell him.

'Then if he has sent . . .' Hugh Bradecote who had been trying not to get overexcited from the mere fact that the only corpse present was that of the monk, could not keep the hope from his voice now.

'Oh yes, my lord, this is not yet over.'

Bradecote let the feeling flood through him for a moment, a rejuvenation so complete, the reeve started at the undersheriff's clipped question.

'When exactly was he found, Master Reeve?' Bradecote asked as Catchpoll, whose discerning nose seemed unaffected by proximity to the body, peered closely at it.

'My lord, it was reported to me by Godwin, one of our cottagers, who has been kept captive here since before dawn yesterday.'

Bradecote and Catchpoll exchanged glances.

'So they were here yesterday, after all,' murmured Bradecote, his fist clenching. 'And our lecherous villager was a ruse. The snow covering aided them, but we ought to have checked.' He sighed, and shook his head. 'Where is this Godwin?'

'I left him back with his family, who, God be praised, were spared by the man meant to kill them. His wife is attending to his injuries.'

'Is he like to die?'

Knowing what had happened before to those who fell into the path of the kidnap gang, Catchpoll was surprised the man had lived this long.

'No, but it is a weird thing.' The reeve sounded mystified. 'The man, the same man who had stayed with the family, pulled a knife across his throat so that it drew blood but not deep or long so that it would take his life. He said he had to do it, but the scar was his "gift".'

'We need to speak to Godwin, injured or not, and to the wife perhaps also,' remarked Bradecote.

'I will fetch them, my lord.'

The reeve left, glad to have the excuse to get out into fresh air and light. The cold had kept all but a vague hint of the sickly, unforgettable odour of gangrene from the barn, except close to the body, but it was enough, and the disfigurement of the body disturbed the man.

'It'll be helpful if we speaks to him, my lord, but I should say the brother died during yesterday or last night, not within the last few hours, and not before he arrived here. The death stiffness is complete. Of course, the cold would make it linger, but there is no sign at all of it leaving him, and if he had died before they got here it might well be easing by now.'

'I wonder they did not leave him in the burning barn, Catchpoll?'

'True enough. He must have become a burden to them, but he was not killed here. Rather he died from the wound of days back. There was time for someone, another religious, presumably, to give him the semblance of decency, even after the disfigurement. The first brother was a sign to us, but this

226

one, no. He was not killed as an example.' Catchpoll was almost talking to himself by now, and paused. Then, with some force required, he lifted the remaining hand, addressing the corpse. 'What have you here, friend?'

Catchpoll took the scrap of linen, itself stiffened slightly by the chill and the dried blood. The hair around it was dark, and long. Bradecote's stomach clenched so hard it hurt.

'That's her hair,' he whispered.

'Aye, my lord, I'd say so. There was no report of another woman in the party, and the brothers would not possess such length.' He looked up at his superior's anxious face. 'It is a good sign, my lord. She was alive yesterday, and from what I see here, this was left for us, and not by the captors.'

He removed the binding of hair, and handed it to Bradecote, who held it as if a precious relic, then peered at the linen. The blood had soaked into the material, spreading so that the marks were no longer crisp and clear. He frowned. It made no sense to him, just stains. Despondent, he handed it back to Catchpoll, who grinned.

'Now here's writing I understand.'

'But you can't . . .'

Catchpoll turned the cloth so that Bradecote could see the marks again.

'I think your lady has kept her wits about her.'

Bradecote suddenly realised the significance of the colouring.

'These marks are in . . . blood?'

'I'd say so, my lord, but think. What else might she have had to hand?'

'Sweet Jesu, she was reduced to . . .' Hugh Bradecote

swallowed hard. It was an unpalatable thought. 'And these are just marks.'

'Aye, but what are the letters you are so proud of, but marks, my lord? Once you know this is a message, you can try to read it. She wouldn't be asking after your well-being and commenting on the weather. She would be trying to tell us what we need to know to rescue her, and that would be where they will be, not where they are or have been. Look close. There's lines, lines for a time, a day.'

'Perhaps.' Bradecote was still struggling with what he held in his hand.

'And the rest, as I "read" it, means sunset and a place. So the second sunset from today, they will be at . . .' He took the scrap back from Bradecote's unresisting grasp and pulled a 'thinking face'. 'Well, the first thing might be a heart, but there's nowhere hereabouts called Heart or Hart something. The second thing is a barn. There is a roof shape and a cross. So a barn belonging to a church or churchmen. Another tithe barn, but where?' He scratched his head.

Bradecote was trying to think clearly. It was so important that he did so, and yet he was finding it nigh on impossible. She had left a message. She knew he would be trying to find her. The message was to him, not just to the shrieval party. The revelation struck him, and he gasped, as if physically winded.

'The monks of Evesham have a tithe barn only a mile north-east from Bradecote.'

He did not need to explain the heart. She meant him, where her heart lay, he knew it, and if Catchpoll thought it fanciful romance, he could not afford to care. Even as his pulses raced, the reeve returned with a white-faced couple, the woman heavily with child, the man with a strip of linen about his throat.

'Godwin and his wife, my lord.'

The woman made an awkward obeisance.

'Tell us whatever details you can about what happened to you, about the men,' demanded Catchpoll, but gently.

'And about the lady also. How was she?' added Bradecote, unable to resist finding out what he could about Christina.

Godwin sighed. His mind was in a turmoil of relief and a vague idea this was all a bad dream. He repeated how they had been taken, how he had remained, convinced he would never see his family again.

'The lady, she was the one who saw me in the wood, the day before, I swear it.'

'In the wood?' Bradecote repeated, frowning.

So he told them about the theft of wood, and his foraging. It fitted with what they knew.

'And the lady, it was she who cared for the dying brother, Brother Augustine she called him. It was she also who cooked the meal, what there was of it.'

Bradecote blinked. He had not imagined her made to undertake menial tasks.

'They made the lady FitzPayne cook and nurse?'

'Nobody called her by that name or any other, my lord, just "the woman" or "the widow".'

Bradecote began to wonder if she had perhaps concealed her identity, and the man's next words confirmed his fears.

'The man who commands, the lord, he was in foul mood last night. I do not know what was going on, what anything

229

of this is about. He was ranting, ranting at the holy brothers, talking about killing a prelate, and then he took the lady—'

'He what?' Bradecote shouted so sharply the woman jumped.

'He took her and threw her on the ground, and told the monks he would show them what they were missing, how a woman filled in time when a man was bored . . .' Godwin faltered at the look on the undersheriff's face.

'Go on,' whispered Bradecote, hoarsely.

'He wrenched at her gown, sat astride of her, but she said something, something very quietly, and he paused, and then the sick brother sat up, wide-eyed and wild. I think we all thought him dead already, and it was a ghost. He shouted something about sin and death, then fell back, and the lord stood up, pulling the lady with him. He hit her across the face and turned away swearing. I did not understand any of it.'

Bradecote swallowed hard, fought his rapid breathing. Catchpoll judged it best to move on.

'And this morning? What about the man with your wife, the one who cut you? What was he like?'

'For all the wickedness, he did no harm to me or the children,' murmured the woman. 'Indeed, yesterday he went out and collected wood, though we had some left, and managed to kill a duck upon the river ice and brought it home for us. We ate well, and sorry I am there is none left for my husband, bar the carcass I left boiling at home. This morning he said his lord wanted us dead, so there would be none to speak about him, but he would not murder us in cold blood. We had to stay indoors and keep quiet and not go to the barn or anything, in case we were seen. I was mortal afraid, but kept the children quiet, and did as he said. He was a man who spoke lordly, at least fluent to the man who threatened me with his knife the night before, the leader, and it was better than his English. He was not well dressed, his clothes were worn, but his boots were good, and he had a close brown beard.'

'So they were here, and departed but this morning.' Bradecote had mastered himself, at last. 'That means we know where they will be tomorrow night.' He spoke almost to himself. 'And we just have to get to the tithe barn.'

'Not wishing to throw a caltrop in the way of this idea, my lord, but you have not considered the Severn.'

'What?'

'The ear of the brother has been removed, so they are clearly sending a message to the lord Sheriff,' Catchpoll could not repress a smile, 'and I would love to see his face when he receives it. They have to allow him time to get it and the messenger to rejoin them, hence tomorrow night. The actual meeting might be for the next day. The river is frozen solid, but we do not know if it is solid enough for a man to cross, let alone a horse, and nor do they. So they will have headed north to cross where it is not quite so wide, and not where they are going to be in view.'

'We are therefore closer yet further away, Catchpoll, if we have also to go north.'

'Aye, my lord, and we wants to get there in advance of the kidnappers, so we catches them afore they gets within the barn itself. Once there, like rats in a hole, it would be far more dangerous for the hostages.' Catchpoll then coughed. 'And you would have to accept, my lord, that if the Severn ain't crossable the meeting cannot happen, and even if it can be done, that when the lord Sheriff gets the message, he will not be a patient man. He will want an end to this, one way,' – he paused – 'or another.'

'But he only knows a meeting place, and it is unlikely to be the barn.'

'We have the advantage that he will not have been sent direct to the barn, my lord, but he has Walkelin with him, and that lad might well think sensible and work out they needs a local barn to shelter in overnight, so he might be there tomorrow also.'

Bradecote groaned. Never had he thought he would want Walkelin to be without initiative. Then he concentrated.

'Where is the nearest point that you think we can cross the Severn?'

'Somewheres south of Hallow, my lord, which is where I suspect the messenger has crossed to Worcester.'

'And the kidnappers also?'

'Probably, my lord, and taken shelter the other side. But they are far enough ahead to have crossed by now. We would not reach near Hallow for the best part of two hours in the snow, and then we would be in gloaming. It would be madness to cross in the dark.'

'In the dark, yes, but by moonlight?'

'My lord you're not thinking . . .'

'I am thinking, Catchpoll. I am thinking we have to make up time. If the night is cloudless and cold, well, it is near full moon.'

'So you are thinking we cross the frozen river in the moonlight, simple as that, and ride into Worcester, waking the gatekeepers with a cheery greeting?' Catchpoll's sarcasm was undisguised.

'Er, no.' Bradecote had the grace to blush. 'I wasn't intending to go into Worcester at all. For a start, we do not know how close the kidnappers are to the barn already. We just have to pray they have stopped before reaching it. They will not be far off, though, and will not want to be waiting in the cold tomorrow, so are most likely to get there good and early. Besides, if we go to Worcester, the sheriff is in command and . . . My plan is to skirt Worcester and spend the night at my own manor. If we set off betimes tomorrow morning, we have a good chance of being there before both kidnappers and the lord Sheriff, which gives us the best chance of securing the hostages.'

'If our bodies are not under the ice, that is,' growled Catchpoll, morosely.

Chapter Seventeen

Christina was cold, she was hungry as she had never known before, and she was scared. Her life seemed to be spiralling to a grisly fate, and she had done the only things she could to affect the outcome. She prayed the blessed Eadgyth was perhaps helping her after all. The remaining Benedictines ignored her, lost in their own contemplations, no doubt. Father Samson looked grave but resigned. Clearly, he expected little from this wicked world, and it had fulfilled his every expectation. Well, she had seen more than her share of sorrow and wickedness, but knew there was good to be found, and happiness, if she could but be permitted to grasp it. She prayed, as her horse stumbled through the foot-deep snow, that the blessed Eadgyth would continue to protect her, and that Hugh Bradecote would find her, and not just her cold corpse. There was no sun that she could follow for time or direction, but when they came to cross the frozen Teme by the bridge near Powick, she realised they must be going north. They travelled parallel to the Severn, beyond Worcester she thought, and then turned to meet the riverbank and the white expanse of ice. The thought of trying to cross it was terrifying. Whether it would take the weight of a person, let alone a mount, was a matter of chance, and a fall could break a bone or send a body to a certain death in the freezing water. The only men who did not look perturbed were Father Samson and Reynald de Roules. Reynald selected one of his own men to go first, an honour that was not appreciated by the man or his horse, which rolled an eye and looked at its rider as if he were mad. Only with a great deal of coaxing and pushing from behind could it be forced onto the ice, and then its own sense of self-preservation took over and it trod, very delicately, head down, behind the man who held it on the loosest of reins lest it disappear and drag him in with it. Once he had got about a third of the way, Reynald set a brother and one of his men, a good ten yards apart, to follow on. Slowly, a few at a time, they made their way across, the later ones heartened by the sight of the first ones clambering up the far bank to safety.

Christina crossed with Guy to one side of her, and Mauger to the other. She told herself that she was lighter than nearly everyone else, and thus had a better chance. She was just over halfway when she slipped and pitched forward with a cry, landing on her hands and knees. Her horse jibbed, but miraculously kept its footing a few paces behind her. Mauger's mount was less fortunate, or sure-footed, pulled up hard and dragged Mauger over as its hind legs crumpled under it and it sat down. He fell backwards, his head cracking on the ice, and lay still. The horse struggled, trying to get its hindquarters up again, while Christina, shaken, crawled forward a few paces and gingerly balanced herself to rise, conscious that if the ice cracked beneath the horse it might send fissures as far as herself. She dared not look back to see how it progressed, or what happened to Mauger, but struggled onward, repeating the Ave Maria under her breath. Guy reached the other side slightly before her, and actually came to reach down a hand to pull her up the bank.

'Give me your hand, my lady,' he said, quietly.

She stared at him for a moment, then held out her hand and let him help her up the bank. She did not know what to say. He might have called her that from some old habit of courtesy, but somehow, no, he knew who she was.

'You know.'

'Yes, from talking with the men-at-arms at the bridge.'

'But you have not told Reynald?'

'No. It . . . It would put you in even worse case if he knew.'

'I—'

'My lady, I would loose you now, but if you knew not your way . . . And without other distractions Reynald would come after you, and outstrip your mare, easily. He will not be crossed, and he is . . . vengeful.'

'I have seen. But, in the end, we are not to be freed. He made that clear last night.'

Guy nodded.

'Knowing Reynald, that is true. And he tires of this "game". We have no time now, for he approaches, but I will try to have words with you. And if not, know that I will do whatever is in my power to see you safe.'

236

He threw her up into her saddle and tied the leading rope from her palfrey to his own mount. Reynald was crossing with Father Samson. Mauger's horse was upright now, and shaking with fear. Reynald had ignored it, but spared Mauger a glance and a nudge with his boot. The red stain from one ear, and the staring eyes, told him all he needed, and he passed on. When he reached the bank, he mounted without so much as mentioning the man, and berated his men for hanging about like washing on the drying grounds. He rode off, not bothering to glance back, as others did, at the pathetic heap on the ice, and the horse, now whinnying at being alone, but fearful of moving.

For a while thereafter, Christina's mind was as numb as her chilled feet. She tried to think. This man Guy, the very man who had chopped off Brother Augustine's hand without so much as a pause, was offering his aid. That he had not revealed her to Reynald, seemed to indicate that he meant it, but should she trust him? Gradually she took in her surroundings. They were unknown to her, masked by the snow, but she knew that she was now east of the Severn and had at least the possibility of recognising where she was. A church, perhaps, might give her a clue. She had expected to turn southwards upon the road to Worcester, which had seen some use and was trampled enough to make the going easier, and then skirt about it, but for a short way they went north, then cut vaguely eastward across country. De Roules clearly thought any pursuers would assume they had gone south as she did, and would be looking for tracks off the road nearer Worcester. She smiled to herself, in the belief that her betrothed no longer needed to track. Then doubts assailed her. What if they actually reached the barn tonight? Would she be drawing Hugh Bradecote to a dangerous stalemate where the defenders had the advantage? She had been praying that he might reach her, but now she realised that to do so he must face the danger of crossing the river, and then taking on an enemy behind wooden walls. She had seen no men with bows among Reynald's 'pack'. She ought to have paid more attention. There might yet be one or two unslung and strapped to a horse's flank. Was she wishing him into danger? She gave herself a mental shake. The ice crossing had addled her wits. He would be coming after her whether she wished him to or not, for he would not abandon her. It was foolishness to worry about it, and perhaps she had an ally.

It was getting dark, and they had not stopped. Not only Christina wondered where they were headed for the night, and when Guy asked Reynald, he received no more than a smile and an injunction to 'wait and see'. A short time afterwards and the squat outline of a church appeared, and signs of a village. Reynald held up a hand, and told Guy to keep everyone back whilst he went to reconnoitre. He returned a few minutes later, smiling.

'I cannot offer much in the way of food, but there will be shelter. Follow me.'

They did as they were told, and came round to the west end of the church. To the horror of the Benedictines, and the discomfort even of his men, Reynald opened the door and led his horse inside. For a moment nobody followed. He stuck his head out, his whisper venomous.

'Bring the horses in, fools. How else can we remain unseen? Come in or stay outside and freeze to death.'

Reluctantly, they followed one by one. Within, the priest, who had been saying Vespers alone, lay gagged. Guy raised an eyebrow.

'You did not kill him? I thought you would not be so . . . charitable,' he commented, as if only mildly interested.

'He will live, so that when de Beauchamp sends someone here tomorrow, he may tell them we have been and gone. Oh yes, this is Tibberton church. His dwelling is next door. The widow can cook. Take her to make the best of what you find, and Guy,' he paused, 'you were ever too easily swayed by a woman. Make sure you are not this time, for it might be fatal.'

Christina wondered if it showed him suspicious, or thinking of last night and merely offering a warning not to take advantage of being alone with her if he thought her diseased. Guy sniffed, looked at her as if she were an encumbrance he could do without, and grabbed her wrist, almost dragging her out of the door.

The priest's house was small but wonderfully warm after their recent refuges. There was a fire upon the hearthstones, the first warmth Christina had felt in nearly two days, and she extended her hands to it with a sigh. Guy closed the door behind them.

'You must at least start to cook, my lady. Could you make your way to Bradecote in the dark, if I let you free?'

'I . . . I do not think so, not in the dark and with the snow. It makes things less familiar. Besides, what you said earlier . . . Reynald would . . .'

'I could delay him.'

There was a finality in his voice, and Christina understood. Guy did not think he would beat Reynald in a fight. She was confused by him.

'Why? Why offer such a sacrifice for a woman you do not even know?'

Guy shrugged.

'I have reached the end, perhaps. I have no stomach for this any more.'

She was reaching for onions, hanging in a string from a beam, but looked at him, her head on one side.

'You are not like the others, not some common criminal. Who are you?'

'I am a common criminal now. Once, years back, I was not. Now I am Guy, no more, no less. The name I had should not be besmirched. I owe it that.'

'Are you declared outlaw?'

'Not in this realm, no. But what I have done these last few years would have me so elsewhere, were there a name to outlaw.'

She frowned.

'You take no pleasure in this. Reynald does.'

'Reynald. Ah, he has a madness to him, one that seems worse since we returned to England. He seeks his own destruction, but wants to destroy as much as he can in that spiral downward.'

'So why have you stayed with him?'

'Duty, in part. He picked me from a gutter, when I had no further to fall, gave me what seemed self-respect again, as a man with a sword in his hand, but not, in truth, just as a man. I was too far gone for that. I am damned.'

'But there is repentance, and forgiveness.'

Christina was slicing the onions, and her eyes pricked.

'Not for sins such as mine, lady. I killed a man, foully, to have his wife, though she forsook me fast enough for another; I have fought not for lord or honour, but for silver; I have killed men, stolen; and now I have even killed a holy brother. God will not forgive me that.'

'Brother Augustine was indeed a man of God, more so than many of his brethren, in my opinion. But if his death brought you to repentance, he would not begrudge you salvation.'

She took a skillet, and cut a slice from a side of bacon, smoked beneath the eaves. A real cook, she thought, would have cooked the bacon first. There was silence, then she asked the question that came to mind.

'But what of that poor woman and her children? That was . . .'

Guy smiled, wryly.

'You do think me that low. The peasant woman, may she be delivered safely come the spring.'

'You did not . . .'

'There are some things . . . No, I did not. Reynald could, I could not.'

'But you cut her husband's throat. I heard you boast of it.'

'I did, and he will show the scar to his grandchildren, no doubt.' He saw her surprise. 'A knife need not cut deep.'

The bacon sizzled, and the smell was enticing. Her stomach, deprived of food, knotted in anticipation, but she hardly felt it.

'So you would end it all, by defending me?'

'You could put it that way, if you so chose, my lady FitzPayne. It has a smattering of honour to it, don't you think?'

She frowned.

'I do not think it would work, as a plan, and – forgive me – had you not thought, if your sins are not publicly upon your name here, could you not just leave this, and go home?'

'Go home?' He sounded as if the word was forgotten.

'Have you none who would not fall upon your neck with tears of joy to see you alive, if they thought you dead?'

'Aye, until they heard what I have done since they thought me lost.'

'There was a prodigal son, was there not?'

'Not as prodigal as I have been,' Guy sneered, but there was a pause.

'For all that is past, you have shown mercy, humanity, charity, these last days. Would it be impossible to go home, confess to a priest, be what once you were, strive for forgiveness?'

There was a longer pause.

'The bacon will be crisped.'

'Oh!'

She pulled skillet from fire, the heat of the handle hurting her hand and leaving it red. Bacon and fat went into the pottage.

'If you cannot escape tonight, then it must be when there is some confusion.' Guy did not wish to speak of himself any more. 'If Reynald makes a show of killing, and the chances are he will take a monk first, then there might be a chance. I will try and keep you bound to my horse tomorrow, or in "my" charge, and if there is an opportunity, I will loose you. The day after, well, it looks as if I will not be left here to watch, but if I am, then you are on your own until my return. I think that is the best I can offer you, my lady.'

'And I am grateful, my lord.'

He looked at her sharply, thinking for a moment that she mocked, but saw she meant her words, and looked at the floor.

'The meal must be ready. I will carry the pot, if you will carry the bread, Mistress Cook.'

If Catchpoll had been praying for heavy snow clouds to occlude the moon's silver visage, he gave no sign of it. They made the best pace they could upon the trackway, hard ground and ruts making their progress through the snow hazardous. The horses disliked it, and had to be kicked hard to keep going, the men rode hunched and miserable, the whisper that they were heading to cross the Severn bringing down curses upon the undersheriff, and prayers to the saints for preservation.

Bradecote himself felt more alive and vital than for days. From Bransford they had signs of their quarry once more, heading northwards, but the tracks themselves were no longer more than a confirmation. He had an objective and a plan, a plan that had a good chance of success, as long as the kidnappers did not reach the tithe barn by tonight, and on the morrow he would be able to do something at last, something other than chase shadows. He would see her, he would save her, if it cost his own life he would save her, and any man who stood between them would die. The pernicious depression that had afflicted him in his frustration was gone, and had been replaced by hope and resolution.

Catchpoll looked, and saw much. That his superior considered the Severn was simply an obstacle that he would overcome without a second thought, was clear. Serjeant Catchpoll was not as sanguine. He had lived on the banks of the great river all his life, and knew it to be unforgiving if treated without respect. He had never seen it frozen hard enough to cross on foot, though he had heard of it being so twice in his oldfather's time. It was not uncommon for the edges to turn to creaking, cracking shards, but, God's truth, this was a colder snap than ever he had experienced. Perhaps it would be hard-iced enough to cross. The only good thing was that if the enemy had crossed safely, then so could they, or at least most of them.

The short January day was hastening into night by the time they saw the tracks turn riverwards. In the gloaming the snow took on an eerie brightness, and when the moonglow filtered between the trees it seemed positively eldritch. They came to the bank, and here the prints of men and horses had trampled a swathe in the whiteness. Catchpoll looked across. There were no signs of cracked ice or filling holes, saints be praised. There was, however, a dark mound upon the ice in the middle of the river. Catchpoll raised an eyebrow. Well, it would ensure the men took the crossing cautiously.

'The river is iced thick enough to cross,' announced Bradecote, in a tone that had an edge of excitement, as if it was the fulfilment of an anticipated treat. The men looked at him sullenly, uninspired.

'So we shall cross,' Catchpoll butted in, 'but we do it careful. Don't bunch up, keep well apart, if the horse goes in, for God's sake let go of the reins, and,' he pointed at the inanimate heap midstream, 'try not to break your neck, or even an arm.'

He sounded less pleased about the 'adventure', which was in accord with the men-at-arms' view, and they nodded. The moonlight – and in this Bradecote had been correct – made the crossing no more risky than in daylight, but it felt other-worldly. They spread out in a line, Catchpoll opting to head nearest to the body on the ice, more from interest than necessity. He had no intention of adding its weight to his own and dragging it to the bank, but if he saw the face, then perhaps, when the river flowed again, and the body washed up, he would know the cause and have no need to ask about kin, or wonder at how he died. Catchpoll did not rush. He disliked the ice more than he would care to admit. It was deceitful, lulling you into a confidence that you could tread onward safely, and then whisking your feet from under you. At very best it was undignified, and at worst, well, the body illustrated that.

He did not linger with Mauger, but contemplated the features a minute to file them in his brain. The man had clearly fallen backwards, and cracked his skull. Catchpoll sniffed, and carried on.

There were a few slips and expletives among the sheriff's men, but all reached the eastern bank in safety. Catchpoll stood next to Bradecote as they prepared to mount.

'And now, my lord?'

'Now, Catchpoll, we skirt Worcester, check there are no massed hoof prints to the doors of Evesham's tithe barn, and if, as I pray, there are none, we go "home" to Bradecote for the rest of the night. The men can get warm and have a decent meal, and will feel the better for it.'

This side of the Severn and within a few miles of his own manor, Hugh Bradecote felt at home again. He left the past few days of misery on the far bank, and felt warm from within, whatever the weather might be doing to feet and hands.

Catchpoll was hopeful also. As long as the morrow brought success, and for the undersheriff that was one thing only, there was no need to ever tell the lord Sheriff how close he had come to the abyss. Nearly every man had a weak point somewhere, and it had not been that surprising that, newly fallen in love, the undersheriff had been very vulnerable. He thought too much, considered Catchpoll. Thinking, when about the who, and how, and why, was good. Thinking, when it meant looking into one's own soul, that was different. He would always look too deep, hold himself guilty for things that just 'happened', think about morality when he was dealing with unemotional law. Keep his woman and his brats out of the business and he would not be the liability he had been in this one case. Catchpoll grinned to himself. He had 'carried' a useless undersheriff for years and been glad of it. Now here he was, fretting that this one had been no help for but a few days, and missed the partnership. Perhaps he was getting too old.

The environs of the tithe barn were pristine, and Bradecote made sure they were not disturbed, lest it advertise their presence the next day. He even kept off the trackway, since he knew the locality well enough to find his way across country by nothing more than moonlight. With a lighter heart than he would have thought possible only that morning, he led the sheriff's men the last mile to Bradecote, with the calming familiarity of every coppice. He had to hammer upon the gate of his own manor for some time, which was met with some murmurs of amusement from men anticipating warmth and food after a very long day. When the gates were eventually opened by a very apologetic steward, Bradecote waved away the apology, urging him to set the kitchen staff to providing a good meal for all his men, and spiced ale to warm them.

'I was not expected, and I would only be displeased if the gates had not been barred this late, and in the dark. No more words. There are men to feed, horses to be stabled.'

Bradecote was striding to his hall, where candles were swiftly lit, and a fire lit in the central hearth. The nurse came from the solar, which was kept warm since baby Gilbert lived within it.

'My lord, Master Gilbert has been laid down to his sleep.'

'I will not disturb him, but would see him, please.'

Shading a candle, she led him into the warm dimness. Gilbert Bradecote lay, fist to mouth, in his cradle. His father looked down at him with pride, and a sudden pang. What if he did not have Christina in this same spot, gazing down at the child, on the morrow? No, he would not think miserable thoughts now. She would be here. He sighed, and returned to the hall, where trestles and benches were being arranged. The nurse shushed loudly, and frowned.

Catchpoll was in discussion with the steward, but turned at Bradecote's approach.

'We think we have worked out who will fit where, my lord, and the spiced ale will be along very shortly.'

'Good. Let everyone eat, drink and get some rest. Tomorrow, early, we set our ambush.'

Chapter Eighteen

Kenelm was not a happy man. Being part of a gang suited him, and he felt peculiarly exposed on his own, though common sense should have told him that a single man passing through the countryside would occasion no suspicion. He had done as he was told, and headed northward before trying to cross the Severn, and had reached the outskirts of Hallow before heading east and to the banks of the great river. Here, his problems had increased. His horse took one look at the expanse of ice and rolled its eyes in fear. He tried clucking and coaxing it down the bank, he even tried pushing it, but when it came to a simple trial of strength between man and horse, there was only going to be one winner. Well, the lord Reynald had told him not to take the horse into Worcester itself, so he would just have to claim he tethered it somewhere and some thieving bastard stole it. He would be the butt of jokes if nothing worse, but it was all he could think of to cover his failing. What it left him with now was a crossing across the slippery ice, and then a very cold trudge through snow towards Worcester. Perhaps he should have tried further south, after all, but it was too late now. Taking his few possessions from the animal, he gave it a malevolent stare, and cautiously set foot upon the frozen water. The edge had been frozen some days, and should be the safest part, but Kenelm was, perversely, more confident as he got further out towards midstream. Then his isolation hit him, as though he saw himself from afar as a single dark spot on the expanse of white. He halted, frightened. His heart beat fast, and a trickle of fear-sweat coursed down his spine. He told himself he could not remain where he was, forced one foot to slide in front of the other, and began to edge towards the eastern bank. When he arrived, he felt exhausted from the strain, but knew it was too cold to stop without shelter. It was only a couple of miles to Worcester, but on foot, and in the snow, it would be miserable and slow. He began to trudge southwards.

There was no decent shelter to be had, no church or stable in which to hide, but he reached Worcester before the gates were shut. His instructions had been to enter first in the morning, and he was still reluctant to deviate from them. Reynald de Roules had shown how he took disobedience, but then, with luck, he would never know of this. That Kenelm might, at this point, 'disappear' and never be seen by de Roules ever again, never occurred to him. Taking a deep breath, and keeping his head well down, he passed into Worcester.

He had forgotten the good smells of a town. The bad were like anywhere, but where produce was bought and sold, bread and pies baked, ale brewed, and all so close together, Kenelm smelt 'comfort'. He possessed a couple of silver pennies and bought a gristly pie from a vendor who thought there were no more sales to be had that day, and Kenelm was hungry enough to enjoy it as if it had been roasted swan. Hunger assuaged, he turned next to his thirst, and settled himself in an alehouse. The comparative warmth made him sleepy, and his coin lasted long enough for him to become half comatose. He was thrust out into the cold by the host when the last customers were leaving, and staggered, haphazardly, along an alley to find himself by the wharfage. An unsecured door gave him access to a shed, where he collapsed upon a bale of linen cloth, and snored in blissful oblivion.

He did not so much awake as was awoken, by a man threatening him with the dire consequences of trespass and theft. That the sleeper had been blind drunk was fairly obvious from the wincing as he opened his eyes, and the bleary, nauseated incomprehension on his face. The agitated owner therefore contented himself with throwing him outside to vomit in the gutter.

Kenelm was in the unhappy position of a man for whom death seemed more agreeable than a head that wanted to explode and a stomach that wanted to repel anything he might choose to ingest. Thinking was, for a time, quite beyond him, but his hungover state was a perfect cover. Nobody spared him a second glance. Women shook their heads, and hoped any wife of his would take their broom to him on his return home, whilst men divided between the sympathetic and the superior.

* * *

Walkelin was at a bit of a loose end, and wondering what excitement was being had with Serjeant Catchpoll and my lord Bradecote. With the dies and silver secured, his tasks seemed at an end. He was in the bailey, in idle chat with the armourer, when a man rode in, followed by two retainers. He was clearly lordly, from bearing and garb, and his left hand was misshapen, all the fingers missing. A few months ago he would have taken no more interest, but now he followed at a discreet distance to find out who the visitor might be. At the entrance to the great hall, he asked a servant, sent to fetch wine. The servant shrugged, and said it was some lord who was an old friend of the lord Sheriff. It might be nothing to do with him, but even so, on the servant's return, Walkelin took the tray from him, and entered the hall.

William de Beauchamp was still engaged in polite reminiscences with his visitor. He raised an eyebrow when Walkelin approached, and the serjeant's apprentice wondered if he had overstepped the mark, but the sheriff brought a blush to his cheek by introducing him as 'my serjeant's right-hand man, and working on this with me'.

De Beauchamp then spoke to Walkelin.

'I want you to hear this, so we will speak English. The lord Audemer de Brescelin returned from pilgrimage a year and a half back. He is a good and trusted friend whom I have known far too long to even recall our first meeting. I sent word to him yesterday, for he was in the Holy Land two years past' – he turned to de Brescelin, who nodded confirmation – 'and might be able to shed light upon Reynald de Roules.'

With which the sheriff then ignored Walkelin, who began to feel invisible as the two men passed from civilities to the matter in hand.

'I am glad you came yourself, my friend. I will learn much more than from some missive on vellum.'

'Indeed, and when I heard of what you suspect . . . That you sent a man so swiftly showed how important it was to you, and it was no great hardship. You want to know about Reynald de Roules.' De Brescelin shook his head. 'A shame upon the good name of de Roules, and Picot never even knew . . .'

'Knew?'

'I am sorry. I start in the middle and you need the beginning. Reynald arrived in the Holy Land some years before me, was there briefly, and left before I had completed my vow and stood before the Tomb at Jerusalem. He had a nasty reputation. Fought hard, could not fault him on that, but they said he . . . enjoyed it too much, liked to take prisoners and kill them slowly, and there were rumours not all he killed were Saracen. He went back to Cyprus, and there . . .'

De Beauchamp's eyebrows rose.

'It was all rumour, nothing proved, until one night he was eating in the company of some French knights, who were entertaining the envoy of the Bishop of Reims. The envoy, who was a cleric of good birth, was introduced. Now, those who knew de Roules, knew he could not abide the religious, but these Frenchmen were not to know. When he heard the name, he apparently went very pale, and glowered at the man all evening. Very brusque and unsociable, yet when he wished to withdraw, he offered to escort him.'

De Brescelin paused.

'And?' William de Beauchamp's grip upon his goblet was so tight, his knuckles were white.

'They found the Benedictine in the morning, thrown over the town walls, his manhood removed and his heart cut out.'

'But why? And was it for certain de Roules who did it?'

'Well, de Roules disappeared, so could never defend any accusation. I heard tell he was a mercenary in France later. A man was found, only a servant, but one who offered his words on oath. He said he saw de Roules take the cleric aside by force, and there was a heated argument. De Roules accused the man of seducing his mother, even though he was already a priest. The envoy at first denied any knowledge even of the name of de Roules, then got very agitated and said that it was entirely the other way round and that Sybilla de Roules corrupted him to get revenge upon her husband. Now, you and I have both met that witch Sybilla, and personally I could well believe it, but . . . Anyway, the envoy said he had gone to his bishop and confessed his sin and left England forever, and God would be merciful because he was contrite. To which de Roules had yelled that there was no God to be merciful, as the envoy would find out. There was a cry, and the servant played least in sight.

The combination of what he almost certainly did, and what he said, got de Roules excommunicated, not that I think that would have worried him, Godless bastard that he was.' De Brescelin laughed suddenly. 'Quite literally, it seems.'

'But nothing has been said here,' mused de Beauchamp.

'No. It was a long way away, and once home, who wants to dwell on "out there"? Besides, what good would it do? Henry de Roules is a decent sort of man, a bit weak, but living with her would cow any man. It cowed Picot.'

253

'If Reynald came back to England, I would say he would tell his mother he had his revenge, and she,' the sheriff shuddered, 'would no doubt think he acted quite correctly.'

'You don't think perhaps she had actually loved . . .'

'Sybilla de Roules?' It was de Beauchamp's turn to laugh. 'She might have had a passion for him, but if he went squealing to his bishop, she would despise him thereafter. I think the only love she ever felt was for herself and for Reynald, her revenge upon Picot, and in his mother's image.'

'True enough.' Audemer de Brescelin nodded.

'The man we seek, the leader, hates the Black Monks, and knows me. He's a cruel bastard, harms for the pleasure of it, I would say. That all fits with Reynald.'

Walkelin cleared his throat. The two men had forgotten his presence.

'Forgive me, my lord de Brescelin, but did de Roules make money in the Holy Land? Did he capture silver?'

De Brescelin frowned.

'Any fight there is not to gain wealth.' He paused. 'But in de Roules's case, quite likely. Some prisoners were exchanged, I believe, and he would have done it for money for certain, not to get back captured pilgrims.'

'And the silver we have is, some of it, from the east, and cunningly wrought, my lord Sheriff.'

William de Beauchamp did not need the confirmation.

'It is de Roules, I am absolutely certain of it now. Thank you, my friend. You will stay and eat, before returning home?'

Audemer de Brescelin thanked him, but declined, and the sheriff left the hall with him to see him depart. Walkelin decided he should remain, working on the assumption that the sheriff would return to make any comment upon what had passed.

Some time about mid-morning, Kenelm remembered his task with a sickening jolt. He fumbled inside his stained cotte. The vellum and the wrapped ear were still there, Heaven be praised. Kenelm, who, unlike Guy, saw no inconsistency between committing deadly sins and a vague observance of general piety, crossed himself. It did not occur to him that if anyone had tried to rob him, neither a piece of a document, nor especially a body part, would have been considered worthwhile taking. He set his mind to obey the last part of his instructions properly. Get an old woman or a child, the lord Reynald had said. Well, Kenelm thought old women far too knowing, so he would pick a child, who would be far easier to intimidate. He made his way, a little more clear-headed now, towards the castle. Before the gatehouse there was open space where children were enjoying the snow and ice, seeing who could slide the furthest, throwing snowballs at each other. He saw a small boy at a doorway. A woman, too old to be his mother, but his oldmother he would guess, was wagging a finger at him. Kenelm wondered if there might be anyone within doors, but decided old women were more likely to live alone than old men, and any husband of hers would not be hard to overpower. He made as if he was just passing by, but suddenly pushed child and woman into the little dwelling. The woman staggered back, surprised and a little scared, but outraged. The boy he took by the scruff of the neck.

'Now listen, brat. I have something I need delivering to the lord Sheriff, see. And I don't want to hand it over in person, so you are going to be a good lad and do it for me, otherwise you won't see your oldmother again, not alive anyways.'

That a scrubby little boy had very little chance of being admitted into the shrieval presence, and would not know how to go about it, was not something Kenelm considered. Reaching the castle gateway was good enough. He vaguely assumed the child would be shooed away, but if persistent would be able to hand over what was intended.

Huw looked to Mistress Catchpoll, who had her lips pursed tight. She nodded. Kenelm took the folded vellum and the slightly stained rag containing Brother Augustine's ear, and placed them in the little boy's hands.

'And you remember, I will be watching, and if you are a bad boy,' he drew a knife, and made a slicing motion. Huw nodded, turned, ran out the door and off towards the castle. He seemed to be let in the wicket gate by a friendly guard, and Kenelm, watching, relaxed. That was a mistake.

Everyone in the castle knew Huw, the castle cook's adopted lad. He was quiet but observant, and seemed to get everywhere and watch people without them realising he was there. The men-at-arms had christened him 'the castle ghost'. He was being taught his new father's trade, in the long run, but at eight or so was too small and immature to help much or learn more than an awareness of the kitchen hierarchy, and, after a few painful encounters, that food on tables was not to be taken and eaten. The snowy weather had meant he had been given furlough to play, and Drogo was surprised to see him back indoors so early. He ruffled the lad's unruly hair, but then an insistent little hand pulled at his sleeve, and a piping treble with a trace of Welsh lilt told him something which made his face grow stern. Huw's pinched features looked worried, in case he had done something wrong, but Drogo, seeing his concern, patted him on the shoulder and led him from the kitchen.

Walkelin was not expecting to see Drogo and his lad enter the hall, and when de Beauchamp himself did walk in, a minute later, he frowned at the presence of the cook. He wanted words alone with Walkelin. Before he could dismiss the man and the brat tucked in close beside him, Walkelin stepped forward, a piece of folded vellum and something, cloth-wrapped, in his hand.

'My lord, there is another message from the kidnappers, and it comes with an ear.' Walkelin glanced briefly at Huw in case this upset the child, but the little boy was too overawed by the sight of William de Beauchamp looking at him.

'Call a clerk,' yelled de Beauchamp, coming forward to take what Walkelin held.

'My lord, before you find out the contents, you should know that the messenger used young Huw here as the go-between, and has Mistress Catchpoll as a hostage.'

'Hostage? But—'

'I imagine once he saw Huw enter the castle he would make off, my lord, but if we are swift . . .'

William de Beauchamp was a big man, but could move with surprising speed.

Kenelm groaned, and opened his eyes. It was like the hangover again, but worse. A very angry face appeared upside down above him, and an equally angry female voice threatened to remove his manhood with a hatchet if he moved an inch. He did not move.

Mistress Catchpoll did not like being threatened in her own home, and took a dim view of men who frightened small children, unless of course the children were their own and in need of a good frightening. A good frightening was an important weapon in the arsenal of parenthood, and had saved many a child from foolhardy and potentially fatal acts. This nasty piece of work had scared her, and if one thing was worse than Mistress Catchpoll annoyed, it was Mistress Catchpoll frightened and annoyed. When the intruder had leant out the door to get a better view of Huw's arrival at the castle gate, and had for a moment forgotten 'Oldmother', she had taken up the pestle with which she had earlier been pounding fennel seeds, and hit him sharply above the ear. He had dropped like a stone.

The arrival on her doorstep of the lord Sheriff, Walkelin and two men-at-arms, she greeted in far from the manner they had expected, thinking they might find her injured and abandoned, or still held captive. Her outrage still at a high level, her first instruction, before seeing the illustrious nature of at least one of her visitors, was for them to stamp the snow off their boots before they set foot in her home. It said much for her air of authority that they all, including William de Beauchamp, did so.

His delight at the capture of a gang member totally outweighed any wrath at being addressed as a nobody by the wife of his serjeant, and once she realised fully what was happening, Mistress Catchpoll bobbed a very fair curtsey, and was as meek as a novice in a nunnery.

The men-at-arms dragged the prisoner, still incapable of walking unaided, back to the castle, the lord Sheriff and Walkelin following on behind. De Beauchamp wanted to hear what was in the demand before interrogating the man, and went straight to his chamber, while Walkelin made a swift detour via the kitchens to assure Drogo and Huw all was well, and arrived just in time to hear Huw asking whether you could make soup with ears.

Walkelin arrived in the shrieval chamber, still smiling, and barely out of breath, in time to hear the clerk who had been perusing the spidery writing of the cold and nervous Benedictine, clear his throat, and read out the demand. De Beauchamp ground his teeth. As far as he was concerned, he knew his enemy, and this was a calculated insult like the rest.

'If he thinks I will give him anything but my sword blade in his gullet, he has another thing coming,' growled the sheriff.

'That, my lord, is what strikes me as odd, in a way. I mean, he knows you, he must know you are not a man to give in to threats. Is it just some strange game he plays? And yet, the forger would be of use to him, so perhaps . . .' Walkelin paused. 'We cannot reach Tibberton by noon, my lord, not with the snow this deep.'

'I wasn't going there anyway.'

'It says a "final" demand for Geoffrey,' offered Walkelin, cautiously.

'Well, he isn't getting him.'

'Understood, my lord. So . . .'

259

'So we find out what our man with the headache from Mistress Catchpoll can tell us. Let us visit the prisoner.'

It was a grim-looking sheriff and his man who appeared before Kenelm.

'Right,' de Beauchamp sounded suitably brisk, 'tell us what we want and you'll die the easy way, keep anything from us and you die hard.'

Walkelin blinked. This was direct, even for the sheriff. Kenelm, whose head still thumped, looked up with resignation on his face. Unlike Geoffrey, he did not think he was clever. Unlike Geoffrey, he did not think any would rescue him. Life had always been precarious, and now he teetered at the edge of the precipice, looking into the nothingness below.

'What is it you want to know?' He thought about adding 'my lord', but was too weary of spirit to bother over much.

'You were sent with the message, but where were you to meet the other men afterwards?' Walkelin knew it would not be the sheriff's first question, but it was the most important.

'At the tithe barn that belongs to the monks of Evesham, just north of Bradecote. Sunset tonight. But he might have said that just to cast me off. I was never sure with him.'

This was the obvious point for de Beauchamp to pounce with what was uppermost in his mind.

'De Roules?'

'You know?'

'We surmised.'

Kenelm was not sure what surmised meant, but took it as an affirmative.

'Are Father Samson and the lady FitzPayne safe?' De Beauchamp had only minor interest in the others held.

'The father and who? The widow woman? Is she a lady? Suppose she was, now you think. She had soft hands, and was a very careful cook.'

'Cook? Are they safe? That is all I need to know.' The sheriff wondered if the man's brain was addled from the blow he had received.

'They were safe when I left them. I can say no more, but if the lord Reynald means to let them go, then it is more than he has ever done since I have known him.'

'And how long is that?' asked Walkelin.

'Years. Not sure how many.'

'Will he be at the meeting point at noon?' De Beauchamp was thinking.

'Not him, himself. He'd send Guy to watch, perhaps.'

'The bearded one?'

'Yes.'

'And how many are there, in the gang?'

'A dozen, more or less. I don't count everyone.'

The sheriff looked at Walkelin.

'I have all I need. Let us get going.'

He strode away, and Walkelin followed. Walkelin wondered what the sheriff was planning. He remembered Serjeant Catchpoll's injunction to keep the lord Sheriff from charging about like a wild boar. Having reached a point where he felt he was almost comfortable in the sheriff's company, but not quite, he now realised how difficult his position might be.

'My lord, what is it we are to do? We cannot reach Tibberton in time . . .'

'Do? Tibberton? Why go there for one man? No, we get to the tithe barn a little before sunset, and we take back our hostages, by force. We creep around no more.'

'What about my lord Bradecote?'

'What about him?'

'Well, if he is also heading for the same place . . .'

'I think we can tell friend from foe.' De Beauchamp was feeling buoyed by the thought of action, of getting his hands on Reynald de Roules's throat.

Walkelin, by contrast, was a worried man.

Chapter Nineteen

Hugh Bradecote broke his fast in his own hall, caught between hunger and a feeling of nausea that stemmed from the adrenalin coursing through his system. He forced himself to eat upon the grounds that the kidnappers might not turn up until sunset itself. This morning he had to think clearly, put aside the urge to be 'doing', and plan. Not that Catchpoll could not do it, but he was aware that he had been 'carried' for much of the last few days, and he wanted to prove he was back in command and capable. He looked towards Catchpoll, and saw he was being regarded in turn. The serjeant gave a smile. Bradecote pushed back his seat, stood and, on impulse, went to the solar. Gilbert was being patted for wind, over his nurse's shoulder. He gazed at his father and blew a milky bubble. Bradecote held out a finger for the baby hand to grasp. He smiled down at the wide eyes and snub nose, and whispered, 'I will bring her home to you.' He dropped a kiss on the fine, silky hair, and went out, thinking of battle.

Reynald kicked one of his men, whose snoring had woken him. It felt too late to go back to sleep, though there was only a faint grey light through the small windows. He contemplated the day, with pleasure. He did not intend to depart until just before Matins, when he could surprise the bucolic peasants by emerging from the church at speed. It was a showy gesture, no more, but it pleased him.

There would be no exchange of captives, he knew, and it did not bother him any more. This dance was done. If by some chance de Beauchamp, or more likely a minion, did come, he would find a bruised and outraged parish priest complaining about horse dung in his church and foul desecrations, and slack-jawed parishioners. Guy would no doubt report back all that occurred. He pondered. Guy was better out of it today. He feared that Guy was getting 'soft' in England, and what he was planning for the barn would not appeal to him. He smiled. When it was all over he would leave a corpse there, and perhaps another, yes, as a gift for his mother, in Bushlea. Father Samson would be most appropriate. Then he would head back to Anjou, where there were feuds enough to keep him busy. He did not want England any more. It had been a good scheme, but even the best were prone to the unexpected. He yawned, and kicked out again, simply out of malice. If he was awake, why should not others be also.

'Wake up, you pathetic heap. We have an interesting day before us.'

Christina, who was already awake, did not like the sound of that, but fought the desire to look towards Guy for reassurance. There must be no sign of collusion, or even connection, between them.

William de Beauchamp was regretting the number of men-at-arms he had left under Bradecote. As Sheriff of Worcestershire he left the majority of law enforcement to his undersheriff and serjeant for the investigating, while he concentrated on the tax collecting and the politics, but when a gesture needed to be made, and there was a good fight in the offing, which would remind folk of his power, he liked to be at the forefront. Bradecote had not brought his own retainers when he had come to the castle, so all that he commanded were sheriff's men, and de Furnaux was already bleating about not having enough for the castle guard rota. Well, today the castellan would have to put up with barely more than a man on the gate for a few hours, until this was over. Donning mail and helm, he strode out to what force Walkelin could gather together. It was not as impressive as he wanted, but would surely be enough.

Reynald de Roules wanted his moment. Waiting in the church had been boring, but not as cold as being outside. He freed the priest's hands so that he might ring the bell for Matins, and had everyone mounted, bar one man peering out from the door. When he confirmed the villagers approaching, de Roules grinned. He looked to the priest, who was still gagged uncomfortably.

'Thank you for your Christian hospitality, Father. The horses are especially grateful – you might say relieved.' The smile grew even broader, as he took in the state of the floor. 'I know you must regret our leaving, but it really is time we made our departure. Open the doors, nice and wide.'

The priest obeyed, and had to step back smartly, as de Roules kicked his mount to bound outside, followed by the clatter of hoof on stone that reverberated through the little church. The villagers fell back in stunned alarm as the horsemen, led by a laughing man wielding a sword, bundled out of their church and set their mounts, snorting and jibbing, into the ridged fields that lay awaiting spring wakening.

Once into the cover of trees, Reynald slewed his horse round, and brought it to a halt. He was still laughing. His captives, who had feared his anger and his morose silences, now realised that there was something worse. His eyes were very bright and wild, as if drunk, but he could be nothing but sober. He spoke to Guy.

'Skirt round the fields, watch and listen. There is as much chance of the forger being brought as there is of me finding religion, but wait until after noon and then come to the barn. We will be there. Off you go, and give your charge to Bertrand.'

He nodded at one of the men, who came forward to take the rope that bound Christina's hands, and which Guy had casually taken as the party mounted up. Guy tossed the end to him without glancing at Christina, but she had felt the slight tug he had given it first. He was telling her she was on her own, but he had not forgotten his promise.

'Don't let her tie you in knots, Bertrand,' he said, jeeringly. 'You know what women are.' Then he turned to Reynald. 'The barn, this afternoon.'

With which he turned away and began weaving his path through the edge of the woodland. Christina felt less brave for a moment. Her message to Hugh had indicated sunset. Would it be all over for her before then?

It was odd, thought Guy, that obedience was so much a thing of habit. When Reynald gave him his instructions, he set off to obey them without thinking, but even before he drew near the village again, he knew he was going to ignore them, once there was time for a gap between himself and the main party to be set and safe. Reynald was in a mad mood. He had seen it but once before, and that had been before a fight. He had admired the bravado, the laughing at fear, as he thought, but been ashamed and disgusted with what followed their victory. Today he had not even the excuse of a battle. The barn, he had little doubt, would become a place of torture and death, and though he could not save all, he would secure the life of the lady. Then he surprised himself. Without thinking, he drew his sword, held it hilt uppermost like a cross, kissed the crosspiece, and prayed.

The tithe barn stood in a clearing. It was really part of a grange, but the Abbot of Evesham had decided that there was no good reason to keep brothers there in the worst of the weather with little to do, and when their bodies as well as their souls would be the better for being among their brethren within the abbey walls. Hugh Bradecote would sometimes ride out with a hare or a brace of pigeon to augment the diet of those there in the warmer months, for it was both a charitable thing and kept him in quiet good favour with Evesham, which held several manors in the vicinity. He judged that the kidnappers would approach from the north, so placing men on the south side was not difficult, except for the problem of cover, which was much reduced by the bareness of tree and shrub. If he kept the horses well back and out of sight, it could be done, but the men would chill if crouching or standing for long, and would have the disadvantage of advancing on foot. The archers would be in good position, though. He set them first and then went to the rear of the barn where the trees grew closest.

'I do not think they would see tracks here. I am wondering, Catchpoll, if we could lever planks off the rear here, at least for men to climb in. It would be even better if the hole were big enough for horses, then we would not leave any tracks in the snow in view, and could ambush them from the least expected direction. I would keep a few men outside, on the western side of the clearing. They will come from the north, to be sure, and once we have them on three sides and they are near to the barn, we spring.'

Catchpoll sucked his teeth.

'Good enough as a plan, my lord, but breaking into the barn might not be so easy. Depends how full it is for a start. Might be no room to get a horse in even if the hole were big enough, and without axes . . .'

'I had thought of this. You did not see I had my steward provide a couple to two of the men.'

'Very forward-thinking of you, my lord,' declared Catchpoll, solemnly, but with twitching lips. 'And how will you explain the hole to the abbot?'

'Mice?'

Catchpoll choked.

'I will send to have it repaired afterwards, never fear, and if we save Father Samson, I doubt the abbot will begrudge us some planks.'

'Then we had best get a move on, since breaking in will not be a quiet job.'

Catchpoll supervised the men with axes, while Bradecote, skirting carefully round the clear white space, set men as best he could to the west, with a line of mounted men further back ready to charge in as the trap was sprung. He returned to Catchpoll a short while later.

'Well?'

'There were enough planks cut away or prised off for a man to get in without trouble.'

'Quite full within, my lord. Can't see horses being practical,' volunteered the man who had been within.

'Pity. It means taking on mounted men at a disadvantage.'

'Not if you strike the horse first and avoid the first downstroke.' Catchpoll held up his hand. 'Oh, I don't like to waste a good animal, but if it is me or the horse, there is no contest. We also outnumber them, and if there is confusion, plenty of yelling, there will be horses jibbing anyway.'

'True enough. I want you, me, and a dozen men in the barn.'

'That'll be cosy.' Catchpoll grinned.

'Yes, well. Two are to stay back and if they can secure any of the hostages, they drag them in and protect them here. Got it?'

'Yes, my lord. The Benedictines would only be in the way, anyway.'

He did not mention the lady FitzPayne, since it was obvious that she was the undersheriff's own 'mark'.

'One thing, my lord.'

'Yes, Serjeant?'

'How do we burst out the front doors of the barn when they are barred?'

There was silence. Bradecote rubbed his jaw, trying to conceal his anger at himself for not taking this into consideration. A man-at-arms clambered back through the hole. Bradecote gave in, and swore.

'I wanted it pristine to the front, but there. We send a man. You,' he pointed at the man-at-arms, 'you look nimble and have not got big feet. You edge round the building as if nailed to it, footprints right up against the wood. You unbar the door without dropping it slap bang in front, and come back with it. They will not be expecting the doors unbarred so will not "see" them unbarred, not until so close it matters not.'

Catchpoll and the man-at-arms exchanged glances, but the man did as he was told, much to the amusement of his fellows watching him from a distance. He did well reaching the doors, but the bar proved heavy and cumbersome, and Bradecote bit his lip, certain it would mar all. However, after some expletives and pushing back and forth, the man-at-arms succeeded, and made his way to the rear with his 'prize'. Bradecote clapped him on the shoulder and promised him largesse as a reward.

Dispositions made, they waited, the men outside blowing on cold fingers and trying to stamp freezing feet without making a noise. Bradecote was peering through a knot hole and was just beginning to worry when he saw movement. He had not heard the chink of a horse's bit, nor the mule's cough, but the shapes of men on horses emerged from between the trees on the north side. The leading group were within thirty feet of the barn when one of the concealed archers gave way to an almighty sneeze. Reynald pulled his mount up sharply, looking to the sound and already reaching for his sword. There was not time for delay. With a single glance at Catchpoll, Bradecote shoulder-charged the door open, yelling, and hoping his archers had a clear target on any man threatening Christina. Even as he ran towards Reynald he was conscious of the fact that he could not see her in what would become, within seconds, a dangerous melee. The kidnappers were outnumbered, and would not escape, but the safety of the hostages was very much in doubt.

Reynald, after a moment of angry surprise, reverted to what he was best, a fighter, and spurred his mount forward even as he brought his sword down with a feral yell. Anticipating the action, Bradecote dropped and rolled sideways in front of the frightened animal, risking flailing hooves to avoid slicing steel. Catchpoll was aiming for Reynald's offside, but a man got in the way, and took the serjeant's slice across the thigh that bit deep to the bone. The horseman screamed and fell, but before the horse was clear, Catchpoll was avoiding a blow from another man. He was aware of two men-at-arms dragging a monk from a mule to his left, and a downed man-at-arms frantically trying to fend off blows, but then was fighting for survival.

Growling, Reynald yanked his horse's head about, as Bradecote rose from the roll, knees bent for the next move, and with a handful of snow that he threw hard into the horse's face. It reared, even as the pressure on the bit turned its head, all unbalanced, and Bradecote lunged up on the blind side in a stroke that would have taken a slower man. But Reynald de Roules had been fighting for years, and his reactions were lightning fast. Blade met blade, as he managed to parry to his left, and, slipping boot from stirrup, kicked out viciously, catching Bradecote in the chest and knocking him backwards, to sprawl in the snow. As he tumbled, Bradecote heard a woman's scream.

Christina, caught totally unawares by the ambush, though she had been instrumental in its laying, had found herself trapped within a fight, her hands bound and the rope still tied to Bertrand's pommel. All about her, men were engaged in bloody combat, and yet she could do nothing but hope a stray blow did not strike her. The archers, whose instructions had been to take down any man who threatened her, had their line of sight obscured by friend and foe alike, but Thomas Wood, biding his time, managed to identify the man who held her, and loosed a single arrow that struck true. Bertrand slumped and fell, and his petrified mount darted to the side, dragging Christina from her own horse into the snow, and bounding off in the direction it saw as safety, pulling her behind it. She screamed as she fell, and was winded by the heavy landing.

Guy heard the sounds of battle enjoined, and did not think to disappear whilst unknown and unseen. He had promised the lady FitzPayne, and it did not occur to him to fail her. He spurred his horse forward to the action, and arrived at the edge of the clearing as Bertrand's horse bolted, almost directly past him. He reached for the bridle but missed, and pulled his horse about on its hocks so hard it almost fell, and lost valuable seconds in the chase.

* * *

Bradecote's grip on his sword broke as he hit the ground. Reynald de Roules considered trampling the man to death, but he preferred to feel the tremor as steel bit sinew and cracked bone, and vaulted from the saddle to end it his own way, lips drawn back in a sneer. His 'victim' was scrambling to get up, scrabbling for his weapon. He shrugged, and lunged. He expected the man to pull back, though it would avail him nothing, but in fact Bradecote did the opposite and threw himself forward, twisting as he did so, avoiding the steel by a hair's breadth, and just grabbing de Roules's ankle, toppling him also. It was not pretty, it was not two lords in combat, it was two men fighting for the right to draw breath. They grappled and tumbled, swords gone, kicking, butting, oblivious to the others fighting about them. De Roules fumbled to draw his dagger, dropped his guard for a fraction of a second, and Bradecote's blow broke his nose. Blood spattered into the snow, and Bradecote pressed home his advantage, grabbing Reynald's arm and twisting it so that the half grip on the dagger broke, and driving it up his back until there was an odd cracking sound and Reynald yelled as the shoulder dislocated.

'My lord.' Catchpoll pulled him off. The serjeant had a bloody nose and was breathing heavily. 'Let me. The lady.'

Suddenly all thoughts of de Roules were forgotten.

'What?' he whispered, catching his breath.

'Dragged off. Horse.' Catchpoll was leaning, hands braced on knees, words at a premium.

Bradecote stumbled to his feet, grabbed the first loose horse and followed Catchpoll's pointing finger. Swinging himself into the saddle he kicked hard, and set off in blind pursuit.

* * *

Guy's horse was a bigger, better, and fitter animal than Bertrand's, and floundered less. He caught up with it within a minute, grabbing bridle above bit and hauling it to a wild-eyed halt, then leaping from the saddle to kneel beside the prone form of Christina FitzPayne. The snow had been to her advantage, keeping her from the very worst bumps of the hard ground, but she was dazed and breathless, too breathless even to sob.

'My lady?'

Guy's voice penetrated her confusion.

'My lady, can you stand?' He was untying her burning wrists, cut where the rope had bitten them, and had an arm about her, assisting her to rise.

Then Christina heard another voice, cold, deadly, and yet immeasurably beloved.

'Let her go.'

'Hugh,' she murmured, blinking, trying to focus.

Bradecote looked at the man with his arm about Christina FitzPayne, a man with a close-cropped beard. His hand went to the hilt of his sword, only to find, of course, that he had none.

'That,' murmured Guy, with a wry smile, 'might make your fulfilling your intent rather more difficult.'

'Though you have a sword and I do not, I will kill you, none the less, if you do not let her go.'

'Hugh, no. He—'

'My lord Bradecote, I presume. Then, my lord, I think you should take better care of your lady.'

Guy raised Christina's damaged wrist to just brush it with his lips, and pushed her gently towards Bradecote. Then his eyes narrowed, and his hand went to his own sword. Mounted men-at-arms were arriving in numbers, and they did not look like men keen to shake him by the hand.

'Hugh,' Christina whispered, 'he saved me, came back to save me. Let him go, please.'

'This man is a criminal. The law . . .'

'Forget the law, my love. Be just. Now, quickly.' Her voice trembled, and she sagged against him.

Hugh Bradecote looked into the eyes of Guy, brown eyes that were those of a man who despised himself, but in whom a flame of hope had been rekindled, the eyes of one who had once been of even nobler birth than his own, and he nodded.

'Go now, with my thanks, but never enter this shire again.'

Guy drew his sword very slowly, raised it in salute, though whether it was to the lady or her lord was unclear, vaulted nimbly into the saddle, tapped the side of the blade to his horse's flank, and lolloped away, as fast as was possible in the snow.

The men-at-arms were forgotten. Guy was forgotten. She was in his hold, safe, alive, and he had so much bubbling up within him, he did not know where to start. Perhaps it was not surprising that, as a parent with a lost child that is found, the first bubble to burst was anger. He held her off from him slightly, looking down at her white face. His voice shook, and he was suddenly shouting.

'I told you not to go; I said it was too dangerous. When will you understand that I—'

'Hugh,' her voice was a whisper, and her face so tragic that he stopped, and there was a moment of silence.

'It's all right,' he whispered back. 'I'm taking you home.'

And then he kissed her, desperately, hungrily.

'Right you lot, stop gawping, and do something useful, like getting back to helping our wounded.'

Catchpoll's voice broke the spell that seemed to have settled on the men-at-arms, and they turned back. Catchpoll waited, and after a suitable length of time, coughed.

'Prisoners secured, my lord. No fatalities among the hostages, three dead, four wounded among the kidnappers and we have two sword cuts, one man nursing a broken head, and one missing a finger.' His voice was deadpan. 'You might care to return and . . . er, take control of the situation, my lord, officially. Looks good.'

Bradecote broke away and turned, trying not to grin foolishly.

'And what happened to the man on the brown horse, by the way?' Catchpoll sounded only vaguely interested.

'He . . . left.'

'Indeed, my lord, no doubt a pressing reason for his departure. Don't tell me, lest the lord Sheriff asks me why.'

He picked up the reins to the loose horse, correctly assuming Bradecote would place his lady up before him. They ambled back to the barn, where things were looking more orderly. The kidnappers were penned against the barn wall by a semicircle of men-at-arms, Reynald slumped and sat upon the snowy ground. He was not a good colour, very pale mixed with smears of blood, which still issued from his nose and spotted the snow and his clothes. He looked up at Bradecote, and something in the way Bradecote held the lady made him screw his pain-filled eyes up even more.

'The widow.'

She looked down at him, without pity.

'Indeed, my lord Reynald, but not for long. I am the widow of Corbin FitzPayne and about to become the wife of the lord Bradecote.'

'That's me,' added Bradecote, dismounting and helping her down. His hands stayed at her waist for a moment, steadying her, then he turned to de Roules. 'Hugh Bradecote, Undersheriff of Worcester, and you are my prisoner.'

'Er . . . not for long, my lord,' muttered Catchpoll. 'Here comes the lord Sheriff.'

Bradecote turned. At another time he might have resented his moment of success being so short, but he had the only prize he coveted, and so greeted the sheriff with a smile. He made his report in similar clipped vein to the one Catchpoll had made to him, but was almost ignored. De Beauchamp was staring at de Roules.

'Pity. I wanted to kill you myself. But there, a hanging is more fitting, and you'll get a good crowd. I wonder if your mother will attend?'

The jibe stung, and de Roules, despite his pain, growled and spat on the sheriff's snowy boot. The sheriff kicked him, and he passed out. De Beauchamp looked surprised.

'He has a dislocated shoulder, my lord,' Catchpoll volunteered by way of explanation.

'Ah. Oh well. Now, I had best see the archbishop's envoy. Where is he?'

'In the barn, my lord . . . leading prayers.' Catchpoll's voice was monotone. De Beauchamp stared at him. 'Exactly, my lord.'

Bradecote had his arm once again about Christina.

'My lord, I was hoping . . . You said Candlemas for our wedding, but . . .'

'She gets into too much trouble without a strong commanding hand, eh?' De Beauchamp smiled. 'Best wed her and bed her before she gets into another scrape. I will take Father Samson back to Worcester with my prisoners, but will ride out to Bradecote tomorrow to see your priest give the church's blessing. She is yours. Keep her on a tight rein, I'd say.'

Chapter Twenty

Hugh and Christina rode in silence most of the way to Bradecote, though she mustered the energy to tell him about Guy. Hearing what he had done, and not done, the undersheriff did not regret his actions.

'Will the lord Sheriff be angry, my lord?' she asked, thinking she might have put him in a difficult position.

'No. He won't even know.'

'But the men-at-arms, Serjeant Catchpoll?'

'You heard Catchpoll, and the men would not volunteer to speak to the lord Sheriff. He is someone who just shouts at them occasionally. If it was good enough for me, and, to be honest, for Serjeant Catchpoll, they will not question it.'

'I am glad.'

There was silence again until the welcoming walls of the manor came into view.

'Oh, the thought of bed,' Christina sighed.

Hugh Bradecote blinked, and then coloured, for the thought that hit him had nothing to do with sleeping. She was not looking at him, so did not see the blush.

'But first, I must wash.'

'I will have a pitcher of water . . .' He was still thinking of the bed.

'No, all over, bathe.'

'What? In January? You'll catch your death.' This shattered his imaginings. He was appalled.

'I have spent a week,' her voice trembled, 'sleeping on earth, in hay, in straw, with vermin about me, human and rodent, tending a poor man dying of the poison from a rotting stump, and the stench of it lingers on me still. I have eaten raw turnip, and sometimes nothing at all. I have—'

'Cooked, so I heard.'

'That too. Seriously, I want to wash it all away. Please, Hugh.'

'I will get the women to find the washday tub, and heat water in the kitchen and over the hearth. You can stand in that and bathe if you must, and they will bring warmed water, but I beg you not to linger over it.'

He was clearly concerned. They rode into the manor courtyard, and he lifted her down once more, and led her through the hall and into the solar. She wanted to pick up Gilbert but would not until clean. Bradecote fussed about, arranging for another brazier to be brought in, for the washing tub and a piece of cloth to line it to be carried from where it was stood after its last use in the autumn.

She removed her cloak and he saw the torn gown. His eyes narrowed, and his voice hardened.

'Did that tear today?'

'No.' She looked at the floor, and then up at him. 'Reynald would have . . . But I told him my husband had given me disease, that gave him pause, and then poor Brother Augustine sort of cursed him, and the moment passed. But I swear to you, Hugh, if I could not have killed him, and he had . . . I would have killed myself afterwards, with my own knife.'

Her face was very serious. He wanted to take her in his arms, but she pushed him away, even as he reached for her.

'No. I want to be clean, for myself and for you, and burn these clothes.'

'Ah. But your others are in Worcester and . . .'

She giggled.

'I hope perhaps Serjeant Catchpoll thinks of them, then, for I would not care to go to the altar in no more than an undershirt of yours and a cloak.'

The thought of her in his undershirt made him swallow rather hard. The nurse, who had handed baby Gilbert to the wet nurse to be fed and kept from the dangers of damp air, shooed him out as she brought in the first container of water, and he went without complaint, and stood by the hearth in the hall with a beaker of mulled ale. Women came and went, and just for one moment he remembered the last time he had been kept from his solar by women. A shadow passed briefly, and benignly, over his happiness. He said a prayer for Ela's soul, emptied his beaker, and brought his thoughts back to the happier contemplation of the present. How much water did it take to clean oneself, he wondered, and then he grinned. The lord Sheriff had given her to him, the Church would bless their union on the morrow. He halted the next wench bearing two pitchers, and trying not to spill them, for both were full, he took them from her, with an instruction that no more were needed.

Christina stood with her back to the door, arms raised, twisting her hair to get the water out, groaning at the use of her pulled shoulder muscles, and the soft curves of her outline stirred him. She had heard the door open. Droplets of water stood out upon her soft, pale flesh, and he watched, fascinated, as a little rivulet formed and caressed its way down between her shoulder blades to the base of her spine. He had spent the last days fearing he would never hold her, living, ever again, that what was about to happen would be left a dream unfulfilled in bitter grief. His throat tightened. He wanted her very much, but there was also a sorrow, for her back told an old tale. The marks were fine lines, but she had been whipped, flogged, in her past, and Hugh knew by whose hand and why. Her first husband did that, and to a girl scarcely into womanhood, for the 'fault' of losing his child early. Hugh could not undo that past, wanted only to give a bright future, but he wondered if she might flinch at his touch.

'Not over the hair this time,' she instructed, and kept the dark veil of hair up from the back of her neck. He approached softly, and did as she commanded, watching the warm water run down over her paleness. He set the pitchers on a bench, then he leant forward and placed a kiss on the nape of her neck. She jumped, and gave a squeal of surprise.

'Clean enough to kiss now?' he murmured, thickly, repeating the deed, but with his arm sliding about her waist. She did not flinch.

'Yes, my lord.' He heard no unwillingness in her voice.

She turned within his hold, offering her lips, and more, and the thought passed through her mind, briefly, that it was the very first time she had ever offered herself, craved what would follow. De Malfleur had only ever hurt and repelled her, FitzPayne had been a duty, but here and now desire burned as fiercely in her as in he who would claim her. She shivered, and Hugh, thinking her cold, reached for the blanket that lay upon the bench, draping it about her. He lifted her in his arms, and her hand caressed his cheek as he carried her to his bed.

'And you . . . will be an . . . obedient wife?' he whispered, half teasingly, between kisses.

'Very. Obedient to your . . . every . . . wish.'

'Oh good . . . because . . .'

Sometimes, words were superfluous.

William de Beauchamp arrived next day, accompanied not only by Serjeant Catchpoll, and Walkelin, but also by Father Samson and his remaining brethren. Having fortified themselves at the priory and collected Brother Bernard, Father Samson was keen to be about his archbishop's business, with a determination that Father Prior found inspiring if somewhat excessive. Catchpoll also presented the lady with the clothing she had left at the castle, which brought an added colour to her cheek, and a glance at Hugh Bradecote.

Sheriff and serjeant found an undersheriff whose face could barely stop breaking into a grin, and a lady whose eyes dwelt with such fondness upon him that the sheriff later told Catchpoll he felt they should have all just gone home and left them to it.

What surprised him though was that at the conclusion of the wedding feast, the newly espoused pair were to set off the next morning, once again bound for Polesworth. It had caused a minor rift the previous evening, during the course of a meal that Christina seemed to enjoy nearly as much as her private hour with her lord beforehand, but not quite. She had explained, as gently as she could, that her vow still stood, whatever her lord said about her trials more than compensating for not attaining her goal, which he did, vociferously.

'Brother Augustine, may he be at peace, told me I would be blessed, said . . . nice things, but I still feel the only sure way is to do what I promised. Please, my love.'

He frowned.

'You are my wife. You must obey me now.'

She laid her hand upon his.

'I am truly your wife, and wish to obey, which is why I beg that you will not forbid this.'

He paused, looked at her. It was difficult to deny her, who had denied him nothing.

'You may go, but,' he kissed her fingers, 'only if I can accompany you this time, and you wear the good thick cloak.'

Her eyes danced.

'Not just the cloak though, my lord.'

'No, not just the cloak.'

Despite the hasty nature of the arrangements, the manor kitchens provided a good feast, and an ample supply of mulled ale, wine and mead. The lord Sheriff got pleasantly drunk, and told several stories that made the Benedictines look austere, but faced with remaining until they could bed down in the hall, or joining the manor peasants about a fire in the yard, they chose warmth and comfort, and after their recent poor fare, might have been considered to have taken more in meat than would usually be accounted appropriate. Only Father Samson turned dishes away.

However exalted a guest, William de Beauchamp loudly and leeringly declared he would not take his right to sleep in the solar, since he feared he would be kept awake all night, and not by the infant. The lady Bradecote blushed, and had thankfully withdrawn before his comments became so ribald that even her lord turned pink of cheek. When Hugh left the table it was to a murmured blessing from the clerics, and loud cheering and table banging from his secular guests. He shut the door on the end of the celebrations, and leant back against it for a moment, before he went to draw back the curtain of the lord's bed. The light of his candle made her skin creamy. She lay waiting for him, smiling, for she knew this, at last, was a man whom she would always welcome.

'My lady Bradecote.' The words were formal, but his face belied them.

'My lord.' She sat up, the coverlet falling to her waist, and held out her arms to welcome him. 'Come to bed.'

With a head not so hungover as would make the short ride to Worcester unmanageable, William de Beauchamp prepared for his departure next morning, with Serjeant Catchpoll, Walkelin, and the escort of men-at-arms he had insisted the Benedictines take with them as far as the shire boundary.

'After that they are someone else's worry,' he had told Catchpoll.

The undersheriff's decision to escort his wife to Polesworth meant that the men-at-arms need not be sent, for Bradecote's own men would do as well, and as sheriff he could still claim that they were under his protection via his subordinate. The two groups parted at the manor gates, the sheriff and his men to turn right, and the monks and newly-weds turning to the left. Catchpoll watched Hugh Bradecote and his lady ride away side by side.

'I'm glad he didn't break,' commented the lord Sheriff. 'He's actually the best undersheriff I have had.'

'Indeed, my lord.' Catchpoll agreed, treating the troubles of the last week as the snow, which was starting to melt and would soon be forgotten. He paused. 'I wonder, my lord, was it fair to lumber them with that sombre-faced monk and his "happy" band, who will no doubt sigh and denounce impurity every time they so much as touch fingers?'

'Fair? No. Practical? Yes.' As the Bradecotes and the Benedictines turned the corner and passed from view, they heard Hugh Bradecote's laugh. 'And I think the Benedictines will find it the most unfair, for our undersheriff and his lady will bill and coo like doves in spring, and hardly notice their presence. Now, let us get home to Worcester. I have some men I am looking forward to hanging.'

SARAH HAWKSWOOD describes herself as a 'wordsmith' who is only really happy when writing. She read Modern History at Oxford and first published a non-fiction book on the Royal Marines in the First World War before moving on to mediaeval mysteries set in Worcestershire.

bradecoteandcatchpoll.com